"Fascinating elements of fairy tales, magic and legend. A fast-moving tale that touches on all the major themes—death, celebrity, love and loss. A gem."

Lou Rhimes,
COSMOS magazine

"A spellbinding vision of the future realized in fantastic detail. This is what the human race is in for. The taste, the sound, the very feel of the future is written here—and it's terrifying."

JC Smith, author,
The Pathless Land

"A great debut. It's rich with detail, utterly convincing and terrifying, too."

Lynne Bryan, author
Gorgeous and *Like Rabbits*

WHILE THE GODS SLEEP

JOHNNY FINCHAM

A VIRTUAL TALES BOOK

While the Gods Sleep

Cover Art © 2009 Michael Leadingham (www.michaelleadingham.com)

Edited by Donald O'Donovan

A Virtual Tales Book
PO Box 822674
Vancouver, WA 98682 USA

www.VirtualTales.com

ISBN 1-935460-08-0

First Edition: November 2009

Printed in the United States of America

9 7 8 1 9 3 5 4 6 0 0 8 4

THIS BOOK IS DEDICATED TO

DAYDREAMERS EVERYWHERE

AND TO LYNNE BRYAN, BRIDGET, CATHY AND JAMES
OF THE "GANG OF FOUR" WRITING GROUP

ALSO TO LAURA, SALLY-ANNE AND JUAN

ALSO AVAILABLE FROM JOHHNY FINCHAM:

THE SPELLBINDING POWER OF PALMISTRY
GREEN MAGIC
PALMISTRY: APPRENTICE TO PRO IN 24 HOURS

COMING SOON FROM JOHNNY FINCHAM:

NEARLY NORMAL

WWW.JOHNNYFINCHAM.COM

ONE

Law and Justice Penal Zone, Near-north Side, Chicago USA.

ABOVE ME, ONLY A SMALL SQUARE OF SKY WAS VISIBLE, enclosed by razor wire and the upper tiers of surrounding cell blocks. It was auburn in color, shimmying with heat though the day had barely begun.

I pressed my face against the securiglass door and surveyed the warren of cells and walkways of the opposite block. Nothing moved, no lights burned, no photons flickered, no motors droned. The penal zone was an escape-proof, sealed-off society. Invisible strands of technology monitored, stalked and bound, but we inmates were forbidden to own so much as a light bulb on pain of death. Here were penned eco-criminals, hacktivists, virus infectors, terrorists, and other potential technology abusers; including, by some bias of the scales of justice, a low-tech, wrench-wielding Neanderthal like me.

A dark moth of fear fluttered in my stomach. Something wasn't right.

The usual gang graffiti was cut into the air-scrubbing moss that clung to communal areas. The same scrawny pigeons squabbled on the walkways. So why did I feel so anxious, so unstrung, so *not safe?*

All the years of sweat and scheming it had taken me to earn full privileges: segregation, a visitor a day, food-growing rights. You'd think I could have found some kind of peace. But fear was a condition of survival. The zone was a bad place. A tumor in the body of the muscular second city.

There, just beside the door frame, were the imprints of my perennial pacing. Worn through the green carpet into the floor-panels, four polished hollows measured the space between the walls. Three steps, turn on the ball of the foot, three steps—the two end holes bigger than the middle ones. I could go at it for hours—back and forth, back and forth, in a kind of walking tic.

I carefully placed my feet in the holes; my bony, white, fifty-six-year-old feet. The shackle around my ankle chinked and winked its position-locating diodes, betraying each footfall to an ever-patient, ever-watchful automonitor.

Death had passed me by, I was way overdue. But death had seen how tenaciously I'd hung on and that winged chariot just kept on going. They owed me, those bastards—fifteen yearning years.

With every snap of stretching sinew of my yoga routine, with every pound of the pestle as I made my herbal potions, with every cent I extracted from visitors, one refrain, endlessly repeated: "live, lie, deceive or die."

The early-morning light softened the angles of the tiny cell. Leaning over the fake-wood table, I shook my puffball of a head.

Just six blocks beyond the tiny window in the back of my cell room was New Orleans Street, the western boundary of the penal zone.

Outside the zone, technology thrummed, electricity crackled, photons pulsed. Out there they had dermal re-growths and nano-probes patrolling arteries like miniature janitors. Out there was temperature-regulating, self-powered clothing, enzyme batteries, technology that talked and learned. Out there, somewhere, was Alvina.

Gulping back a whimper, I sensed the lightest possible touch of her, moving through the room like a zephyr. It was in the hunt for her that I'd got myself confined and she haunted me constantly.

If only I could see that gap-toothed smile of hers once more this side of eternity. If only I could get out. Only then could I know the how of it, the why and the where of it, whatever it was that swallowed her. There'd be a spoor somewhere; everyone leaves a mark, even in the chaos after The Changes.

The paraphernalia of prophecy covered my little table: the cracked porcelain palm, the wooden-handled magnifying glass, the chipped, green-tinged crystal ball.

I looked down at my feet, at the network of veins under the white skin of the instep like strands of blue hair and the notion came: she'll be a Cosmique, today's visitor, from that blue-haired, blue-veiled tribe.

That's how my glimmers of knowing arrived, the brain's synapses sparked on, chinking and winking in the space between thoughts.

But there were more important things to consider. A new escape strategy was needed. The last one, Escape Scheme Thirty-Two (abandoned like all of them in the late planning stage), involved getting a light-refractive suit smuggled in, so I could slip invisibly past the ward guards. But the problem of the exit gate's DNA scans remained.

"Live and lie, deceive or die."

Light flashed from the opposite cell block

I slid open the cell door and stood on the walkway, sucking hot, foul air. "Who's there?"

"Hey, Zach!" A voice ricocheted around the ramparts. "Is me. Long time pass. You keeping 'em cold?"

"What's up, Pembo?"

He stepped into view, lank hair, tribal tattoos, rack of bones stretching the skin of his bare chest. A small mirror in his left hand flared with reflected light. "So wha' happen with you parole?"

"Usual shit." I spat. "How many hearings now? Eight? Nine? Murderers walk free, I don't even get a sentence review. The official "no's" not through yet, but it's a fix."

"You hear about 'em guys down on North Town Street? Bubonic strep virus got 'em."

"I heard."

"Yeah." He lowered his voice to a murmur but the concrete acoustics carried every word to my ears. "There's somethin' else. Maybe trouble."

Feigning calm, I turned, stretching my thin arms upward. For one horrible moment my reflection was captured in the door glass. My haunted, hollow face stared back, skin wrinkled by years of unprotected exposure. With the wine-stain birthmark swathing my nose and my torrent of gray hair, I looked like some primordial, featherless bird about to take flight. I swivelled back to face Pembo.

"So what's the word?"

He spread his palms wide. "Hey, kindred. We walk a long road—we longest surviving inmates in 'ere, eh? All 'em visitors you get, payin' you for 'at witch-doctor spell you put on 'em. This'll cost."

"You gonna bill me for every whisper on the wind?"

"Hey. You got advantages. We all got to get out and under."

"This some scat about another battle for turf and tribute down there in the concrete undergrowth?"

"No. This significo. Mine good info, you know it."

I groaned, fished around in my pocket and found a grubby fifty. Then I had to scrabble around the rubbish-strewn walkway for an unbiograded bottle top. I squashed the note into the top with my thumb and threw it over.

He snatched it easily from the air with his free hand. "There's some people data-dredgin' on you. Visitors from outside. Tribe people."

Shit.

"Visitors give me no grief," I said, curling my lips in an attempt at a smile. "It's inmates I get stressed about. Visitors have too much to lose."

"These two big bastas, they give out bad atmospheres. They bin ask all sorts of questions abou' you. Wha' apartment you at, wha' sentence you serve— everything but your dick size, man."

I gripped the balcony rail tighter. "Probably just curious."

Pembo shook his head. "No, is more than tha'. They wanna know about your cell-access door, what kind of lock you has, what you routines are, when guards patrol. All 'at stuff. Looks like trouble."

Something inside me buckled. The heat from the furnace sky seemed to beat down on my head. "But I..." *Who'd ever heard of visitors breaking into a prison cell?*

Airships crawled across pink clouds like caterpillars, their undersides emblazoned with providers' names: Merchantainment, Datacom, Artemis. Stinging streamers of light speared my eyes. The air was closing in like the fart of a giant god, a sulphurous soup of corrosive acids and ozone, swimming with vengeful viruses that probed my defences, eager to vent their instinctive rage.

When I looked back, Pembo had vanished.

I hauled the heavy cell-door shut. The air in my cell was a stew of wet heat.

What the hell now? I shuddered as I locked the door. Had some inmates recruited outsiders to get at me? They hated segregated zeks more than they hated the guards. I'd have to be extra vigilant.

I thought about my illegal hoard of magnet-and-coil generator technology—if anyone found out... Cables were concealed between the floor-panels, running from the exercise bicycle to the battery. I shoved the table to one side, mounted the bicycle and pumped the pedals, cranking the generator hidden within the frame.

This was the secret of my power.

The sound of the pedals turning filled the room, ca-chank, ca-chank. Eventually, a soft gurgle was just perceptible as the unseen battery charged. The battery was made from an old aquarium, its plates forged with lead off the roof. It took me a year to make and a further four months to acquire and build the coils for the generator. For this crude device, I risked life itself, but without the cash it earned from visitors, the zone was unendurable.

Stepping off the exercise machine, I whispered the words to myself like a prayer, "Live and lie, deceive or die."

As I settled my frame to the floor, I sensed the passage of years weighing me down. Time's deadly chariot was hurrying near, not gently, but with ropes of smoke and sparking wheels and a roar of flailing wings.

TWO

"OPEN UP—OR I'LL USE THE OVERRIDE KEY."

I jarred awake. A ward guard of uncertain gender stood with a blue-haired woman the other side of the door. Holy arseholes! All my life a bloodshot hunter of sleep, but now only a moment of warmth or comfort and shoom! Sleep came unbidden.

The woman leaned forward, pressed her lips against the speech vent. "Orion D'Angello. Nine o'clock appointment."

I liked them to come upon me sitting cross-legged in meditation, not slumped on the floor, dribbling like some enfeebled cretin. Her sing-song voice had an edge of anxiety; the features in her round face were mismatched. The top lip too large, the nose curved and sleek like a rudder with slits for nostrils. It was all wrong, that nose. It looked like she'd borrowed it. The scraped back, near-fluorescent hair was in the classic Cosmique-tribe style. I felt in my lead-heavy limbs a dread foreboding.

I adopted my "serene wise one" look, unlocked the cell door and flattened myself against the wall as she entered. The guard stood, tweeting and glimmering with weaponry and sensors.

"I'll be jest twenny feet down the walkway. Bang on the door when you want out, ma-am," the guard said.

"Yeah-huh," she chirped, her mood spray slapping my senses as I locked the door behind her. It was a vile mix of vanilla and citrus megapheromones that made me swoon with lust till I pinched my nose and mouth-breathed furiously.

She moved around the tiny space with a peculiar step-stagger gait, inspecting everything. She ran her fingers over the backs of books, scrutinized the jars of herbs, spun the cracked, outdated globe that still had Antarctica on it.

"So," she crooned, "you're he."

"He being?"

"Zachary Crowe. The Shaman."

Her right leg was much thinner than her left, and twisted, so the knee turned in and the heel stuck out. A minicam-embedded pearl droplet dangled from her right ear. It tracked me as she see-sawed confidently around to perch herself on the stool on the opposite side of the table. Her blue huna suit was in venting mode—she'd be warm after the steps. Its fibers had separated till it was almost transparent, in diaphanous, blue material with gold-trimmed cuffs.

I nodded. "I suppose I am. Tea?"

Her eyes flicked to the low ceiling as she considered the question. "No. I only consume foods sourced by my provider."

A faint seam followed the line of her jaw where a new dermal layer had been grown in with replicated scrub-cells. She was oriental, with lifted eyelids and perma-red lips. Her face was lit by purple-tinted irises, made more striking by double-length lashes and the blazing blue of her hair.

"You're looking at my nose," she touched the tip as if checking to see if it were still there. "It's in transition, I'm in the middle of juving treatments, having it resculpted by non-invasive cartilage modification. I wouldn't have come, but it's been a long wait for this appointment—getting a visitor's pass, the security clearances and all."

'I'm in no position to comment on appearances."

She looked into my creased pouch of a face, frowned, blinked, looked away. "Tell me, why do they call you confined people DATCHOs? I mean, I know the "DAT" bit is "Denied Access to Technology', but the other part?"

"Criminal Holding Order." I noticed the morning chorus had started—shouts, jeers and bursts of song, underscored with the continuous pound of footsteps on the lower walkway.

She nodded. "Your accent, Canadian?"

"English."

"Yeah-huh. Forgive me, but I get this energy from you, like you're holding some hurt." She touched her sternum. "The Cosmique are allied to the Adroit lifestyle brand. Our provider's optimizers and software enhance higher awareness. I'm no natural psychic like yourself, but I *am* developed."

She moved her palm, placed it on top of the other on the table. "It's hard for me to remain open here. This place, it's scary, so primitive. The criminals wandering freely around the communal areas. How do you survive among these people?"

"I am to a great extent self-sufficient. Only visitors with a pre-booked pass and ward guards can access this building. You've recently moved house?"

She had a sort of rootless look about her. Tiny fibers of fake hemp lingered on the toes of her boots from a new floor covering. Her long lashes flittered while she processed the information.

"'Ya–huh, hey, you're good. I'm newly installed in the GoLightly Building, north end of Lake side Drive. That's so valid. What else do you know?"

I gave her my astute look. "One never can know enough and to know enough is too much to bear." I'd long stopped wondering at my capacity for the fatuous phrase, but it seemed to impress. She swallowed. "The stuff they say about you. Is it true? That you've forgone food? That you live only on chi, on pure energy?"

My stomach answered with a long gurgle of hunger. I'd slept when I should have been preparing breakfast. "It's a question of correct breathing."

"Wow. That's so real. My network's files suggest you've been imprisoned on faked-up charges, 'cause you kept curing people without drugs or immune programming. Were the medical providers out to get you?"

God's teeth, if only.

"Indeed so," I said, my smile thin as a blade.

"Ya-huh. Now, I know you don't guarantee any kind of cure or anything. But I've been drawn to come. The moon's in my sign, Leo. I have a trine conjunct Pluto, currently retrograde, so some kind of metamorphosis is imminent. It's my leg, of course and also I'd like a brief reading, not a complete life story or anything."

Jeez, another needy-me. I swallowed a groan and picked up the magnifying glass. She silently presented her hands, splaying the fingers wide. Minute cracks covered the fingertips; the palmer lines were faint, as if partially erased. The hands are traitors to anti-ageing treatments, even clone grafting doesn't hide the signs. She watched me press the loose, deflated skin at the thumb ball, her pupils bloated by ability-augmenting drugs.

"What sort of hands do I have?"

I pursed my lips, affected a wistful tone. "Refined hands of extreme sensitivity. Obviously a creative spirit."

Dimples appeared in her cheeks. "Venus in Aquarius with Jupiter ascendant. I feel life itself is an art form, I try to live creatively."

I nodded, waiting for inspiration but there was no spark, nothing in my head but ashes.

Her eyebrows lifted fractionally. "What else?"

"How old are you?"

She lurched back as if scalded, knocking over the little photo of Alvina in the center of the table. She frowned, tried to speak, gulped, squeezed her lips together, tried again. "That's just so *male*," she hissed. "That kind of testosterone-fuelled, comparative-destructive thinking went out with The Changes. The Goddess rules now."

"Forgive me. I wouldn't ask unless I needed to know."

"Forty-one," she lied feebly, staring fixedly and dropping her bottom lip in a blatant give-away. "And it's disgusting of you to ask."

"Your true age would be useful..."

"Have you no respect?" She stood awkwardly, bumping her head against one of the shelves. "Generational stereotyping is illegal."

"I need to ascertain the time values on your palm lines." My voice sounded scratchy and plaintive.

She stuck out her chin defensively. "It's sickening to be valued in chronological terms."

"So. Fifty eight?"

She shut her eyes for a second, and then lurched back to the table. Her fingers found the pearl droplet at her ear. She touched the tiny lens with her index finger. There was grace and vulnerability in the gesture as she exposed the fine line of her neck. She leaned closer and whispered, "Sixty-one."

"I see."

"Well into middle-youth."

"I don't know," I said as brightly as I could, "sixty, they say, is the new thirty."

Her nostril sluices shut. "I'm on my fourth skin re-growth program. When they've been scrubbed of defective DNA enough times the cells start to lose telomeres and suffer replication errors. With my leg needing gene-specific drugs and endless auto-immune bolstering, my problems are financial as well as physical." She sat back down, drew a long, even breath, touched the tabletop gingerly with both hands. "Is it true that you're over a hundred years old?"

I brought my hand to my forehead, covered my eyes. How sick I was of these myths. "One hundred and nine, actually." I dropped my hand. "It's a question of purification."

"Wow. Even mega-rich rejuveniles barely make it that long. And you've had no immune programming? You're unmodified?"

"Yes." I offered my most indulgent smile with this rare truth. "Death and disease are an insult to the American way of life. They're so anti-aspirational."

She hesitated for a moment, gave me a peevish look. "You're a true holy man. Please, Shaman, use your powers, help me."

Her right, shriveled foot was planted in a hole in the carpet. I got a glimmer in that moment: footprints, sandy soil, movement; a roof garden with a little swing; delicate hands pushing a child back and forth; water falling somewhere. "You're thinking of having a child, a boy child. You're planning to move again... let's see, north, somewhere cooler ... Seattle, I think."

It was there, so I said it. Without pre-thought, chink, wink, the ejaculated truth. Awake at last.

She leaned forwards so our odd noses were almost touching. "That's totally cosmic. In this world of imitations, you're the real thing. The child, yeah it's what I want." She brought her hands together, entwined her fingers. "Tell me, when will this all happen, the baby, the move and everything?"

"Hmm," I tried to shrug, but my shoulders were solid, as if waiting for a strike. "Nothing is cast in stone. If you believe in that future enough, then it will be yours. Nothing is more powerful than belief."

"Ya-huh." Her eyes met mine. "There's a lot of karma around the mother issue. I still have my menses of course. But my leg, it's Ebola B. The retrovirus process caused some auto-immune problem. It destroyed the nerves in my lower spine. They managed to get some re-growth going but it failed in this leg."

We both looked down at the leg accusingly.

"I don't feel it's part of my karma to suffer this," she said.

"Take off your shoes," I intoned gently, "sit in the healing chair and close your eyes."

As I wriggled my feet into rubber-soled, insulated slippers, she got into the chair, smiling beatifically like a martyred saint. "I know you can help me," she said. "By the pale goddess, I know you can."

I checked the ward guard wasn't snooping around outside. Said a silent prayer that this wasn't the day I got found out. Then I stood behind and slightly to the side of her, so the earring-lens couldn't see me. Using the old bath salts dispenser, I "anointed" her with perfumed water. She shuddered as the droplets fell on her face. I made sure plenty of water dribbled over the metal plate at her feet to draw the current, keeping my own feet dry. I found the tiny transformer lever on the chair leg with my foot. I spoke reverently. "The power of spirit moves through you, child. Open your heart to receive."

Touching her withered leg, I pushed the switch, upping the current as far as it would go. The hidden battery gurgled beneath the floorboards. She tensed with the surge, stretching her toes downwards. "Holy mother. I can feel it!" Her eyes bounced, opened wide.

"Close your eyes," I said. "Relax." She reluctantly squeezed them shut. "There, there, that's it. What is sundered shall be joined. All shall be well and all manner of things shall be well."

Her foot began to quiver, the toes splayed out, then her leg joined in. Too much current. I moderated it quickly.

"Gaaah!"

"Heal your child, Great Spirit; let her receive your blessing."

"I... I, by the... Oh, heaven's light."

I let her ride the current for a moment longer, then bumped the switch and walked around the chair to face her. As I came close, her head fell forward, her forehead hitting my chest with a thud.

"Thank you..." The voice came from somewhere deep inside her. "Thank you, thank you."

Dampness, tears on my shirt.

"Incredible." She raised her head, looked around as if seeing everything anew. "Unbelievable, the power, it was like an electric shock, like being hit by lightening. I knew you'd do it. I knew."

I tried out my authoritative voice. "Your faith has cured you, child. Walk!"

She stood confidently and strode around the close confines of the room. Her leg faltered once or twice, but her walk was practically normal. I should have been glad, the joyous look on her face. But I felt only an urgent need to be alone as soon as possible.

She looked beyond my head to some far place and spoke in a child's voice. "Are there words you could give me?"

"Words?"

"A personal mantra, you know, for my meditations. To help me develop, to give thanks."

Jeez. "Oh. Ah, yes. 'I'll follow my heart when I find it.'"

"This will help?"

"Yes, yes. All will be well. When you're ready to... the donation box is just by the door, there's no obligation. I won't know what or whether you gave. It won't be emptied till the week's end."

She nodded stupidly, blinked and nodded again.

"It's over?"

"Yes."

I squatted down, crossed my legs, closed my eyes, and pretended to meditate. I heard her breathing close, as if she'd bent near my face. Then a groan, footsteps, a sigh. The donation box lid clacked, a knock sounded on the door, the rattle and squeal as the door was unlocked, opened and closed.

I heard her and the guard's footsteps moving down the walkway. I made myself hold back, counted four minutes in my head, till they would have descended the stairwell and left the building. Then I jumped up and rushed over to the box.

Three fifties and a twenty! One hundred and seventy dollars, more than generous. How foolish my intuitions. It was going to be a good day after all. Now, time to climb the ladder to the roof, where my string-and-glass hydroponic grow-dome waited. Nothing but the scent of leaf and the feel of burgeoning life; it would calm my shredded nerves. The sprouting barley would be drying out and the beans...

I yanked open the door and stood transfixed in a surge of heat and sound. Heavy footsteps were pounding up the steps.

THREE

TWO MEN EMERGED FROM THE STAIRWELL—NOT inmates. They had mock-silk suits, muscle-aid torsos and faces glistening with new flesh. One was tall with multicolored stripes of stubble across his skull, the other medium height with a nude scalp and a wiry beard like his head was on upside-down. They bore blazing bindis in the middle of their foreheads.

With clumsy hands, I slammed the door, secured the lock, stood back.

The slick-skulled one yanked at the door handle, his pebble-like knuckles clonking against the glass. "Open it," he ordered.

"No. I don't think so," I said, wondering how they got through the ground-level door without pass or escort. I dragged the curtain across the door. Let them disappear, be gone, vanish, I wanted none of them. The glass was bullet-proof, bomb-proof, DATCHO proof. I'd sit tight and wait it out.

Acrid blue smoke swirled around the room and in one grinding crunch both door and curtain were hauled aside. Where the lock used to be was but a blackened hole dribbling bubbles of liquefied metal.

Snatching the magnifying glass from the table top, I pointed the handle at them, stretching myself to full height. "I'm armed with a stun device and will defend myself if necessary!"

"Don't get yourself excited. It'll set your shackle off," crooned the rainbow-haired one, a wad of muscle slung around his shoulders like a lifebelt. Their bulk filled the room, the tall one's head almost touching the ceiling. They ignored my pointing fist, took an elbow each and lifted me easily into the healing chair. It was alarming to be handled, so long since I'd been touched by anyone.

"Who are you?" I said, swallowing spasms of fright.

The one with multi-hued hair said, "You're Zachary Crowe?" his forehead jewel burned a deep yellow, his purple pupils iridescent.

"No, I'm David Melbury, inmate number three, three, nine, eight, seven, two. I demand to know who the hell you are." I said this with clenched, furious sincerity. They exchanged looks.

"It's not him," said slick-scalp.

Rainbow-head picked up the magnifying glass from the table. "Wait."

He barged around the cell-room. He pulled books from shelves, wrenched open drawers, spilled potted herbs, threw everything to the floor.

Finally he found a paper transfer-request form with my name on it. "It's him. We got him all right."

"What do you want?" I said.

"Relax." His smile a cold-eyed baring of teeth. "We bring you a pearl beyond price. Listen." He curled his hand around his ear. "Liberty is calling."

"Liberty?" An express train clattered through my brain, flashes of faces, names, escape plans plotted and put aside. I remembered a slot-eyed, stick-limbed Bliss addict named Cleo, years back, selling me a tale of connections and favors. Only five thousand dollars and I'd walk free. I gave her a couple of hundred and she promptly disappeared. That was what? Four years ago. Could it be? Could it possibly be?

"You've been sent by Cleo?"

The men exchanged glances again.

"Cleo. Yep, Cleo. She arranged everything," Rainbow-head said, too glibly. "Rejoice! You're going outside."

Outside? Meaning outside the zone? I thought of the display by the fence, the names of the dead and the means of their escape attempt: tunnelers, flyers, ID fakers; they'd all been fried. I tried to grip my solar plexus, to breathe deep and dissipate the panic.

Suddenly, I didn't want to escape. It was impossible. I belonged in the zone with the primitive, the ravaged, the unredeemed.

"We'll all get zapped," I said. "Monitors are thicker than mosquitoes here, no one's ever escaped. You'll be DATCHOs yourselves any sec..."

The slick-skulled one who'd hardly spoken pursed his over-plumped lips in concentration as he blasted a spray of Bliss in my face. I glimpsed the yellow lotus-flower label, the red nozzle and in one long hiss I was melting in euphoric tenderness.

How beautiful they were, these glossy Adonises. Rainbow-head's eyes were like cracked violet ice. My leg was lifted upwards, straightened, stretched out. They bent over it, heads almost touching, examining the shackle like doctors scrutinizing an injury.

"It's okay, take it easy."

Of course it was okay. What a young voice of green sap and youthful mastery. Everything was A-OK easy. I nodded benignly, kept nodding as shimmies of sheer luxury rolled down my neck.

Slick-skull unbuttoned the front of his suit and revealed a slab of belly pork strapped around his middle. In the far-out state I was in, strange things came to pass, things not normally possible. Such resource-inefficient food I believed had died in The Changes, with cow's milk and ocean-born fish.

"No bacon sandwich for me." My voice seemed to echo. "I'm a vegan."

But when the meat was peeled away, taped around the sculpted torso were an array of goodies: bundled photon tubes, a pliable paper-thin display screen, an input device. The meat would fool the scanners of course, a layer of false flesh. There was ingenuity here, planning and method. These people were serious.

They taped the screen to the wall, wired up the tubes and input unit, connecting both to the motion battery pack under the lapel of Slick-skull's jacket. The raised swirls on his sleeves seemed to ripple and flow like oil. Within seconds, multiple maggoty lines of data wriggled across the screen while the crystals within the tubes glimmered to life. As the miracle unfolded, as a virtual keyboard of green light was illuminated on the tabletop and his fingers danced over it, my limbs oozed languorously.

Ha, such folly, I thought, *no data stream here.* But as each objection floated in my head it sank, subjugated by another trick. A green balloon was inflated from a little canister, lighter than air, light as my head. A gold fiber-optic wire was hitched to it with a little hook; they forced open the window and out it went. It wanted to be free, bobbing eagerly skywards. It had never occurred to me that up there the photon beams might still thrumming with data above the jamming mechanisms of the zone.

Now the screen had my name on it. "Segregation criminal code 5. Inmate 339872 Crowe, Zachary. Full privileges. Offenses: (a) Attempted murder of a national guardsman. (b) Accessory to multiple hacking attempts into forbidden systems (c) Intrusion into secure government quarantine area. (d) Illegal overstay in the U.S. (e) Fraudulent assumption of U.S. citizenship."

I wanted to point out that the guardsman was trying to kill me; anyone would've done what I did. But it didn't really seem to matter. I was dangling in empty air, nothing below but light years of space. At every breath I unfurled like a flag.

A well-manicured hand carefully wrapped my ankle in silver paper. Slick-skull's face was green in the screen's light as he caressed the virtual keys. Fountains of deranged digits poured out, engaging the stream in its intimate song.

A silvery chemical was poured onto the shackle. *Liquid fire,* I thought, *this must be what they used on the door.* I could smell flesh burning and something acrid, like ammonia. There was no pain. My palm was stretched out and my fingerprints appeared, all ten of them on the screen, then my eye was reflected there, huge and pulsating, like a planet. The eye froze. My DNA was scanned. This was real, this alchemy. Maybe I'd get out! *Oh God, Great Spirit please save me, this is the day, let there be light, let me be free, imagine!* But I couldn't imagine and the hope was gone in another blast of spray and black night.

❧

"You don't want to come to the shops? It's okay. That way I can take my time, I promised to stop by at Nancy's place."

Alvina had her back to me as she spoke. Beyond her shoulder, the kitchen window awash with light from a sky almost navy blue, shot through with purple and red. Even with everything sealed, there was a pervasive smell of sulphur, like old cinders. I spoke to her mass of black curls. "It already seems years since we've seen white puffball clouds and blue sky."

She turned from the window, her large, pale forehead like a wall. "It's only been three months. The Ecological Science Institute says it'll be over fifty years before the atmosphere clears and we'll see the sun again."

I put my cold hand on her warm shoulder. "Mister Daedelus from over the road says they've decided on a name for this eco-collapse or whatever the hell it is. The Changes. Like it's a global menopause or something.

She sighed. "These new diseases, the riots, the shortages. Maybe it's the end of the world, a divine punishment or something."

"I'd better come with you," I said, "just in case."

She pressed herself against me, her hair whispering over my cheek. "It's fine, I'll manage. It'll give me space to think. I got my auto-alarm and portal. Anyway, all the looters have been locked up. They're building new no-tech zones to keep the bad people in."

"Yeah. I suppose I could stay put and brew up another infusion. I could distil the last of my Chinese herbs. Got to keep in good shape, there's no chance they're gonna give me immune boosters with my ID."

"You should have got yourself authenticated with a proper citizenship when you had the chance. I couldn't bear it if you got ill. I couldn't bear..." She pulled back, shaking her head, covering her face with her hands.

"I'll be fine," I said, holding her by the elbows. "Have you ever known me to be sick? I'll make my own medicine like always. Anyway, I got good genes."

She took her hands away from her face. How tired she looked. "You're right. I hope you're right. I hope... I don't know anything anymore."

Since the curfew and emergency control laws we'd been more or less confined to the house. There'd been weeks of waiting—for the power to be switched on, for water, for food rations. We were still waiting for the next raft of her inoculations. I thought of the luxury of ticking silence, solitude. "Keep your portal linked in," I said. "Okay? Then I can check up on you."

She gave me a wry look. "I'll be good. You've got to worry about yourself for a change." She looked beyond me at the distilling apparatus I'd built from bits from an old washing machine. "You and your amazing contraptions. You're much happier when you're doing something. I'll be back in a couple of hours."

The gap between her two front teeth made her smile roguish. I didn't argue. She needed space, movement. It would be fine.

She grabbed the shopping bag she always used, the one with an illuminated tomato on the back. The image was dying, the light diodes fading with wear. "Bye, angel."

"Love you."

Only after she'd gone did I realize we hadn't kissed. We would always kiss on parting. It was a thing with us, a ritual; but not this time. The door's soft click finished my life with Alvina. She vanished from the earth like she'd never drawn breath.

FOUR

PAIN. I WAS BACK IN 3D LIFE AND IT HURT. THROBBING temples, eyes boiled in the stove of my skull. My leg was stretched straight, my ankle, pink and bloated with the last inch of trouser leg burned off. The shackle was gone.

Slick-skull's face came into close-up, precision-cut grooves in his eyebrows, a heart of pink pigmented skin on his left nostril.

"Overdid the chemistry a little. You okay?"

"Who are you?"

"Name's Josh." He pointed to the one with hair who was carefully cutting through the antennae wire. "That there's AT. Don't think we've had the pleasure."

He offered his hand. Hairless wrists from testosterone neutralizers. Palm hot and hard. I sensed physical power, impatience. "Why are you doing this? Remote sensors can pick up photon flow, you're taking an appalling chance."

"And you're whinging about it?"

"'I'm not... ungrateful, it's just..."

The split-open shackle lying on the floor. I felt the loss of it. It had been part of me for so long.

"I changed the master codas," said Josh, standing. "You're Mick Tarn as of now—a visitor on a temporary pass. Your new ID will hold long enough to get you through the gate. We got to go, this instant."

AT stood waiting by the door while I changed my pants, pulled on shoes, donned the old white jacket with big lapels like this was all normal, like I was taking a walk. No one could change the master codas. If it were this easy, the whole security network would break down.

I dug out my stash of dollars embedded in the soil of a pot of geraniums. I put nostril filters in, strapped on my ancient wind-up watch. Time couldn't be stopped or slowed down; this was real, it was happening.

Alvina's little framed photo had been knocked to the floor, a lock of her hair in the back. I snatched it, held it to my chest like it was life itself. Josh grabbed my elbow to support me. They thought me feeble, I could use that.

Staggering to the door, forcing a wheeze as I leaned against the door frame. "I'm not strong," I gasped. "Can't hurry."

Over the rooftops in waves of heat, a black speck appeared, getting bigger. I knew immediately what it was, even before the thrum of wings was audible.

The hornet arrived in an instant and hung in the air, its onion-dome head and polished black proboscis only inches from my face. Its minuscule antennae implanted behind the bands of yellow and black, the glint of its grafted-on lens lending it a third, overlarge eye.

"Shit," whispered AT, his forehead crystal turning red. "They've picked up something. Watch your body signs, relax, and remember you're Mick Tarn on a visitor's pass."

As if. With my ruined features and ancient suit I may as well have had "DATCHO" tattooed on my forehead. No one moved as the all-seeing eye buzzed about us carefully, and then it hung in the air above our heads.

AT's hand pressed the small of my back, propelling me through the door and along the walkway towards the stairs. Our footsteps echoed thunderously. The insect trailed behind us, manoeuvring drunkenly, as if its on-board chip hadn't quite mastered the impulses of its minute brain.

The battered street-access security door winked its eye and opened without complaint, obscenities scratched over every inch of it.

We emerged into the communal prison area. Even through filters the wave of hot air was like bad breath—hashish, rotting fruit, home-brewed hooch, horseshit. We were immediately ambushed by another swarm of hornet monitors. We moved in single file—Josh behind and AT ahead. We made for the super-surveyed safety path, the blue-painted strip in the center of the road for visitors only.

I gritted my teeth as I put my foot on the blue area, tensed for the sirens, for the zap beam that would turn my bones to powder. Nothing happened. I took another step and then another with no consequence other than an odd weightlessness in my left leg, relieved of the shackle. The distance quickly opened up between me and my cell block. Oily streamers slithered behind my eyelids.

The noise was deafening as we skirted cell blocks and passed by the mass of mangled humanity on the sidewalks. Wrinkled faces, bad dentistry and balding heads marked each their length of sentence estranged from cosmetic enhancement. I cowered as they ogled me on the safety strip. Five years since I'd mixed with the general prison population. I was a bulging artery in a vat of vampires.

Yellow-eyed lookouts and gibbering derelicts crouched in doorways, glass crunched underfoot. Acoustic music banged out from bars. Crudely-painted boards advertised all manner of toxins unavailable on the outside: potato-sticks boiled in the fat of some dead creature, sugar-based ice cream, tobacco. Strung across the street above our heads a ragged banner, "Raging bull—shots—20 dollar." A dancing bull triumphantly held a glass of red fluid aloft, tottering on two delicate hooves.

On walls and cell blocks the gang emblems were carved. Along side-streets, feral-faced men loitered, yellow t-shirted Tigers, black armband-wearing Disciples and other gangs I failed to recognize. The acrid air twitched with tension.

We marched towards the eastern gate, down Park Street, deep into the clanging chaos of hell. Our movements were marked by our posse of flying bugs and a battery of monitors that studded walls, street-posts and buildings. Through Wells and Lincoln we marched, through the whole length of the zone.

A female inmate with a shock of red hair and stitches painted across her lips squealed as we strode by, "Hey, ain't you the shaman guy? Don'cha know that strip's for visitors only? Who you tryin' to piss on?" Her voice died in the din. On the front of her T-shirt, the words "Gagged, tagged, zone hag."

"This is suicide," I shouted to AT's hindquarters. "A ward guard's got to walk visitors in and out. They'll recognize me immediately at the gate. We've got to go back!"

AT stopped dead. My forehead smacked against the wall of his back. He turned, cheeks muscular hollows, eyes like spikes.

"Wait up," he said over my head.

"Whassup?" Josh stuttered to a stop.

AT's hair seemed to bristle in alarm. "He's panicking. He's gonna give us away."

"Too late," Josh said. "Keep going to the gate. It's all arranged. It'll be okay."

As they hesitated, I stepped off the blue strip, sprinted across the street and dodged around a corner. A line of jeering Disciples were too slow as I squirmed through them and around a trio of hawk-faced hookers. I kept going, crouching low through an alley to huddle in a piss-reeking doorway.

I kept my back to the street as slurry-voiced lowbrows lumbered by. Fear spread in a stain of sweat down my shirtfront. I dug my nails into my palms, fought to work things out. I had cash. I'd wait for five minutes then try and bribe a couple of meatheads to escort me back to my cell block.

The door before me opened and I was gawking at the rusted point of an arrowhead. It was stretched back from a crude bow made of strips of bound wood. Behind the bow was a collapsed face with all the front teeth missing.

Out the corner of my eye shadows moved closer.

Pucker-face looked delighted, like it was his birthday. "Here, chicky-chicky. Come you inna 'ere,'" he grinned, gray gums behind obscene wet lips.

From the darkness behind the door, a tattooed hand snaked out and clutched the lapel of my jacket. As I was dragged forward, I clung to the doorposts, uttering a tiny cry of alarm. A heavy forearm appeared around my middle and began hauling me backward, bending me in half. Pucker-face's features crumpled, my lapel was released, unseen hands forced the door shut.

Josh carried me bodily through a gang of gloating onlookers and back to the blue strip where AT waited. "Don't try it, dipshit. You'll get through. There's no going back now."

This nightmare I knew would end at the exit-gate screen. It performed hundreds of checks: ID authentication, brain scan, body scent, facial recognition, deep tissue DNA. Thousands of DNA particles were shedding from my skin every second. No one had ever escaped. I knew I could signal the monitors, call out for a ward guard, tell them I was a DATCHO. Maybe they wouldn't kill me, maybe just take away my privileges, put me back on the street. But I knew I wouldn't. I couldn't go through it all again. All those years of guile, of second-guessing the shifting sands of gang hierarchy, of fear in the night. Over to our right, the barrier, pylons of filament punctured the sky and between them a grid of vibrating sensa-wire. We followed the barrier, buzzed constantly by our host of hornets and already the main gate was in sight. Pillars of steel curved gently outwards forming the giant "O" of the exit shutter.

Involuntarily, my feet stopped when I saw the cluster of blue-sheathed ward guards waiting by the screen gate.

"C'mon!" Josh's fist in my back.

I took it all in, the puce blotch of obscured sun, distant vultures spiralling in a vortex of heat, the orange stained sidewalk scrawled with tribal markings like runes. I felt my final moments falling away. The monitors closed in to a "V" formation as a ward guard approached.

"Wait!"

The guard wore ludicrous amounts of body armor, the blue plates overstating the curves of her body like some fetishist's idea of a mechanized Venus. Her elbow creaked as she put her hand on my shoulder.

I brought my hand up, pinching the bridge of my nose as she scanned me with lupe-sheathed eyes. I heaved hard at the air, trying to drag down the speed of my maddened pulse. When I glanced into the polished black face I searched vainly for the eyes behind the blue-tinted lenses. Those spex could sample DNA from a hundred feet, could input monitor feeds, read my body language, and, in particular, smell bullshit, with lie-detecting hardware built in. Her voice was surprisingly soft.

"You people are in trouble. Your movement patterns display erratic configurations. You haven't followed normal procedure and you aren't accompanied by a ward guard. I'm extremely concerned."

"We're leaving," Josh barked uselessly behind me.

I kept my hand over the middle of my face. She was so tall I could see the honeycomb air filters in her nostrils. She bore the scent of something oily and dark, like graphite. "I haven't done anything wrong," I said with an edge of apology. "These people are responsible. I'm just trying to stay out of trouble."

Her expressionless visage turned to AT. "Anthony Taldori, why did you tell your escort you would remain for three hours, when you actually stayed for only twenty-five minutes? What was the purpose of your visit to block E?'

"Ah, I had an argument with my proposed inmate...The guy I was visiting wasn't in his cell. I was kinda lost."

That was *three* reasons and clearly crap, but it didn't stop Josh adding, "That's correct."

Her blue-glazed gaze returned to me. "Why did you run off the safety strip?"

I said nothing, rubbed my nose as if to wipe its stain away. I must have looked the shiftiest shyster in the zone.

"I need to cross reference your signs with facial recognition," she said. "Take your hand away."

Hot prickles ran over my cheeks, a thunderous pulse in my ears. My ankle throbbed. How unexceptional these last moments, no transcendental insights, no divine visions. Just the mundane sensations of the body.

"We got passes, we're within the law," Josh was getting agitated, panting heavily, his brow blinking red.

Data fluttered briefly in the blue lupes. She knocked my hand away, grabbed my chin and wrenched my face up, inhaling sharply as she saw the birthmark, the ravaged skin. A full minute passed while more data blinked under her brow.

Now.

She hesitated.

"Why didn't you explain yourself earlier, Mister Tarn?"

Mister Tarn. Maybe the trick was still holding.

Instinctively I repressed the lie give-aways—any exaggerated gestures, blinking, shuffling feet. I'm Mick Tarn, I told myself, a putty-faced, personal lifestyle consultant, from Chicagoland. I love shoes, blues music and near-milk coffee.

"I don't know what my situation is..."

"Fascists!" Josh leaned forwards and rapped his knuckles on the seam around her armored shoulder. "You think all men are criminals? You think you can do with us what you like? We're not DATCHOs!"

Her arm flicked up like a signal, catching Josh under the jaw, knocking him backwards.

"Josh Christos. Your recent activity patterns are suspicious and your words of dubious verity. Both of you are detained here for examination. You." She brought her hand back to my shoulder, grip like a grape-press. "What is your relationship with these people?"

I tried to stay light, like this wasn't happening, like I wasn't about to become dust. "They're friends, sort of, they're here looking for a healer."

She pulled off her helmet and became human. Her ebony face beautiful in an average sort of way but her furious eyes and the emotion in her tight jaw made her quite stunning. She scratched knotty fingers through the silver stubble of her scalp and turned to Josh.

"You know what the DATCHOs call you people? 'Popeyes.' You get a pass to 'broaden your knowledge of human difference' or for 'inspiration for artistic projects' but you're just rubbernecks. This zone is dangerous, inhabited by violent and unstable elements. It's not a theme park or a place to seek a quack cure off some faker. You will be subject to a full data trail analysis and security code check. You have, of course, the right to appeal, or to consult a legal team. Transgression code fifty-four. Do you wish to dispute this ruling?"

"Yes. No. Go ahead," said AT looking as if he were about to explode.

From the freeway came a whine of distant traffic like the cry of some dying creature. The scene—guards, gate, graffiti-daubed houses—all melted into a lake of fire.

She looked at me and pointed a finger at the gate with a kind of violence, "You. Go."

Josh shouldered his way between us.

"Not you." Up came the barrier-like arm again, blocking Josh's path. "His speech, scent and body sign patterns run true. Yours do not. I told you, you and your accomplice are detained here while monitor and data logs are examined."

A similarly armored male ward walked over, ushering me to follow. I tried to slow the ticking bomb of my heart, to mimic the serene stroll of a visitor. I was in the space between breaths. I couldn't keep up, the man's stride was for a world on a larger scale, one I'd never get the measure of. How come everyone was so damned big? I used to consider myself tall. Now the world was full of giants. My time had come and gone.

"Hurry." There were two of them now, waving me to the screening gate. They watched me approach the screen. Red lettering danced in the air.

DATCHO ZONE GATE EAST.
PASSES MUST BE VALIDATED
BEFORE ENTRY AND EXIT.
EXCEEDING YOUR PASS TIME
WILL INCUR A PENALTY
CHARGE—MINIMUM 900 DOLLARS.
CRIMINAL CODE 46 APPLIES.
INMATES: IF YOU ATTEMPT
TO PASS THROUGH THIS SCREEN
YOU WILL DIE.

A skull with crossbones leered obscenely. Hair-fine lasers pulsed from post to post, uttering a faint hum. A silver harp, singing a death song. Had I spun out my days to end it all like this? The beams crackled with excitement, bounced outwards to find me. I saw in the spray of phosphorescent light, the moment when I brought the long night of incarceration upon myself.

"'Alvina," I cried. "The waiting is over. I'm coming to join you."

❧

Time to act, no more waiting. Fifteen deranged days and no sign of Alvina. I stalked the night, cold, toxic air in my lungs, and it felt good. I'd tried everything and now there was no option but this.

The previous day I'd been in the garage of a ranch house in Halden, where a nervy young hacker by the name of Earl had supplied a possibility that burgeoned into certainty in the hothouse of my brain. Earl's garage throbbed with screens, fiber optics and gadgetry like a mad scientist's in a bad 2D movie. Earl's frankfurter fingers danced over his keyboard.

"If she's out there, dude, I'll find her."

But Earl found nothing. Eight hours of scrubbing data and—just like the police—he'd found no trace, no transactions, no security monitors or faze ads reflected her passage on the earth.

"Hey, wait a minute. You checked the quarantine center at Bakersfield?" Red veins in Earl's eyes were enlarged by old-style spectacles.

"I called every quarantine center in the country."

"Yeah, but have you been out there and looked? On the day she was headed for the Wal-Mart, there was a virus outbreak, right? They shipped all the locals from the outbreak there and some of 'em still ain't come back. Just 'cause she don't show

on the records don't mean she's not in there. Maybe they're usin' people for donor milking or something. There's things going on, man. Plasma stocks are low, there's a donor organ shortage, a stem-cell famine. Word is, the military has gotten control the donor system, usin' it for their own personnel 'cause there's a war coming. It's the Chinese that started The Changes, you know that? They put a bomb in that volcano that started it off."

He switched the computer off, sat on the fender of his pick-up. "Friend of mine, Dave Adams, lives out of Sleaford, he was in there at Bakersfield, told me folks are locked in a kind of pressure chamber, like divers with that thing they get, the bends ain't it? They speak in bubbles. No one can go near 'em. What if she's in there?"

Waiting had been a kind of dying, every nerve, every feeling closed against the awful certainty of loss. Now a slow burn of resolve warmed me. Alvina at thirty-six was in vibrant health. She hadn't even considered enhancements. They wanted her. She was there, in the quarantine center. People were shunted there compulsorily if they'd been within a hundred yards of an outbreak.

Another tar-black night. No moon nor stars lit the velvet dark, the sky had fallen. Bolt cutters in my hand, carving a hole in the fence for my tight- wound torso. How wonderful it was at last to do something. Once I was in, they couldn't let me out. They'd quarantine me, but who cared? As long as I was with Alvina, I'd survive.

The crunch of gravel loud in the cold air. Something rustled in the bushes. I walked for what seemed like miles, making for the lights ahead. I blundered into a low fence of razor wire that snagged me in a spiteful embrace. Cursing and cutting through, I knew I was making too much noise but didn't care. An unearthly hum emanated from a cluster of squat buildings lit by sickly yellow lights. Insulated pipes ran over the roof and down the walls, steam spewed from funnels, doors were double sealed behind transparent flaps. The building itself seemed sick, like an intensive care patient hooked up to tubes and catheters.

An explosion. A roar of pain. Lightning illuminated a face, bulging eyeballs, big teeth. They'd shot me. My right arm hung shattered and useless. I was deaf, acrid smoke in my nostrils, burned skin on my cheek. A hand pushed my head down into the earth, dirt filled my mouth. A shout, muffled spasms in my chest. My left arm flailed and touched something hard. I grasped it, lashed out, turned my head. I could breathe, the pressure gone, heaving lungs. I struck again and again. I pounded away at the uniformed official that kept me from her, from everything good. One by one the searchlights came on, picking out the bloody bolt cutters against the night.

FIVE

MY BLOOD SANG, MY UNDYING BLOOD. THERE WAS more to do. I lived!

I stood swaying on the sidewalk of North Michigan Avenue, shivering from the shutter's cold rays that miraculously, released me with a feeble bleep. The dolts had done it. Incredibly, they'd altered the master codas. I was new made, new named, reborn—a miracle. Mick Tarn. The words strange in my mouth, an abrupt name, someone young, precise, tech-headed. I was someone else, not me.

After crossing the eerily silent no-man's land of warehouses in Union Street, I felt like some long-lost explorer come upon a new civilization. In the over-stuffed zone, everything was crowded together. Here every building, every figure had separateness, the air itself seemed to breathe. There should be flags, crowds, a band. But the news of my liberation reverberated only in the buzz of cicadas.

Three women strutted by, identical skin tones and similar scooped faces, big eyes, long necks, graceful as gazelles, unaffected by the heat. Their conversation mingled with the prattle of other pedestrians as they mumbled into portals, or blathered into blog-files.

"But not my previous life, I was a Navajo then, up in Nova Scotia."

"The bird represents my mother, and the rest of the dream is obvious. He's great, we have a good time. But I don't want to meet him in the flesh..."

Sparse trees lined the sidewalk, some kind of cinnamon leafed, air-resistant hybrid. Vehicles passed on a whisper of air. They'd got uglier—lurid colored, small wheeled, huge windshields and mean little headlight eyes. Opposite me, a dolphin shimmied across the window of Bandera's Fish Restaurant. The building was alive, the walls writhing. Maybe I'm a ghost. Maybe I got atomized after all and this is the otherland.

Down the street other buildings were swathed in quicksilver facades. Suits danced together on the lower floor of Bloomingdale's, cocktail glasses chinked on the wall of Andy's Bar and a line of elephants trampled over the Antiques Mart. A gaggle of brown-toned girls crossed the street towards me, their saris iridescent with color like a flock of hummingbirds. Over to my left, the silo-like Tribune tower stabbed a boiling larva sky so vast it stretched forever.

"Shit!" I sprawled onto the sidewalk, banging my head, grazing my hand. All balance gone, nothing to lock onto, just acres of space. So long since I'd been anywhere that didn't have a damned roof on it. People's eyes snagged on my old-fashioned clothes, my face. My hands found a reassuringly solid trash bin. I used it to pull myself upright. The sky still rocked gently. A mosquito needled the back of my hand, kicking my brain into gear. Get moving, idiot, don't stand about waiting to get arrested.

Walking the avenue, I felt self-conscious, out of shape. My ankle throbbed. The landscape seemed, too, serene, like a stage set. Any second, the scene would freeze, the film would stop, I'd awake back in the zone.

A black creation of a car slinked along the street. Some kind of exotic, gas-guzzler replica, globular headlights, running board, chrome pipes wriggled from under the hood. It slowed and came to rest beside me as if I'd willed it so. The bonnet badge read, "Uniquely created by Josef T. Farango."

A little man had the steering wheel in a two-armed embrace, all angles, bony elbows, sharp face, an orange gemstone twinkled in his brow. This guy didn't look so good, his face fractured with regrowth ridges and purple capillaries. The window shuddered, slid down. The pink tip of the man's tongue flicked in and out like a gecko's.

"You're him ain't ya? You're the one."

I stood mute, not knowing at that moment who the hell I was supposed to be.

The jagged head bobbed in annoyance. "You. You're the one who Josh and AT... they got you out, didn't they?"

A bolt of hope, a flicker of the most incredible, impossible happiness.

"Alvina? Is this anything to do with Alvina?'"

Two folds appeared between his eyebrows. "Who in the... Yeah, Alvina. That's her. That's right."

On the back seat, a can with a yellow "Bliss" logo, a set of chromed handcuffs. His little fists gripped the wheel furiously, the pin-prick pupils were closed against me and I felt a ripple of alarm. This was no divine intervention, these people, this plot. They meant me harm.

His eyes followed mine to the back seat, his tongue testing the air. "Get in!"

I turned and ran. Some hopeful child in me, some romantic idiot, had against all the laws of time, space, science and God, expected Alvina to be waiting. As if this miracle of freedom had undone the chains of logic.

"Get back here, you old retard!" he bawled.

I pushed through perfect, far-away faces, crossed the road in a cacophony of screeching auto-emergency brakes.

Loping headlong down North Michigan, the breath ragged in my chest, water fell, stinging my eyes. It seemed criminal that rain fell on the outside too, even if it were the rainy season. I wasn't ready, not for running, not for liberty, not for the rain. It fell harder. Pinging bullets of yellow-tinged drops rasped my face.

A shop, "Aristos—instant perfection," opened its doors in welcome, the walls ablaze with reels of rainbow polymer. A sales assistant's overwrought jaw dropping slack. Mood spray tainted the air, strangulated music played somewhere close. A dummy wearing a black, layered coat changed shape, chest deflating, shoulders moved together then its arm came up and beckoned with a hand at an impossible angle.

"Hey Mick, you'd look fantastic in this!"

I made for the exit on the opposite side.

The dummy took on my own shape even down to my knobbly knees. Its boiled-egg eyes held mine till I was out into another street, this one quiet. Around a corner, I slipped ahead of a clump of smart-dressed men under umbrellas.

I knew if I didn't act natural I'd set off body-sign surveillance. I turned another corner, wondering how many times I'd been ID'd already. Every retail outlet and ad-sensor sucking in bits of me, broadcasting, storing, sifting. I wouldn't last long. I turned with locked shoulders onto a vehicle-free zone crowded with uncreased faces in vibrant daywear. I needed to merge, to disappear. Rainwater burned my eyes, enraged my raw ankle, soaked my thin suit.

Shop fronts rippled like mirages. My reflection was captured momentarily in a window, a scanky scarecrow in a sodden suit.

I was the loneliest soul on the planet, no one to run to and nothing...

"Joy to you." A tall man in theatrical dress, like an extra in a DHD movie. White cotton shirt buttoned to his round, comically bearded face, big-brimmed hat funneling water. I stuttered to a stop.

"Are you well?" he beamed. "Spiritually fulfilled?"

An Amish, a proto tribe, some kind of Christians, been around for centuries. Weren't they one of the first tribes with their own networks and values? Well, they got competition now.

His circular face was youthful, unmodified. The face of a blameless life. I visualized men bent behind stomping horses, maidens in cotton shifts bearing baskets. The smile seemed to promise renewal, peace, wholesomeness.

"Afraid I've got to run," I said.

He frowned. "Let me help. You seem lost."

"I've been away for some time," I mumbled, moving on.

"Mummy! Mummy! Look at the funny man's nose!" The little girl's own nose wrinkled in disgust. Her elfin mother thrust her umbrella between us.

"Leave us alone!" she said, gripping it fiercely. She looked about twelve.

"It's okay," I said, "I'm harmless."

To my right, violas cranked out Mozart on the wall of a café. Way ahead, between mammoth towers was an edifice of concrete so vast and ugly it could only be the lake front.

A police siren sent a tremor down my backbone, spurred me onward. Maybe up there by the water there'd be no monitoring. I crossed streams of spray-drenched traffic, leap-frogging islands of raised asphalt where lampposts bore buzzing insect traps. Mosquitoes swarmed around them like devotees sacrificing themselves on an altar.

I saw a gap in the barrier wall where steps had been cut.

As I climbed the steps the rain eased and then stopped. The steps uttered innumerable warnings about invalidated health insurance as I went up. From the top, the sight was heart-stopping. Lake Superior lay prostrate, the color of weak tea, twitching its surface lazily to the far horizon. Above it the sky was a vast pink cauldron in which gold clouds were burning. A line of flamingos glided just above the water. The faintest of broiling breezes flapped at the lapels of my steaming jacket, cooking my neck.

I looked back in the other direction, at traffic moving in shimmies of heat under arcs of floating ad frames. Who'd give me shelter? I sat against the dyke wall, hidden from the road. I needed a network, a helpful companion, but didn't have a friend in the world. I'd been a loner so long; the veil of the seer had kept all human company at bay. Only Alvina had got close and look where that had brought me. Love was a disease, a sickness. You could put up walls, close yourself against it. But once love had singled you out, there was no defence...

♣

My backside was perched on the edge of a stool in a massive, ice-cool trailer in the desert of New Mexico. The walls were festooned with clothes, wrapped in cellophane packaging like presents. A part-eaten salad on the table, tomatoes sculpted into flower heads.

"I've been there with the relationships thing and now I avoid the commitment-trap process." Go-A-Junior pulled her famous overlong gash of a mouth into a smile. Her palm small and cool in my own.

"Well," I said, "if you come back to the broken life line, what it means is that you've never felt secure. You've never felt anyone could love you for yourself."

She twitched on the stool. Like all actresses, she was dosed with fat-reducing Redox and had the bony, muscular body of a racehorse. "It's kinda odd. I knew you were going to say that about my lifeline." She lit a no-harm cigarette. Took a puff and stubbed it out. "I mean, I didn't know I already knew until you said it."

"Let's talk about your extraordinary talent," I said.

Afterwards, as I emerged into the baking oven of the desert, I was thinking about celebrity. The sheer desperation of their lives, crammed on that narrow ledge of fame, never knowing how long they could hold on because they had no idea how they got there.

A woman ran up with a clipboard. She had golden skin and an amazing black bush of hair. It was as if I knew her already from some distant memory.

"How is the divine one?" she said. Her lips were marked with minute kissable crinkles. Amongst the anxious faces, she burst from her skin, spurting an aura of vitality.

"In a state of grace," I said. "She'll be ready to start shooting again soon."

"You must be quite something for her to send her private jet."

"Yeah, it's a long way to the Holy Land."

Her laughter was ready, like she just needed an excuse. Her lusty, life-giving laughter filled me with longing. I was sure that if she were in my life my happiness could make the desert bloom.

But she was talking again. "Alvina's the name. Guess you don't have enough time to read my palm too? The car won't be taking you back to the airport for another hour or so. But hey, it's okay. I mean you probably don't do these things without an appointment ..."

A torrent of words tripped over my tongue—I wanted to flatter, amuse, inveigle, but I'd said what I was thinking before I remembered who I was. "If it means spending time with you, I'll do anything."

⚜

I lingered by the water till I was cooked in my own sweat and near-blinded by the lake's glare. As I negotiated my way back across the road, a smear of black caught my eye. A long limo prowled in a phalanx of slow-moving cars. The chromed fake exhausts seemed to writhe, the bulging lights like all-seeing eyeballs. It was the gas-guzzler replica. The black shape trembled impatiently, jerking each time it moved off.

I lowered my head, turned to the glossy wooze of warped glass fronting Mitzi's café. A stainless-steel cow stood vacuuming up bluegrass mulch from a rolling feed tube. The udders oozed multifarious flavored milks through glass tubes. A genie ad confided "One hundred percent natural process."

Fumbling in my pocket, my fingers found my cash wad. At least I had money. What to do? The cafe promised refuge, a cool drink, a place to plot my next move. But I'd leave purchase and preference information. I'd be probed, measured, marked. Oh for a plan, a map, a course of action. The ward guards would soon find me missing and I'd be meat.

As I stood there, blinking away the blur in my eyes, pedestrians gave me a wide berth, drilling me with their stares. Best to keep walking, I reasoned. If I followed the lake side north, it had to take me out of the vast city eventually. It was amazing, really. Ten minutes of freedom and already I was acting like I had half a chance.

I upped the pace, walked for a mile or two, till some instinct made me turn and look back. A way off, on the other side of the road, a shiny dome head was hurrying through the press of people on the sidewalk. The colored dot in his forehead, the suit, the bulk, it had to be the quiet one, Josh. His head nodded as he walked, his powerful legs moving like bob-weights. What did they want? The purpose in those powerful strides had my name attached, but not my welfare.

A junction ahead, an underpass, welcoming darkness. I scurried down into it, folding my collar up. "Access tunnel sponsored by Datacom," a voice said in a frenzy of 3D ads that yowled like banshees.

When I emerged at the other end, I bolted, turning at every corner, first left, then right, not daring to look around. Only when my legs complained and my breath rasped in my throat did I slow down.

I found myself in a broad six-lane avenue lined on one side by tall structures with white marble facades like tombstones. On the other, the lake wall, its presence somehow reassuring. Above a flower boutique, a sign, Lake side Square. A connection clicked in my synapses—Lake side. I knew someone in this vicinity—Orion, the reading I'd done earlier on that never-ending day. I trawled embossed addresses further along the street to check this actually was Lake side Drive, and then stalked its plazas of polished buildings looking for a name.

After what seemed hours, footsore, sweat-drenched, anxiety like a blade in my ribs, I found it, The GoLightly Building. A metallic tube of tiered apartments and angulated solar screens. There, by the entrance in a lozenge of pastel glass the name among a host of names, D'Angelo O. The Cosmique legend, a pentagram of stars on a blue background beside it. I leaned on the button and stared up at the battery of monitors imploringly.

SIX

THE NICHES OF ORION'S NOSTRILS QUIVERED AS SHE threw wide the door. "This is so real!" she yelped. "I was thinking of you when my entrance-viewer showed me your face."

Her place was five floors up, serviced by a see-through elevator that sang through the air with no visible means of support.

I pretended not to notice her arms splaying wide as I slipped between her and the door post. The room had a sense of newness, low-rise seating in fake leather without a scratch on it, gleaming shelves displaying projected 3D ornaments. The floor had a fresh covering of fake hemp. The largest wall was all glass with a view over the tan hide of the lake. The back screen-wall had the planets projected over it, moving and ringing with strange majesty—Mars pink, Venus orange, the silver moon with its craters and mountains.

"How can you be here? How can you be free?" She stood in the center of the room in a billowing blue puff of a dress that didn't so much cover her as follow her around.

"By thought transference in a deep meditative state." A seat folded out from under the shelves with a sigh of compressed air. I pounced on it gratefully and, as I did, a polite purple plant turned its leaves aside to make room. "I submitted a parole application and by focusing on the thoughts of those that made the decision, I was able to influence them to a positive verdict. All these years I've been building my powers, waiting for the right moment. I need a place to rest, somewhere to orientate myself." I hadn't prepared an explanation but this sounded so plausible I almost believed it myself.

"It's an honor. You're a spiritual warrior. You healed me and I owe you. I'll do anything." She held up her hand and the room filled itself with a soothing piano concerto. "This is the most dazzling day of my life! Am I the first person you've connected with since you got out?"

"Yes." I sat looking around the room, trying to look as fazed as I felt. "The world seems to have moved on since I was imprisoned, I'm a little disorientated."

"Of course," she crossed her hands over her chest. "You must have been through so much—it must be like coming back to life again."

I watched the red planet revolving over her shoulder. After my long excommunication from such things, the effect seemed miraculous.

"We call it a grand trine," she said, following my gaze. "The present conjunction, of moon, Mars and Jupiter." She stood close, rested a foot on the other seat, gave me a long look. "You look exhausted, if you will excuse me for saying so."

"Thought transference, when done for long periods, is exhausting."

"Allow me to get you something." She disappeared through a door in the screen-wall and came back with a "Revive" mood spray and a glass of purified water. "I don't know if you bend to such chemistry," she said, proffering the canister.

"Go ahead."

A blend of mango-scented mood-lifters engulfed me, stiffening my blood. I was instantly sharp, centered. *Alvina.* One thought, one intention. Here was a chance to know at last. I sat bolt upright. "My main wish right now is trawl the stream to see if there's anything out there on the fate of a certain person."

Orion stretched herself upwards, squeezed her lips together. "Really? You don't wish a news and culture update?"

"No. Alvina was a priestess, a highly evolved soul of my tribe. She disappeared a few weeks after The Changes. I have long sought to know by what means she was stolen away."

Orion snapped her fingers, the music shifted gear, the ornaments and planets disappeared, the room's surfaces appeared to pucker and warp to lively guitars.

She bent down so her round face was close to mine, gave me a quizzical look. "I didn't think you belonged to any tribe. You can change matter, heal the sick and live on chi. Can you not look into the akashic records and discern this information for yourself?"

Jeez. I didn't answer for a while, distracted by the action of the seat pan massaging my buttocks. "I could, with some effort. But all my energies have been devoted to the cause of release till now. It would be a considerable drain on my resources."

"Well, I could trawl the Cosmique network's archives." The music seemed to soften my limbs, the room melted in its pool of sound. Orion leaned even closer, reached a hand out towards my face, then pulled it back. "You honor me with this task."

"You are a soul of great compassion." Some kind of after-shock was setting in. I shivered, my teeth chattering. "Can we do the search now?"

"*We* won't do it. Lone Bear will. He's my digi-assistant. I got to warn you though; he's got double-human capacity reasoning and can be a little tetchy." Her eyes glossed over as she stared at the screen-wall. "Wake up, Lone Bear."

The wavering musical effects continued as a flare of orange flicked across the screen, forming a thin face which looped around in liquid motion. The nose was daubed with blood-red ochre, black circles covered the cheeks, a strip of porcupine quills flopped under his chin like a bib. This comic-book Native American only needed to say "How!" to complete the cliché. The face looped and spun, expanded and shrank, eventually stabilized. His grimy palm came up in front of his face. "How!" he said.

"Stop it, Lone Bear," Orion said with an indulgent smile.

It struck me how similar the face was to my own—the red nose, the hollow face. "Lone Bear," she said. "Allow me to introduce Zachary, The Shaman, the wizard, the man who healed me this morning."

Had it really only been earlier that morning? It seemed a lifetime ago.

"Now this is very strange," Lone Bear's bass voice picked words like they cost money and he was short of cash. "This is indeed the same man according to my data files whom you saw today, yet his physical data now identifies him as Mick Tarn. Clearly his ID file has been altered."

Orion peeled her eyes from the screen to look at me. "Is this true?"

My buttocks clenched against the rhythmic pulses. I necked back the cold water. "I've not been myself lately."

"Why would someone as famous as you change your name?"

"The reason is obvious. Fame is but a bubble I want to be free of. My history is behind me. That unfairly incarcerated person I was in the zone is gone. I want to be someone else, to make a new start. I was allowed to change my ID as part of the parole process."

"You're walking away from that priceless media penetration you've accumulated?" Orion's neck seemed to elongate. "Abandoning the celebrity endorsements, the stories of your spiritual ascension in India, the healings? Only a true holy man could do that."

"He's a fraud," said Lone Bear. "This Zach, this mystic, Mick Tarn, or whoever he calls himself. His body signs and voice analysis indicate extreme anxiety and probable duplicity. Mistress, suspecting this is an escaped DATCHO, I've already checked the wanted persons profile. He's not listed. However, I warn you he's likely to take advantage of your impetuous generosity."

Under Orion's and Lone Bear's prolonged gaze, I donned my hurt/innocent look—down-turned head, lips slightly parted, wallowing eyes.

"Lone Bear, please." Orion sighed, sat on the floor beside me. "This man is guiltless. I know you're trying to protect me, but please place your faith in him as I do. Be nice."

"Ah, my ever-trusting mistress. If you wish it so. But I would remind you of your vulnerability to gurus and elderly authority figures. You have experienced a spontaneous healing process as a result of an intense psychosomatic wish-fulfilment fantasy. Remember your liver enzyme reading this morning? This is all a part of..."

"Please!" Orion closed her eyes, covered her ears. "Not now. Be nice. We want you to initiate a search."

Lone Bear's dried-mud complexion cracked into a smile. "Of course. What is your wish?" The hooded eyes glittered with intelligence. This damned injun was too savvy for my liking.

"Tell him," she said, turning to me. "Tell him the ID details of this woman."

"I want a trace," I said. "All you've got on Alvina Rohanna Khan, born Walnut Creek, California."

"ID reference?"

"Four-oh-eight, nine-nine-six, slash, two-seven-three, slash, forty-six."

The face froze for a half-second, then, "I have a full set of records until June third, year zero. What do you wish to see?"

"No. That's when she vanished. I mean it's after that date I need data. There must be something beyond that?"

"Only a missing persons report," Lone Bear said. "In the absence of physical DNA, I have performed a deep search using all known biometric information, including facial, fingerprint and retinal scans."

Both Lone Bear and Orion watched me expectantly.

"There's got to be more. Can't you find a way into the logs of the security services or the blog-files archive?"

Lone Bear's six-foot face darkened. Orion inhaled deeply. "Accessing a blog-file other than your own is impossible," she said. "And Governmental records are not to be trusted. " She got up and circled the room, blue hair bobbing. Not a trace of her old limp was detectable. "I can see you want this information badly. But your chances of getting any further are virtually nil. You cannot have faith in any data outside of the Cosmique network."

I had a sense of a great weight flattening the husk of my life. Over the years various clients had searched their tribe's source files fruitlessly on my behalf, so this was a foregone conclusion. I should have been prepared, should have known what to expect, but some residual glimmer of hope remained.

"Is there any other way I can help you?" Orion said, kneeling before me. She placed her hands on my wrists. The age-thinned skin of her inner palm contrasted with the re-plumped flesh on the back of her hand. "I want to help."

"I don't see how you can. I can't find peace until I know the means of her going."

The ripe tang of her mood spray enclosed me, I felt an urgent stirring. Her hands slid up my forearms, then dropped onto to my thighs. I watched, pliant in loss, unable to respond. Lone Bear's head wafted around, regarding us impassively. She kneaded the stringy flesh of my upper legs, working slowly higher. The folds of her flimsy dress revealed her bare, mismatched legs.

A light glimmered in the back of my mind, something I'd missed. I placed my hands on hers, trapping them.

"Hey, ah, how does Lone Bear check my stats so efficiently?" I said, pointing to the screen-wall. Still kneeling, she dropped her forehead onto my knees.

"The sophisticated screening took place at the door-entrance security scan." She looked up, pointed to a line of slightly darkened circles in the screen-wall. "That's where your body markers are cross-checked and analyzed."

She dropped her head again, pressed her forehead against me, pulling her hands from under mine.

"I've been thinking," she muttered. "Maybe you'd like to join us, the Cosmique? We'd be privileged to have someone of your ascended nature with us. You'd instantly have friends, a community, a lifestyle and a network. We'd give you a chunk of on-line real estate. You gotta have a tribe, otherwise you're nobody."

I sat upright, pushing back into the chair's embrace. "It's tempting. I've been out on my own so long."

Her hands moved higher up my thighs, stroking, squeezing. "You're very special. And your face isn't unappealing. Your anti-aestheticism intrigues me. We're so alike. It's been such a long time since I was intimate with anyone. I haven't had a commitment-bond relationship for more than two years."

Something glinted in my inner eye. I saw a square of metal, a face. I fumbled for it, just out of reach...

Orion's voice echoed around the room. "It's so rare when two people really find themselves in attunement. You're a Scorpio, according to your profile and your Libra moon is opposite my ascendant."

Her right hand came up and touched my cheek, and then it dropped back onto my thigh.

"I love the honesty of your face."

Something fell away; a long-tethered hunger broke free. Our lips met, our teeth clinking together. I seemed to be disappearing into her face. I pulled at her dress, which parted open down the front. Her rebuilt breasts were upturned.

Around her navel were crosshatched streaks of cell deterioration. She bit my earlobe.

The picture. Alvina's hair in the back of the frame.

"Wait!" I pulled away, half stood, leaned against the wall. "I've got a DNA sample. Can we do another search?"

She reached, wrapped her arms about my legs, spoke through gritted teeth. "Not now."

"Sorry," I said. "I'm not ready, I can't."

"I've got some Virilo to get you in the mood. My immuno program is up to date for all known STDs including the newest AIDs variant."

I shook my head.

Orion's round pan of a face was suddenly expressionless. "It's okay. I understand." She fastened the front of her dress.

This time when Lone Bear appeared, I pulled apart the picture frame and offered up the dry strands of Alvina's jet-black hair.

"I fear this is futile," Lone Bear intoned. "But please place these DNA materials in the scanner." An aluminium plate slid from a rail running around the base of the wall.

As the tray slotted home, Lone Bear blinked once. "I have a trace. No name confirmation, but a single DNA profile of this person exists, tracked to a recent image file. Do you wish to see it?"

My heart stopped beating. "Recent? Hell, yes."

Though only a black and white 2D still, the image blazed with light. Alvina's broad, familiar forehead, the pronounced cupid's bow. The mess of warlocks had gone; her hair was straight and boyish. I stared, transfixed.

"I—I. Alvina." I lunged at the screen, clawing at her face. My nails squealed over the polished surface.

Alvina stood in a group around a statuesque woman, the roiling sea behind their heads. Then I saw the words "Star Gossip Newslink, July 4, 0014" on the bottom of the screen. Less than a year previously. The number hammered through my head. I pressed my fingers to the screen wall as if I could pass through it to her. Blood was shooting through my veins, blasted by a series of explosions in my chest. I was incapable of speech. The headline "Exclusive— Pink Lady in final floatation," drifted by, then, "Motox head and socialite, Maxine Pink, made a dash for a Triton yesterday, just weeks before her eighty-eighth birthday. She joins a number of high-profile exiles on the notorious floating mini-states. There she'll spin out her years with illegal life-prolonging treatments, beyond the laws of decency and morality."

The statuesque woman was being welcomed by the little crowd. Alvina was looking to the right of the lens with her bright, living eyes. A tall man appeared to be leaning against her, with similar eyes and a full face. Then I saw the hand, just visible at Alvina's side. The man had his arm around her.

"An insect-based spy camera with attached DNA profiler infiltrated this vessel's security screening," said Lone Bear. "This particular Triton reputedly inhabits the North Sea, obscured by year-round acid smog. The bug was operated by the Starlight News Agency."

Orion said, "I don't have 3D available, but the image can be rendered in sensara, if you wish."

"Yes. Yes please."

"Do it, Lone Bear."

The screen softened under my fingertips. I felt the strands of Alvina's hair, the firm contours of her scalp beneath.

"Oh my love."

The skin of Alvina's neck was cool, a hard, round object at her throat. I felt the letters engraved around its circumference I knew what those symbols were. Lifting my finger, opening my eyes, I saw the pendant.

"I'll never take it off. Never, ever," she'd said.

I continued to stare, not daring to blink, not daring to think, lest the image vanish.

The dry stone of my throat cried out soundlessly: impossible, incredible; she's alive; alive and breathing. Fifteen years. Fresh and as lovely as that day she left...

"I want to contact her. Now," I whispered. Nothing could have prepared me for this moment.

Lone Bear's voice was inscrutable: "No connection available to the Triton network."

"Please don't take the image away."

I'd ceased to exist. I could only stare, mesmerized by the blazing sun of Alvina's face.

SEVEN

ALVINA WAS THE ONLY WOMAN I'D KNOWN WHO wanted the man and not the mystic. She was an oasis in a desert of aloneness.

She was hopelessly untidy, while I was positively anal in my orderliness. Her feminine flotsam of jewelry, shoes and make-up would be strewn all over the house. I loved this evidence of her. It was a reminder that she belonged.

"Hmmm, yes," she'd say, narrowing her face, mimicking my voice and staring into my palm. "Yes, you would have had a long and interesting life, were it not for that crazy woman you took for a wife."

Remarkably, of the two of us, she was the more insecure.

"Why do you love me?" she'd ask.

As if there could be any doubt, any question.

"Because you're intelligent and funny; because you're unpredictable and strong-willed. Because you're the only one, when I was lost beyond hope, who saved an impossible loner and brought him into the fold."

She was superstitious, wary for any signs portending bad luck, forever collecting talismans and charms. We had shelves of crystals, stones with holes in them, miniature deities. One day she announced that a rune spell had come to her in a dream that would render our bond unbreakable—A+Z=♥∞. Alvina and Zachary equals love infinitum.

"The beginning and end of the alphabet," she said, "and everything precious in between." It was ridiculous, childish, the scrawled code of the playground. Yet she'd scratch that rune on shopping lists, mark it in secret places of the house—the garage, the basement.

On our third anniversary, I presented her with those very symbols engraved on a gold teardrop. She wore it on a chain around her neck.

We were both loners at heart, tentatively treading the new paths of love. I'd always hidden inside myself, always drawing back. Alvina hid in gregariousness. She could make the dullest person feel fascinating, collecting friends effortlessly.

We moved north to the backwoods of Marlborough in Massachusetts away from the smog-bound summers of California.

At night, I'd lie chasing sleep, watching over a slumbering Alvina. My great-est happiness was then, holding Alvina while the clapboard house creaked and groaned, seeming to tear adrift as we'd roll in the storm-wracked ship of the night.

❧

I came to in a hit of scathing spray that made the blood fizz in my temples.

Orion's index finger released the "Revive" dispenser's button, then she placed a bottle of "Enzo" enriched water in my hand, the bubbles hissing furiously.

"You okay? You go into a trance or something?"

Her anxious face swam in and out of focus. I noted the light in the room had changed. Through the window the lake's surface seemed leaden and lifeless.

"I was in meditation," I stammered. "I went somewhere beyond. I'm all right, I think."

She turned to look at the wall over her shoulder.

"Can I turn the screen off now? You've stared at it for half-an-hour. It won't make her materialize you know, even for you."

"No... okay, turn it off."

As the screen warped into curtains of orange, the date burned in the back of my eyes—July 4, 014. Less than a year ago. There was every chance she still lived.

"Jungle!" snapped Orion. The wall took on a thousand shades of green, great trunks bowed beneath the weight of leaves, animal calls resounded, the scent of leaf mold and earth permeated the room.

"This woman wasn't only a highly evolved soul? She was special to you?"

"Was. Is." Blinking sore eyes, I swallowed the whole bottle of water, effer-vescence hissing on my tongue. I pieced loose thoughts together carefully. "I was sure she'd fled the land of the living... and yet she's still alive. I should be happy but..." A hollow pain of longing burned in the center of me.

Orion passed me another bottle of Enzo. "How did you lose her?"

"I didn't. I mean, she just disappeared. I don't know why she hasn't tried to contact me. How can I get to this Triton?"

Orion shook her head. "The Tritons don't exist." She looked at my dis-traught face and continued, "Oh, other tribe's info-sites will tell you the Tri-tons are the most elitist, unattainable network going. That their ships are a kind of earthly paradise where they push enhancements way beyond the frame so that no one ever dies." She sat cross-legged beside me. "They're allegedly into illegal extruded-cloned organs and humano-pig hearts and stuff. No one that goes to the Triton is ever allowed back, it's said, in case they introduce some mutated virus or warped genetic material back into civilization."

"We just saw Alvina on a Triton. There it was in a news link, a spy camera captured the image. How can there be any doubt about its existence?" It was hard to squeeze words past the dry gag of my gullet.

Orion's eyes trailed a jaguar slipping through the trees. "According to legend, the Tritons started out as city-sized luxury ships, floating in international waters as tax-havens for the mega-rich. When The Changes came, they evolved into life-prolonging, floating laboratories where ultra-advanced medical interventions are practiced outside international law."

I held the pale blue moons of her eyes. "So she's on one of these ships somewhere off the coast of the UK? There must be some way I can verify the info?"

Orion scowled. "Who's authority would you trust?"

I spoke with palms outspread. "But I saw Alvina on a Triton. It's a fact."

Orion's voice hardened. "The data you saw was from some provider-sponsored news service. Hardly a fount of integrity."

She folded her legs up, brushed carpet fibers from her shins. "You know there are governmental and corporate sources that list you as a fraudster and illegal immigrant, aged fifty-six? That you're an attempted murderer? Is that the kind of facts you want? You think they really put a man on the moon back in the nineteen-sixties? Or that Nine-eleven wasn't staged by U.S. arms traders?"

I tried to hold her eyes as if this would stop this evidence of Alvina being spirited away. "What is your truth, Orion? Is she out there?"

She sighed. "Jeesh, I don't know. Four fifths of the population of the U.S. are tribe members. Half of them believe The Changes were God's day of judgement. Babylonian tribes-people believe we're all Martians, the Divine Messengers say Elvis Presley was the Son of God. There's no agreed pattern to events. We live in a permanent, ever-changing present."

"I'm so confused," I said, squeezing my eyes shut, "nothing makes sense. Is she alive or not?" When I opened my eyes, my fingers seem to stir the air to dance. I felt corrupted, like some time-line of reason had shifted beyond reach.

Orion's far-away voice weaved in and out of my head.

"I'm a Cosmique. I believe only in my tribe and our truth, and it is this. The Tritons are a sort of fantasy, a utopia, promising everlasting life and happiness but unable to deliver." She spoke more quickly. "Probably they exist in some virtual realm with no physical existence. Or maybe they're just off-shore place the rich go to die, who knows?"

"That doesn't make things any clearer."

Orion's foot tapped frantically. I thought of her leg trembling during the healing, she seemed to crackle with impatience. "Look, the image you saw was traced through a DNA match, so you can probably trust this Alvina of yours had a physical existence on the date and time stated. Maybe she's simply moved on to a new tribe, a new provider."

"So she could be out there, somewhere?"

She gave me a hard look, then sighed. "Well, yeah-huh. But even if these fantasy ships existed and she's somehow got herself onto one, you'd never get on one yourself. The Triton network itself is incredibly exclusive, heads of state and corporate leaders get turned down, so you sure will be."

She touched her unfinished nose. "Permanence has gone. That's the how the world is, now. We got to learn to let go of relationships when the time comes, don't you see? We can't expect that another remains the same. A spiritually ascended soul like you must be aware of this."

I felt I had to convince her, to convince myself. "Me and Alvina had a love not to be changed by place or time."

Orion leaned closer, narrowed her eyes. "There was a guy with her, you must have seen that. She's moved on. This lovelorn grief, it ill becomes you. You're above this..." She examined the fake fiber floor, tugged at her blue hair. "We've got to make the most of the present." She shook her head, whispered, "'I'll follow my heart when I find it.' I'm looking for another whose heart can help me find mine." She softened her voice further. "Your eyes are amazing, like muddy emeralds. I could..."

Orion was interrupted by Lone Bear's voice. "Lower secure door entry-system breach. Anthony Taldori, Josh Christos, Siddharta Baston inside building. Also a multi-headed hydra worm seeking biographic detection of Mick Tarn has accessed security system files. Perpetrators originate in the Great Ascension network."

Orion's face blanched of color. "Someone's violated my space." Her voice caught with terror, "Lone Bear, call the police!"

"No." My voice sounded stronger than I felt. "I don't want to be linked with any illegal incident so soon after my release. I know what this is about." I stood, moved towards the door. "I'll leave. Your entrance security will check me out. It's me they want."

Orion remained crouched on the floor, azure eyes raised, voice warping with hysteria. "I'm prone to anxiety attacks. Don't get me involved!"

I yanked open the door and stepped into the corridor, then ran for the fire-escape stairs at the far end of the hallway. As I grabbed the chromed fire-exit handle, the door burst open, banging against my hip. AT filled the door frame, his face edged with color. The little man who drove the car and Josh were behind him.

"There we go, ole fellah," he cooed in a mockery of concern, snapping my hand behind my head till I gasped in pain. "Pray accompany me now, and do not protest, for I am an agent of good."

AT and the driver bundled me down the stairs while Josh went past me and back to the corridor. I tried to resist, but any move from me resulted in a wrench likely to tear my arm off.

I seethed silently as they hauled me down the chalk-white steps. Each had an arm around my middle while AT applied the arm lock with his free hand. My feet barely touched the ground.

Outside, the long chromed snout of the car waited.

EIGHT

I WAS THRUST HEADLONG INTO THE BACK OF THE
vehicle. AT forced me face-down onto the seat and snapped handcuffs on my
wrists.

I turned my head to one side, sucked air. "Where are you taking me? What
do you want?"

AT slammed the door shut and lifted me into a sitting position. His eyes
spat fire, a diamond glinted in one of his incisors. "Be silent, or pain will result."

The car's pink mock-leather and walnut interior smelled of oranges. The
cold air conditioning hit me like an ocean roller. They didn't bother with the
Bliss spray.

AT sat beside me, silent and solid as a building. Rain began drumming
down on the car roof. As we moved off, only the driver was animated, rolling
in his seat, stabbing buttons on the dash, driving nimbly as if the vehicle were
weightless. The car splashed up a waterlogged North Lincoln Avenue behind
a line of traffic. I craned forward, desperate to capture every impression before
my freedom ended.

We shunted through an underpass, crept beneath the shadow of towering
buildings, then the skyline opened up and a mass of diluted colors filled my
eyes: balustrades of frothing foxglove, rooftop gardens spilled violets and bou-
gainvillaea; pergolas burgeoned with every tint of oxygen-emitting, sulphur-
resistant succulent.

A few miles on, the rain stopped abruptly. An illuminated sign over the
road said the pollution index was eight point two.

We eventually pulled up in West Ridge, four hundred and nine, Greenleaf
Avenue. An old Victorian brownstone with windows like polished onyx, sand-
stone columns, steep steps.

They pushed me before them. The entrance scanner checked us, opened
the door wide.

In the gloom of a spacious hallway, the driver looked at AT. "Where?" he
said, a line of perspiration trickling down his thin neck.

"Wait." As the entrance scanner clunked and locked the door behind us,
AT went down the hall and through the first of two panelled doors to my left.

The driver and I stood together in silence, an antique clock ticked loudly nearby. The banister rail was fashioned in jade-like material, embedded with pearly strands. The doors looked to be real hardwood with glass knobs. The front entrance panelling was obscured by steel truss rods and a series of scanner plates. It looked the sort of deep-secure device that could ascertain what you'd had for lunch.

AT returned down the corridor accompanied by a woman with green lantern eyes, an exquisitely molded face and short blonde hair. She brought her face up close to mine, so close I thought for a moment she was going to kiss me. My shoulders tensed, but she merely stared. Here was a glossy glamazon at the blue-chip end of cosmetic enhancement. A palette of dewy, regrown flesh was artfully stretched over sculpted facial bones. This wasn't the standard job for sale in any clinic. The languorous lilt to the eye corners, the inferred strength in the jaw. It was the tiny, naturalistic imperfections made her truly lovely— uneven nasal flares, an indentation on her forehead, a mole at the corner of the long, full mouth. Subtle purple pigments emphasized her eyelids, while a cherry tint suffused the lips. This face cost big dollars.

"So, you're he." Her voice sounded incredibly loud, like she was making an announcement. I was getting mighty bored with this line.

"Ben D Sherman, dental technician, at your service."

Her gaze was intense, as if trying to penetrate my skin. Her luminous face seemed to float in the shadows. She nodded as if confirming something to herself. "By the tree, age and incarceration have withered you, old man. If your face is your fortune, you're destitute."

She bore the scent of oranges. As I sniffed, I got a giddy sensation. "Do I know you?"

"Nowhere near as well as I know you, but I'm kinda out there. My music gets sampled a million times a day. I'm the singer, Roxanna DeLancia."

"A singer? It's you that got me out?"

"Yes and yes. Follow me." She nodded at AT. "Take off his cuffs and wait here."

"Watch him, he's tricky," Josh warned, eyeing me as he keyed in his biometrics to release the cuffs.

"Yeah, well," she turned back to me, smiling, "so would you be under the circumstances."

She led me through the same door that AT had previously entered and we were in a room pulsating with music: "Baby maybe, maybe I can ho—ld on, ho—ld on." The sound bounced between my ears, seemed to emanate from my internals.

"What is this... the music?"

"You like?" She draped herself over a bamboo chaise lounge. "It's from *Siren*, my 'Elevation' series, in wave sound."

"Wave sound?"

"Sonic stream harmonics just above and just below the human acoustic range in fractional pulses that play through your bones. Good, yes?"

"Hmmm."

The room was enormous, furnished sparsely in the Japanese style: wood and cane furniture, reed matting, stone ornaments. A tank seethed with fluorescent fish in the center of the room. Some kind of modified plant with hairy yellow leaves sat in a silver pot. The walls emitted diffuse pink light. Through the window, the street seemed remote and lifeless, like a bad painting. She flicked her long fingers, beckoned me to sit opposite her in a cane chair while she poured alfalfa juice for both of us from a glass jug.

"My favorite," I said.

She gave me another of her stares. "The juice? Yeah, I know." She wore a cream ribbed bodice top, her long legs sheathed in loose-fitting pantaloons, "Sansara" brand etched in fine stitch-work effect down one leg.

I donned my incredulous face and whispered, "Your voice is exquisite."

Her smile was a foot wide. "Thank you. People are sick of random generated echoes, beat shimmer and soul-emote bass. They want real songs, sung by real people, accompanied by real instruments." Her hand went to her throat. "I've recently had a voca elaborator implanted for extra timbre. It's extended my range nearly an octave." She sighed, even her sighs were resounding gales. "In this business you got to upgrade yourself continually to stay in the game. People call me 'The Voice.' In South America, I'm bigger than anyone, even Cha-Cha Whitey. They got music in the zone?"

"No. At least, only drums and screams. I hope you didn't harm Orion?"

"Of course not. She's fine."

"Why am I here?"

The glass chinked against the glacier-white glaze of embossed, titanium teeth. "You're a shaman aren't you? A healer? I want you to heal me."

"Is that what all this is about? My powers have been somewhat exaggerated. Anyway, I'm stressed. I can't perform healings when I'm stressed."

"You can heal me all right. I know all there is to know about you, Zachary Crowe. I had a team trace your sorry life from way back when to last week. Believe me, it wasn't easy and it cost plenty."

As always when alarmed, I touched the mark on my face and feigned off-handedness. I stretched, yawned, looked around the room. "I'm flattered. My life, as you must know, hasn't been terribly exciting. Apart from today that is."

She watched me carefully. "Oh but it has. Let's see. You were born Dean Lemar, some fifty-six years ago. Your mother was a gypsy palmist working the last travelling fairground in the UK. She drank. You never knew your father. You were a difficult, withdrawn child with no friends. You got expelled from four schools. You changed your name to Zachary Crowe at age nineteen and followed your mother into the family business with a little peddling of quack potions on the side. After a short jail sentence for fraudulently selling Dong Quai, a common oriental herb, as a miracle cure for impotence, you came to the U.S. on a visitor's visa. You overstayed and eventually acquired the ID of a reclusive Kansas farmer who'd died at ninety-two and who had the same name as yourself. You adopted his great old age and told the world you lived on breath and chi. You impressed a few minor movie people with your fabrications and wangled your way to being the shaman of the stars—need I go on?"

I sucked air, tried to stay calm. "You seem to have gone to an awful lot of trouble."

"When you were arrested for breaking into a quarantine center," she continued, "the authorities discovered your phony credentials. By that time, however, the myths about you had grown stronger than the facts."

I kept smiling through gritted teeth. "We all need a little embellishment, do we not?"

She took another mouthful of juice. "About the only thing about you that *is* true, according to medical files, is that you've survived this long with no immuno treatments whatever. That's pretty amazing."

"Actually, I've got Patau's syndrome. It's not fatal, but it's notoriously infectious. Have you been programmed against it?"

She leaned forward, unperturbed by this lie. She pressed her palms together beneath the contoured chin. The moons of her nails had an unhealthy bluish tinge. The fingertips were crisscrossed and puckered with indentations where the sebaceous tissue had broken down. This beautiful woman was not merely old, but ancient, older by far than I. As extreme an example of perma-youth as ever you'd find. She was talking again.

"... mast cells eventually break down and the worst are the species jumpers, the new mutations. According to your medical records you've developed some kind of natural immunity from all of it, Ebola B, plague four and five, malaria, airborne AIDS, everything."

"All over the world," I said. "We are dying of abbreviations."

"Oh." Her face flushed, minute drops of moisture beaded her forehead and upper lip. She sat back, dabbed at her cheeks with a tissue snatched from a pocket at her hip.

"Listen." I tried for my sternest voice. "I won't be able to fix you. You've gone to enormous trouble to get me here, I'm very sorry. Clearly you're ill in some way, but I can't heal you."

She stroked back her hair, crossed her arms. "Oh, you can heal me all right. You will make me well. I'm a Great Ascension tribal elder. My success is due to the flowering of my god essence invoked through the rituals practiced by my tribe. Within the tree of life we believe certain shoots are made for immortality. I'm an old soul brought to fruition of my purpose, one who inspires others to fulfil their destiny."

"AT and Josh and the other guy, what's his name? They're Great Ascension too?"

"Siddartha? Uh-huh. The Sansara provider is linked with us. Our movement began in Rockwell, New Mexico when some higher beings came to earth to pass on certain codes. Our founders used these codes to create a new vision of humankind's destiny. The jewel at the forehead is a smart-crystal implanted to heighten activity of the third eye and pineal gland. It's worn by all members except for enlightened elders."

"Since The Changes it seems everyone's got a god to suit their lifestyles..."

She narrowed her eyes, waved my words away. "There's a hegemony in the tree of life. Those on the lower branches can be redeemed by making sacrifices to more elevated spirits. Redemption is possible no matter how badly they've conducted their lives. This is a basic truth. You, for instance, can enhance my life and in return I can give you immortality. I can compose a song, filled with your life experiences, your thoughts. I can make you live forever." The sheer resonance of her voice made each word final.

A chorus of sound filled the silence, roamed the room, occupied every space inside me, "got nobody, got nobody, got nobody, but me-ee-ee."

"Tell me," she said, topping up my juice even though I hadn't drunk any. "Your face. Couldn't you have got it fixed? Before you were incarcerated, I mean. Cheap skin jobs have been available for decades. It must make relationships difficult?"

"No, I was married. Am married."

A twist flickered across her lips. "Yes. You had five years of marriage. Yet you seem a natural loner."

"Well, marriage suited me fine."

"And your face?"

I touched my mottled features with my left hand. "My face isn't about affordability. It's a birthmark formed from nodules of venal tissue called haemangioma. It's my revenge on superficiality, I suppose."

With a start I realized that what I'd said was true. Her immaculate features regarded mine soberly.

"You're a brave and uncompromising man." She rubbed her palms together. "It must be a relief in a way, not having to keep up appearances—all the endless consultations, makeovers, treatments. In the zone, I guess you're free of all that."

"Yeah, life there was sweet. It's a wonder they aren't queuing round the block." I stood, suddenly eager to bring the situation to a conclusion. "I want to go now."

She didn't move, merely brought her hands behind her head. "Where will you go?"

Good question. "I have things to do," I said, "a purpose."

Her eyes rolled. "You have a purpose here. A divine destiny, in a manner of speaking. You're a convicted criminal. Your disappearance from the zone will have been noted. On the street, you'd get vaporized in minutes. There's nowhere for you to go. You have no choice but to stay with us. I guarantee you'll be safe."

Most people lie repressively, that is to say they inhibit the minute physical expressions in some way, but she was an exaggerator. She met my eyes, blinked, held mine. My heart flailed in the flickering shutters of her lashes, sensing the anxiety behind the lie.

The door opened and Josh lumbered into the room. She stood. "You're exhausted. Rest now, we'll get started with the treatment in the morning."

"I won't be able to heal you..."

She touched the tip of her finger to her lips. "In the morning. Meantime, enjoy your time with us. Are you hungry? You can have anything you like. Your room's smart activated, you could enjoy an immersion game? Maybe an interactive erotic? It must be years since you..." She leered. "For security reasons, no communications are possible, but hey, you can have some fun."

I realized I was starving, that I didn't have to pretend to live on air.

"I'd like a salad of unmodified ingredients if possible. With say, organic tofu and sprouted barley grass."

"Okay, rest now."

I followed Josh's broad back upstairs to a room crowded with furniture, eight chairs, a big pine table and a smaller one, high ceiling, gray carpet, books in a glass case. It had the stale, still aura of a room unused.

Josh departed, banging the door shut, but almost immediately it was opened again by AT with his massive, colorful head.

He stuck a thin tube against my lips.

"Blow," he ordered, "your health is important to us."

The tube was attached to a device with a display, probably some kind of health status analyzer. I wheezed into the thing, forced a rasp in my chest.

He smiled. "Faker."

This time when the door banged, it was secured with an ominous second clunk.

NINE

I EXAMINED THE DOORKNOB. IT HAD AN EMERALD-winged butterfly embedded in it, intricate patterns of veins visible in its wings. The books in the cabinet were valuable looking, leather-bound tomes, Dickens, Twain, Tolstoy. But when I removed one for closer inspection it was a fake, a polyphedral look-book with a distressed finish.

The windows were sealed, one-way chromatic glass, incredibly strong. Outside, the street was deserted, no sound, nothing moved, something sinister in the blank, reflective stare of the windowpanes.

Behind me an ornate mirror with golden cherubs around the frame sat propped against the bookcase. A porcelain green frog squatted by the door as if guarding it.

A rush of raw emotions slowly evaporated to be replaced by tentative, more familiar ones: fatigue, an ache in my lower back, a slight chill in my hands and feet. The room's sensors responded to my presence with a rise in temperature, invisible sound pipes made gentle music and greenish light irradiated from all surfaces.

How do these room computers work? Maybe the room's linked to the house console?

"Hey, computer. Er, what's happening? Are you there?" It felt ridiculous, addressing the wall. But the machine answered after only a second's pause.

"Welcome, Mick Tarn. NCBC news upcoming," it whined in a female, nasal, New York voice.

"No. Give me a search engine, or a digi-assistant or whatever you use to find things out."

"Only ambient utilities and entertainment facilities accessible to current operator."

Great.

"So what can you give me on Roxanna DeLancia?"

"Complete music archive of the Elder is available. The upcoming surround scheme has been selected as most appropriate to your current mood state. Do you wish to change it?"

"Yes."

The room's surfaces flashed, liquefied and heaved with the runnel and eddy of storm-whipped waves. The air became salty with spray. Gulls cried as they skimmed over my head, sea thundered against rock. The wire-walls illusion seemed more tangible than the dead scene beyond the window.

"Having fun?" AT stood in the open doorway, a tray in his hand and a napkin over his wrist. He put the tray on the smaller table, left the room and closed the door. The food and herbs were exactly as ordered, in a china bowl complete with a fat tube of tofu pate, hot water and an infuser for the herbs.

Devouring the food in mouthfuls, reeling in the blur of the day, I seemed to melt into the room's effects. I swirled with gulls over gray water, rolled with leaden waves.

Why was I here? I needed to anticipate their next move. I replayed the conversation with Roxanna. All that stuff about sacrifice of branches of the tree was ominous. My bones ached with fatigue.

"Off. Turn the ocean off."

The room instantly returned to a soft green glow. My fists were folded tight. I opened them and stared at the searing red lines that crossed my palms. I stared and stared at my outstretched palms, looking for a sign, some kind of answer till my eyes throbbed. It was like a silent scream.

I looked up, focused, breathed deep. I had to impose some kind of order on myself. I forced my weary limbs through a series of yoga postures, starting with downward facing dog. Head dropped, I ignored the pain at my ankle, the hollow ache at the back of my knees. I worked my way through a dozen moves, driving the breath, forcing myself on.

Later, calmer, I stood by the window, pressing my forehead against the cold glass. There was only each moment to get through, second by second. The next day waited over the horizon, but now outside the light was leeching from the sky. Curtains of shadow flittered in my eyes. So tired.

As I slumped down the wall and curled on the floor, memories pounced, memories of the zero moment, the first seconds of The Changes I'd thought long buried. So magical, memory, triggered by a whiff of scent, a touch, a few words of a song, or perhaps not. Perhaps memory is a curse, a quicksand waiting to drag you down when you're too weak to resist...

I swore and wrestled the blue-tinted, gel-filled, doubled glazed nightmare of solar-protective glass down to the floor. It simply wouldn't fit, no matter how carefully I'd measured up. It was just too big.

Alvina's head appeared around the door, apprehension in her eyes. "We should hire a specialist. You've always got to fix everything yourself, mend the boiler, cut your own hair. Ever thought a professional might know something you don't?"

She came into the room, pressed her copper-colored fingers against the pane.

"But it's satisfying," I said, "to be self-reliant."

"It's trust." The gap between her teeth just showing on nearly closed lips. "You don't trust anyone."

I trailed my fingers gently across her face, then turned and hoisted the pane back up to the lip of the frame.

"I trust you," I said, pushing the base of the pane into place. "Anyway, I let Mr. Daedelus do the plumbing when the pipe burst last winter." I lined up the top and banged the glass with the heel of my hand. It snapped into the surround perfectly. "Hah."

Alvina laughed, clapped her hands, stood back. "Thank the Gods."

We both looked around the room. The glass cast a violet tint, the table seemed to be in soft focus. But I couldn't resist. I leaned against the glass with both hands and gave the pane a last, satisfied push. "Great job!"

With a sharp pop, a crack seared end-to-end across the pane. Blue jelly began oozing from the crack down onto the carpet.

"Oh."

I looked at her.

She sighed, reached for my hand and kissed it. She pressed my palm against her forehead. I turned, full of teary, unexpected happiness, pressing my cheek against a section of cold glass.

Alvina put her arms around me. "You're so funny. Funny eccentric." She began stroking my neck, humming softly. "Let's go to the bedroom."

There were only two stages to life—being without Alvina and being with Alvina. She would reach upward when we made love, like trying to hold on to something.

"Come on." She opened the door.

'Coming."

I heard her feet on the stairs, but didn't move. I felt a tremor, a disturbance like thunder far off, whether inside or outside of me I wasn't sure. The air seemed thicker than before. I peered through the fractured glass, looking beyond the Peterson's house opposite, to where the sky was a mountain of cloud.

Then the glass bounced under some monstrous force, smacking my cheekbone. The pane warped and fell outwards, dribbling fluid and shards all the way down to the lawn. Fetid air filled the room. The little Buddha leapt off the shelf beside me, metal clattered downstairs and my first thought was: I'm being possessed. Everything around me banged and rattled, as if taken by some almighty hand.

Alvina was back in the room, wrapping herself around me, her fingers digging into my flesh. "Look."

I followed her pointing finger. I saw the garage roof had collapsed. Slates, like enormous red leaves, littered the lawn.

"It's started," she said.

But, I wanted to say, thank Jehova, the demons haven't got me. It had started years ago, the unheralded heat of summer, floods every winter, chunks of Antarctica melting and a pollution haze on the horizon.

Incredibly, realizing that it was an earthquake or some kind of natural disaster, only old Gaia venting her frustration, I was at that moment, relieved.

We rushed downstairs to the DHD viewer and waited. Some channels had gone down. Most sources gave the cause of the shock wave as Combre Vehiecha, a volcano on one of the Canary Islands. It had blasted its top away, fountaining ash and sulphur dioxide. The chance of a mega-tsunami was high; they were evacuating the whole Eastern shore of the States.

We sat to watch the most spectacular movie in history, one that ran and ran.

⁂

In the darkness, the air twitched with the tense, too-hot atmosphere of the zone. I sensed the confines of my apartment cell, the coarse fibers of the sleeping mat. I listened for the familiar sounds of the night: the sirens, the screams. As I raised my head, the room was illuminated. Strange furniture, gray carpet. My shackle gone. I lay in a heap on the floor, fully clothed. The escape, the car, Roxanna's face; the events of the previous day flared though my mind.

I'm out. I'm free. Alvina's alive.

Was I? Was she? I realized none of those statements was necessarily true.

"Computer," I said, "what's Roxanna's health status?"

"Only ambient utilities and entertainment facilities accessible to current operator."

"Who's granted full access?"

"Default setting is to access all persons admitted by door-entry master system. Mick Tarn, however, granted only ambient utilities and enter..."

"How do you identify me?"

"Body-sign scan, including scent and voice recognition."

I got down on hands and knees and examined the screen-walls, shifting chairs, clearing furniture, heaving the bookcase away from the wall. A series of faint circles were just perceptible a couple of inches off the floor on every side of the room.

I trawled the place looking for something to frustrate the scans. Orion said room sensors weren't sophisticated, but would that apply here?

I paced a cleared area around the room's perimeter, step, step, step, turn, waiting for inspiration. Smoke would do it, perhaps, or dust, or... I almost stepped on the tube of tofu paste and paused. I squeezed the tube, rubbed the paste between finger and thumb. The gray goo was slightly oily. Before I could question the wisdom of it, I'd bent to floor level, begun smearing gunk over the sensor spots.

When I'd finished, the room looked like the aftermath of a wild party—the walls smudged with congealing paste, chairs and furniture thrown around. I lay face-down in the center of the room. "Shut down," I whispered, closing my eyes, pretending to sleep. Nothing happened, the room remained illuminated. Was this good or bad?

"Great Ascension member, he require data access," I drawled in a feeble mime of Pablo's strangled spanglish.

The room exploded with white light, "An error has occurred at recog, biof, alt net points three, four, nine, seven, two. Do not proceed. An error has occurred at recog, biof, alt net points..."

Inwardly cursing, I continued, "This me, man. I need access some files on Roxanna, her health status."

"Unable to establish ID. Sensor processing dysfunctional. No access."

Shit.

"I gotta tap the mains. This urgent."

"Password protected."

"Password. Really?" I gave up on the accent. "This password... Er, let me see, is it Great Ascension?"

"Access denied."

"Tree of life?"

"Access denied. Unless the correct password is rendered within ten seconds an intruder alert will be triggered."

"Shit, piss. Wait, no I... Holy horseshit..."

"Five seconds."

Only one word came, so obvious, so inane, but I'd said it already: "Siren," Roxanna's song title.

"Access granted to grade-two data. Do you wish information on the elder's health status?"

I sighed heavily. "Hell. Yeah. Please."

"There are two-hundred and five health references to Roxanna DeLancia in news streams, notice boards and fan-base interact rooms posted in the last four days."

"Anything about her needing the services of a certain Zachary Crowe?"

"None."

"Is there anything that suggests serious diseases or some reference to her needing the services of a healer?"

"There are sixty-two messages relating to rumors of Roxanna having a terminal illness. One of these messages claims to be hacked from her personal blog-file and is of a medical consultation. This was posted two days ago in the chat room of Alia Gloriana, an official fan web-site. The message was deleted twice and re-posted each time, the latest posting only ten minutes ago. The posting originates from the Authentus network. The author of this file is called the Scarecrow."

"Is it reliable? I mean, how do I know it's accurate?"

"The Scarecrow has posted stolen blog-file revelations on various networks causing much controversy. Though often strenuously denied, all his postings have so far been found to be genuine. Data tracking indicates the Scarecrow is based in Cambridge, England, also the home of the Authentus network."

"Yes, okay. I'll take it."

The words "Mount Sinai Medical Center, Miami, Florida. 11.36 am. May 9th 015" flicked across the largest wall. The words reshaped themselves into the figure of Roxanna, lying on a gleaming white examination table. Her naked body was dappled with sweat like tiny glass beads. Banks of projected colored columns danced gaily above her head.

A short, Latino woman came on screen, her face glowing in the yellow antibacterial luminescence of her uniform. She wore metal-framed spex that curled around her face. She lifted the spex to give Roxanna a long, unsmiling look.

"Hold on sweetie, nearly done."

Roxanna's familiar, fine-boned face puckered. "Don't call me sweetie, doctor. I'm not a child. The probe was injected ten minutes ago, it must be finished by now." She glared out of the screen, her green eyes imperial.

The doctor turned, examined the colored columns for a few minutes more, then she sat, removing the spex and leaning forwards to look Roxanna in the face. "It's not good. Explains your low blood count, better prepare yourself."

Roxanna stiffened. "Prepare... Mother of Jesus! Please no. I've been, I am, fine. Never better."

The medic was silent for a moment, then she let her breath go in a long hiss. "I'm going to shoot it to you straight. Sooner or later, after repeated auto-viral immunization, the system weakens. Something comes along and finds a way through. You've got a new variant of acquired D-L type leukemia, your lymphocytes aren't responding as they should. The virus is mutating its surface proteins faster than your weakened system can counter..."

Roxanna sat up abruptly, restructured breasts pointing accusingly. "Half a million dollars I shucked out to you people last annum, and you... how can you not do anything?"

The doctor's pupils were black as oblivion. "Roxanna, you must've anticipated this. You're eighty-six. You've had a partial colon renewal, two new heart valves, bone bolstering, arterial re-growths, a kidney replacement. You've got your dollar's worth in dermal recellular treatments and anti-oxygenation enzymes alone."

"Death is for the unenlightened. I'll find a way. What about the Triton network? There are supposed to be gaspers out there stuffed full of modified cells shifting weights way into their hundreds."

The medic shook her head. "Has anyone you know got themselves on a Triton? And besides, the illegal stuff they're supposed to do, like creating modified, cloned-incubus donor cells, it takes time. Time you don't have."

"You're absolutely sure? Great Goddess above, I don't care, legal or illegal, this disease, this... this thing in me. Give me something, give me a chance. It's so unfair. I'm not ready. My primal song series is being re-released on wave sound, soon." A single tear trickled over her cheekbone to nestle at the corner of her mouth. "There must be something?"

The medic reached for her hand, squeezed it briefly, and then let go. "This may seem beyond imagining now, but it's the same for everyone in your position. There are three stages—fury, recrimination, finally, the dawning of acceptance. With that, there's a kind of peace. It will come, Roxanna. Truly it will."

The medic smiled gently as she stood, stabbing buttons. "If there was a way, I assure you we'd find it. Only thing in your case would be a matching bone-marrow donor, someone who's survived to at least middle-age without immune programming, so they had substantially active trigocytes. If such a person were to exist, which I very much doubt they do, they'd have to be willing to sacrifice themselves, to yield up every drop. You've got no time to wait for batch cells to renew themselves. It's not worth running a search. I'm really, really, sorry Roxanna."

The image melted into a sea of green. My knuckles cracked as I curled my hands into fists.

TEN

MORNING. THE ROOM RADIATED GREEN LIGHT FROM every tangent. Around me mundane objects sat solidly indifferent to my continued existence—the glass-fronted bookcase, the short-legged table, the line of matching chairs. Unsleeping, scratchy-eyed, I sat propped against the wall, waiting. The porcelain frog weighed heavily in my hand. When the door opened, I'd attack, strike hard and fast.

Faint smudges were visible around the walls where traces of tofu remained, the mirror was slightly askew, the carpet creased where I'd pushed things back into place.

Something pinged, far away, like a string snapping. My scalp tingled. I gripped the frog tighter, hesitated. Would it be AT? Or Josh? Should I hide behind the door and attack from behind? They were so tall; maybe I should get on a chair and drop the weight from above?

The door opened noiselessly. AT pounded in, hands like shovels and feet of iron. In a half-crouch, I shifted the frog behind me, letting it thud heavily to the floor. Cursing myself, I looked up at AT's smiling face, third eye glinting gold. He seemed so indestructible, so *meaty*.

"This is a great day."

I straightened. "What?"

He leered. "You may regard me unkindly, but I serve the Great Ascension with joy in my heart and you will serve, also."

"I'm so glad," I said, stepping backwards onto the frog, almost tripping. "What's happening?"

"You'll see. C'mon, we'd better go down."

We—him and me—as if we shared something.

"I'm coming."

I followed AT out.

Opposite my room, a frosted crystal door hung open, revealing an ornate shower unit.

"I need to use the bathroom," I said.

AT waited outside while I entered a palace of white marble, shutting the door. The seashell style shelves gleamed with an array of instruments: breath monitors, skin-stims, dental devices. I declined the toilet's offer of a fecal analysis and leaned my head into the shower cubicle, pushing the faucet full on. The shock of cold water did nothing to revive me. I urged my brain to action, tried to think rationally. I knew something they didn't want me to know, that was an advantage. Now I needed another—a weapon—something that cut or harmed, something easily concealed.

On the shelf, a stainless-steel cylinder with a button in the base and a flexible projecting arm with a buffer head. When the button was pressed the arm spun with an insect whine. A tooth polisher or nail burnisher or something. I snapped the head off by trapping it under the faucet and pulling. The buffer disappeared down the plughole. The device now had a jagged stem where the attachment had broken off but it looked neither threatening nor robust. At least it fitted into my inner-jacket pocket.

I felt my guts tighten into a ball as I followed AT's fat neck down the stairs into the same room of the previous day. Roxanna was waiting in an aura of orange scent. She stood by the window in a navy-blue suit, black boots. She nodded at AT, who departed, closing the door quietly.

"'Sit down and help yourself to juice," she said, turning to gaze through the window.

I sat, leaning forward, grasping the base of the chaise lounge, thinking about her throat. I couldn't mess up this time. If I pressed the device against her neck, saying it was a laser scalpel, I could maybe force them to let me out. I had to risk it. Just let her get a little closer...

"I'm pleased to tell you your breath analysis gives you an excellent health status," she said, turning. "You really have had no immuno programming."

"Pleased for you or pleased for me?" I heard a sound behind me. Two shapes loomed. I glanced around at AT and Josh. They must have crept in through the other door. Roxanna pulled up a cane chair and sat with knees almost touching mine. I leaned back, stretching my arms, trying to look unfazed.

Her eyes gleamed, matching the gem in her ear. "Pleased for both of us." She glanced over my shoulder at Josh, nodded. "There's a medical team arriving at 10:00 a.m."

"Why?" I said, swearing inwardly, scratching my birthmark.

A pair of heavy hands dropped onto my left shoulder.

Roxanna smiled. "It's a pity you had to find out the way you did. About my illness, I mean." The hands gripped my trapezius then one paw lifted away, brushed my hair and dropped to the other shoulder.

I donned my incredulous expression. "Illness?"

"It's astounding you managed to access that hacked file last night. You really are a resourceful old bastard."

If those hands would release me for just one second. I tried to look defeated, dropped my hands to my lap, blinked. "I should have known better than to try and trick you."

"Yes." She stretched her lips into a smile. It was a smile so dazzling, so warm, I almost smiled back. "I ask you now, knowing what you know and with no chance of survival. I ask you, with no reason or purpose to your life and a death sentence over your head as an escaped DATCHO. Will you, Zachary Crowe, join our tribe and offer yourself to me, to save an elevated soul? Will you do this, and erase your past crimes and gain hugely in spiritual merit? Will you..."

She said more, but I missed it, fear and rage roaring through my arteries. "Do you expect me to throw myself in the grave to save you?"

She squeezed her lips together, leaned back. "Why not? Thousands are inspired by me. You have no one."

"I have Alvina. I have a wife."

"Your wife died on June twentieth, year zero, of the highly contagious Strep Five Virus in the Jessop Hills quarantine center in Bakersfield, New Hampshire. You're over. You were rotting in the zone, waiting for death with your mumbo-jumbo shaman routine..."

I lurched forward against the restraining hands. "Alvina is alive. I'm not a criminal. Let me go, or believe me, you'll suffer." Two more hands grabbed my elbows, pinning my arms to my sides. Hot breath gusted in my ear.

"At least this way you're worth something, contributing something," Roxanna went on. "Think how it'll enhance your media aura, to go this way, to save an elder."

My shoulders were released, but my elbows remained pinned. Behind me, the crackle of stiff material unfolding. Something popped in my head. I found myself sprawled forward over the table with my hands behind my back. A smashed glass lay on the floor, bubbles of green froth hissing into the carpet.

Roxanna leaned over me, her lovely face tight. "This is your fate. Your karma. I got you out, that means you belong to me. Next incarnation you'll come back as someone better."

"You'll get nothing from me," I gasped, as the air was forced from my lungs, as I was gripped in a bear hug and lifted off the floor. AT dropped me back down, holding my arms aloft as Josh wrapped me like a parcel in yellow material. I was bound into a restraining suit, my arms crossed over my chest and strapped to my shoulders. I inhaled desperately as my torso was trussed ever tighter.

I turned to Roxanna as she stood, her eyes locked onto mine. I looked hard at her smug, refurbished face, burned into the anxiety in the heart of her and mouthed, "What a sad, sorry, old crone you are. Your spiritual path is nothing but self-serving bullshit. Death sits waiting at your shoulder."

Three chevrons folded between her eyebrows. "I see your aura. I see the darkness there, the evil. Take him!" she bellowed, teeth glinting, breath loud in her nostrils.

They dragged me from the room backwards, my head lolling against my strapped wrists. I watched the ceiling as they carried me face-up into the hallway.

Roxanna's voice rang out, "Not upstairs! Put him in the basement. There's no console down there."

I was hustled through two doors and down a flight of stairs. My eyes followed a series of silver runes on the ceiling all the way down to a door set deep in the wall. They put me inside and placed me on the floor. The heavy door scraped shut, leaving me in darkness.

ELEVEN

DARK SHAPES DRIFTED IN MY EYEBALLS. I COULDN'T focus in the poor light. My physicality seemed an intrusion in the gloom—the faint breeze of my breath, the ghostly outline of my hands.

When I tried to get up, my ankle buckled, my hands straining uselessly to break my fall as my forehead struck the floor. I waited quietly for the pulse of pain in my temple to subside. Objects sluggishly took on tangible form. I lay in a heap in the middle of a square room—a place of shadows and angles. The concrete floor was faced by painted-over brick; the walls on two sides had boxes stacked high against them. Two large battered suitcases lay open in one corner next to a pile of clothing. In the opposite corner a dank reek emanated from a decomposition tank. Yellow light came from a small window of opaque glass.

My watch ticked loudly, counting down the seconds, hidden beneath the wrist straps. Roxanna said the medical team arrived at ten. That gave me at most a couple of hours. My skin gave off the sweet, sticky smell of fear. When I closed my eyes, velvet black beckoned. I rolled over to the wall under the window, sat up against it and forced my eyes to fix on the tough yellow webbing of the straightjacket. My hands were fixed to my shoulders by restraining straps of black fiber. I could feel more straps running down my spine. Useless trying to force my arms free, I'd need a hundred times my normal strength to break the straps. This would require patience, persistence and thought.

I tried pulling down hard with my elbows. No good. Twisting my arms to each side. No movement. I pulled upward with my wrists while drawing my shoulders in, lifting them almost to my ears. This was a little better, the jacket slipped fractionally. Filling my lungs as they strapped me in had made for a loose fit around my armpits. I flattened my shoulder blades and repeated the action till my arms flagged with fatigue. The jacket had slipped perhaps two inches. Already it felt like I'd been scrabbling at it for hours.

I tried lying flat and squeezing out every trace of air, collapsing the scaffold of my ribs and wrestling my arms up in a series of jerks. The jacket moved up my waist another inch. This was some sort of progress. I continued the action doggedly, over and over, until the jacket jammed solidly halfway up my rib cage. So far and no further. More precious minutes had elapsed. Upstairs, doors banged, voices echoed, laughter, footsteps.

Out of sheer frustration, I began wriggling eel-like around the rough floor, hauling upwards, using the floor to drag the constricting coat up my trunk. Every movement crushed my chest further. Every movement gave me less air. Sweat oiled my back and arms. Panic made me want to cry out. There was a burning pain on my lower back where the concrete tore exposed flesh. The struggle went on and on. It was like trying to be born.

After an agony of time, I'd wrestled the wretched jacket under my armpits where it bunched in a tight, immobile band. Gulping air like a beached fish, I fought for every breath. Sacred piles of shit. Now what?

Starving lungs, agony in my lower back. There could be little time left. The jacket had such advantages of tightness and toughness, my efforts seemed a futile display of rage.

How hopeless it all was, I hunched over onto my side to get my back off the concrete.

"God," I gasped, "you bastard, give me something, do something."

The stainless-steel device I'd stolen from the bathroom fell from the compressed folds and rattled along the floor.

I rolled after it, heart beating too fast. I lay, face-down, fumbling for the smooth, cold cylinder with my right hand. As my thumb found the button on the base, my foot caught something, boxes fell crashing to the floor. A pile of shirts flopped on top of me. Sweat drooled in my eyes, hair, mouth.

Over the ratcheting of my breath, came the grinding scrape of the door. I lay still, held by the jacket's crushing embrace.

A shadow was framed in the doorway. A patina of light glimmered on a bald head, a third eye blinked orange. Josh. The silence seemed to go on a long time.

"No use getting impatient, my friend. They'll be here in a moment."

There was a subdued tone in his voice. I took little sips of air, praying he couldn't see me properly in the near dark, half covered as I was. The metal cylinder was still in my hand.

"Don't stress it," he said, "there'll be no pain. It'll all be over soon."

He withdrew and slammed the door.

Faintness took me. I saw in my mind's eye Roxanna's puckered fingertips, the stars embedded in her fingernails. The sound of rushing water in my ears.

After what may have been seconds or minutes, I recovered slightly. It seemed to have got darker. I found I was still holding the device in my hand only inches from my face. I stabbed the button on the base with my thumb. When it whined into manic life, I turned it awkwardly towards me. I pushed the spinning arm against the material using my index finger, imploring to every deity.

It was pathetic, the material was totally unmarked. My eyes strained to focus, my lungs ached, my fingers floppy and useless. I couldn't apply sufficient pressure. I saw then I was bleeding from somewhere, a track of dark blood smudged the grimy floor.

On the ceiling, a black spot seemed to move when I turned my head. My vision was deteriorating. I closed my eyes, tried to blink the spot away, but when I opened them it was still there. Yawing my head back, forcing my eyes to fix on the yellow fuzz of the jacket, I saw a circular black spot like a cigarette burn.

Not daring to hope, I worked the device against the material again, drilled the spot while I counted to a hundred.

"Ah!"

The shaft bit the skin at my breastbone.

I made another hole beside it, only stopping at the welcome pain, then another. I made a line of holes, joining the dots. Come on, come on, I urged myself, impatience drying my mouth, breath a series of shudders. Burning smell in my nostrils, eyeballs bulging from my head, nothing visible but black holes. I pulled the material by wrenching my hands apart, hearing a harsh, tearing sound. The section under my chin began to split. Hurry, hurry.

The next time I pulled upward, there was a series of popping noises. My breastbone undulated with new air. "Come on!" I pulled, wrenched, wriggled and swore, ripping apart the fabric that bound my wrists, my body, my accursed life. The tear lengthened reluctantly, almost imperceptibly. As I writhed with frustration, the crumpled jacket refused to cooperate, perversely snagging for long minutes at my chin, my nose, my forehead.

At last, with an explosive gasp of air I slipped it up and over my head, leaving the thing dangling inside out off my arms. My shirt and jacket were sodden rags.

I got up, sucking swathes of oxygen into starving lungs. I had to pick the wrist straps apart with my teeth. Finally, I threw the thing off, kicking it viciously around the floor, gagging, spitting and coughing.

Nine fifty-two, according to my watch. No rest for the dying. I jerked the lids off storage boxes. They were stuffed full of crisp white shirts and emergency stock: food in hot cans, heat-retaining blankets, seeds, air filters, water purifiers; a set of silver dining forks; a heavy pot from the days when cooking required flame heat. There was nothing I could force the door with.

Stretching up, I examined the window. It was old, opaque glass encrusted with grime. Thick and strong, but not unbreakable. Sickening that it wasn't wide enough for my skinny frame.

I paced the floor in my cell-block fashion—three steps turn, three steps turn, as familiar as breathing.

As I marched the manic rhythm, the problem of escape tumbled through my mind, spun through thousands of permutations. Three steps, turn, three steps turn. I juggled a chain of cause and effect as sweat cooled on my skin.

Step, step, step, turn. Step, step, step, turn.

"Live and lie, deceive or die."

A shard of possibility presented itself. Utterly pathetic, but it was all there was. Escape wasn't possible. But deception was.

Time moved in ragged jolts. Everything was in place. My hands shook. Ominous sounds came from above, footsteps, heavy objects being moved.

Most of the boxes were piled against the door. The rest were stacked under the window, forming a crude staircase. The heavy pot hung from the excreta tank pipe by a "rope" of twisted, knotted blankets, reinforced by torn-off shirtsleeves. The swing of the pot aligned with the window as best I could get it.

I threw stuff in the pot, anything heavy—cutlery, brass ornaments, bags of seeds. Again, I checked its alignment with the window.

"Please Great Spirit, God, or whatever you're called," I prayed, "guide my hand, gimme some slack, you cruel shit."

Pulling back the pot, hearing the rattle of cutlery. Hauling the ungainly mass as far as my straining arms could bear, joints wrenching in their sockets. I steadied myself, then shoved it forwards with all my force.

A deafening crash as the pot smacked the window, bounced back, the glass unscathed. "Shit."

The ceiling trembled, paint flecks fell, feet pounded, an earthquake of activity above. Sharp pains in my heart. Again!

I grabbed the pot, wrapped myself around the thing, threw myself through the air with it. The glass exploded. A million shards flew, slicing my face, cutting my hands, littering the floor. The room flooded with foul outside air. Boxes trembled and fell, spilling their contents as the door was rammed with huge force. I used my elbow to clear the remaining glass from around the frame. The room reverberated with sound, filled all the space in my head. Placing my feet in the largest suitcase, I saw with horror it wasn't big enough to hide in.

As the door was pushed from outside, a trio of boxes were pushed from the stack, forks skittered across the floor tinkling a demented tune. With stuttering breath, I hunkered down into the case, pulling the lid down, rolling to one side and drawing my knees to my chin. My feet and head wouldn't go in. Shouts and thumps, more boxes fell. Pushing against one side with my hands, I worked my back flat, managing to slip my feet inside, but the side of my head was still jammed against the rim. I heard Josh's muffled shout. Twisting, gripping my ankles, I pulled my legs in tighter. Skin was being scoured from my cheek as I forced my head down onto my chest. With a final wrench a chunk of hair was torn out and my head flopped inside. The lid closed and all was darkness.

"Bastard!"

AT's voice. I had a momentary vision of myself, eyeballs rolling, a mad beast in a trap.

Thumps, yelps, the sound of slapping feet, a low animal howl so loud it could only be Roxanna. The crackle of broken glass unbearably close, like crunching bones. Something sharp cut into my knee, a weight on the lid. Blows rained down. A roar in my ears, more pounding. They know I'm here! I'm finished.

The violence stopped. Somewhere nearby, a scuffle of feet, the chink of metal, then nothing.

A tremor above, a door slammed. Silence settled like dust.

TWELVE

SIGNALS TRANSMITTED TO RANDOM LIMBS FAILED TO get a response. Only my right hand could move, prodding feebly against the lid. I imagined boxes, cans, clothing on top of the case, interring my bones. I pushed the lid again, curling my hand into a fist, twisting slightly. A slat of light, a minor avalanche as objects fell. I repeated the action, braced my other hand against the case bottom. The lid opened fully, my head popped free of the neck-breaking clinch. I could see, move. Uncoiling slowly, I emerged onto all fours. Apart from a sharp pain as I dropped my head downward—a raw patch on my back—I seemed to be intact, every joint and limb functioning.

Split boxes spewed their contents, glass fragments, cans, seeds, clothes and air filters littered the floor. The room reverberated with the aftershock of violence. Stinking air, the sound of the occasional vehicle passing outside. The pot swung on its juddering chain. The thick door hung wide open. Some fearful urge tempted me to remain, to stay concealed, but I knew I had to move.

Padding up the stairs, up into the illuminated hallway, the only sound that of my own breath and my heartbeat somewhere behind my ears. I saw with a jab of frustration that the front door was shut. My hand reached for the handle, turned it. The scanner bleeped, said, "Sealed, no exit."

Wonderful. As a bonus it'd probably send out an intruder warning.

Now there were voices echoing down the hall. Excited, passionate voices, not English—Spanish maybe. I went up the stairs to the first floor, feeling insubstantial as if made of smoke. Beyond the bathroom and the room I was held in the previous night was a third room with the door open. It looked like a hospital—two beds, instruments with dancing digits, gleaming surgical tools. This was for me, I realized. Yet another door at the end of the corridor, inside, a bed shrouded with angled drapes of glossy purple. A reek of oranges—Roxanna's bedroom. The bed was tilted upward, racks of medicinal sprays sat on a dispenser at the side. Fat candles were arrayed on a shelf in the corner. A contraption of stimrays was suspended over the bed, leaking feeble light.

I hesitated in the doorway. Roxanna could appear in the flesh or some virtual form at any moment. I moved tentatively, pulled out drawers of dazzling clothing, opened cupboards of smart coats and suits. I didn't know what I was looking for but hoped to find something, some tool, some knowledge.

Finding nothing of use, I sat on the bed, unsure what to do next. The bed adjusted itself to my weight and tilted further as I stretched my feet to the floor. The room took on a darker hue as the computer adjusted the light. The computer. Of course.

"Hey, computer. Open the front door. Now."

"Cannot comply. You have non-tribal guest status. Only ambient utilities and entertainment facilities accessible to current operator. Security alert in progress," the familiar whine.

"You betrayed me when I accessed those hacked files, you shitbag."

"I am programmed to report all unusual activity."

"What kind of unusual activity would it take for you to open the main door? What if there were some kind of emergency?"

"I am programmed to cope with any emergency."

"So what happens when there's a flood or toxic chemical spill?"

"Appropriate measures will be taken."

"What happens if there's a..."

Fire. Yes! There had to be something to light the candles with. I began opening more drawers, scouring the shelves.

A sound, a muffled thump, like something soft falling. I stood immobile, listening intently.

Then the faintest squeak on the stairs. I visualized Josh creeping towards the door. Opening myself to the sound, I listened, strained for a minute... two minutes. Nothing.

The fear of imminent violence made me aware of various sensations: slippery hands, burning cheek, a dull pain in my neck. I looked around. A chunky red crystal on the windowsill, sharp-angled and heavy. How many potential weapons had I already acquired and not used to fight with? The frog, the spinning device I'd left in the basement. Would I use this one?

Closing it in my fist, my thumb found a chink in the base. A tongue of yellow flame spurted from the side, almost burning my finger.

The flame licked at the drapes, but they merely shrivelled away from the heat. The ultra light bed cover did the same.

Another creak, louder this time.

The room became brighter lit.

"Certain materials have indicated exposure to naked flame," said the computer.

In the corner, a phial lying on its side. The label read, Eau d'l'orange. Among the warnings about modified pheremonal agents and heightened mood states the word "Flammable." The orange reek saturated the room as I blasted it over the bed. This time the bed cover burned like an offering, a silent blue pool of combustion. The flames blossomed quickly, licking at the drapes, deciding they could consume them after all. The purple wings of silk disintegrated in a flower of sparks that spiralled slowly to the floor. A siren honked. The ceiling cascaded pink fluid, saturating the room, the fire and me in a cold curtain of liquid.

When I hauled open the door, a man was frozen in place, halfway up the stairs. It was the driver, Siddharta. He was staring up at the ceiling, one hand on the banister, his face folded in shock.

Crashing down the stairs, siren blasting, I hit the wall, bounced off.

"Fire! Fire!" I shrieked, louder than the siren, louder than the roaring in my head. As I closed on him and raised the crystal, he flinched, raising his hands. "What...?"

He didn't get to say it, whatever it was, I'd already run past him. At the bottom of the stairs, the front door gaped open. The hall was flooded with light, bad air, street noises. Out! Out!

Out the door, tripping on the steps, dropping the crystal, almost falling into the street. I looked up into a parched blood sky, the air scented with fire.

The big black car sat parked out front. The street was quiet, apart from an occasional passing vehicle and a couple of figures in the distance, one dressed in red the other in black.

They won't take me again, I swore. No one would chain me again.

I shambled off in the opposite direction, spitting blood. I'd bitten my tongue, fat and unfamiliar in my mouth. I was full of vague pains, incomplete.

The street seemed to go straight on to forever with nowhere to hide, the houses high-walled, gated, and shuttered. Eventually, on the opposite side, a gap like a missing tooth, a low house with a short hybrid hedge around it. I crashed through the hedge, trailing leaf and twig, crossing a lawn of purple grass. A whirring, grille-mouthed, mower robot appeared, with swivelling sensor eyes that nibbled impatiently at my heels. Head down, I dodged through thorn and thicket to the back gate, where a battery of recycle bins pointed skyward. I clambered over the gate, landing on my backside in an alley. Turning right, I dashed between two villa-style houses, then left again into an avenue of hair-thin trees. I expected Josh and AT to appear in a heartbeat.

The sidewalk steamed, the gardens blazed with color. House doors signalled tribe loyalty—Masonic eyes, yin-yang doorknockers, crescent moons and stars.

I checked my watch. The hands had stopped moving.

Two vultures on a pantiled roof, idle as thugs, watched me. How come all the scavengers survived The Changes? The rats and cockroaches, the mosquitoes and vultures? Not just survived, but multiplied, thrived.

A riot of traffic ahead, streams of people; a parked car's windscreen mirrored my approaching figure—a derelict in a torn suit, splattered with grime, blood and anti-flammatory spray. Only the eyes in that ruined face hinted at signs of life. I needed a network, filters, skin protection, new clothes. I needed Orion.

THIRTEEN

A CLUMP OF PEOPLE STOOD WAITING TO CROSS THE road. I tried to merge, aware of them studying me covertly. I sensed blood streams loaded with lifestyle optimizers, mood-lifters, leukocyte boosters riding their aortal highways. A jangle of light effects cascaded down shop-fronts. A short woman stood opposite me, waiting across the street with fancy spex, blue hair and cheeks studded with an intricate pattern of silver swirls. Her blue dress skittered with moving images.

Lights changed, autobrakes locked, traffic halted and the mob moved off. I remained on the pavement.

The blue-haired woman came close, a cockatoo or some such bird shrilling away down her front.

"Excuse me. Please wait a minute."

She jerked back from some realm behind her mirrored spex. Her little mouth closed slightly, she half-turned, carried on.

I ran ahead of her, blocked her path. "Please! You're in the Cosmique, right? I need to connect to one of your number."

She stopped. The spex gleamed coldly. "My daywear is alarmed. I am recording this action, any attempt to obstruct me will trigger your instant arrest."

"No. I only want... Orion. Orion D'Angello. She's in your tribe. Can I use your portal to speak to her?"

The lips momentarily pressed tighter together. "Orion is no longer one of our people. She has left the path."

"I assure you she's definitely a Cosmique member. I was with her only yesterday. Can you call her for me?"

The spex tracked me carefully up and down. "By the spirits!" she said. "Why are you in such a condition?"

Someone's elbow thudded into my kidney. Two white-robed, priestly types stopped to watch the show.

"I've been attacked. Please, call Orion, tell her it's Zachary. I assure you she's on your network."

"She's not." The reflective glaze of the spex remained steady. "Do not delay me further."

"I... Forgive me. I'm not mistaken. Do you know her personally?"

The woman hissed loud and long. She mumbled something into her spex and stuck her blue-clad arm out. A panel of liquid color flickered on the back of a fat silver bracelet. Orion's head was framed in miniature, a bright spot burning between her eyes.

"... to tell you now of my enlightenment." Orion's breathy voice came from somewhere in the folds of the woman's dress. "Following the instincts of the artist I am, I've accepted an invite to join the Great Ascension. By divine grace, my development will be liberated to new levels. No longer inhibited by inti-mate-destructive issues I will find new creative outlets, and..."

The screen went blank.

"When the police arrive," the woman said. "I won't instigate legal proce-dures if you allow me to pass unhindered."

"Please, no police. I'll leave."

I stepped aside, almost knocking into one of the robed rubberneckers. The woman swivelled on her heel and walked off.

Could this data be trusted? That "intimate destructive" stuff, the words sounded like Orion's. And the reaction on the woman's face at Orion's name. It had to be true. Data wasn't trustworthy, it was the signs and signals of the heart that betrayed the truth.

I stood, trying to discern what instinct would guide me now, where my heart would lead me.

"Jeez. What happened to you?"

The cop's spex were encircled with scanning scopes and DNA detectors. Her uniform a patch-work of badges, body armor, weaponry and display panels.

"Why did you interfere with a citizen's freedom of movement?"

I crumpled under the photon-powered might of her scrutiny. My backside slumped to the hot pavement in resignation, pedestrians trampling around me.

"An offense has been committed," she said.

I saw the wedge-shaped police vehicle parked half-on the pavement, saw the streams of statistics running across her shielded eyes.

"I never had a chance, did I?"

"Mister Tarn. You better explain yourself fast, or you'll be arrested."

Mister Tarn? Was I still him? A bolt of hope shot me into a standing posi-tion, donning my "baffled" expression. "I really am most terribly sorry, officer. I can't tell you how stupid I feel. I thought I knew the lady, but didn't." The cop stepped back, listened to a data feed for a few seconds. "You demanded Stellar Hevan connect you to another Cosmique member—she's just uploaded a record of the event."

"Yeah, that's what I mean. I wanted to connect to a fellow Cosmique, but she wasn't a member any more. I mean, it doesn't matter now. I hope I didn't cause any trouble. I'd hate to have alarmed her in any way."

The cop stood, processing. She looked back to her car, tapping her gloved hand against the stun-stick at her hip.

"Your actions have been logged and noted. Any further aberrant behavior will trigger instant arrest. Go now and transgress no more. Enjoy your lifestyle."

I sloped off in a state of near elation. I felt... honored, accepted, blessed. Quadrillions of data was downloading every nano-second, recording every shade and hue of human experience: transactions made and wished for, urine analysis, observations, speculations, meditations, affirmations, knowledge shared and bared, great slabs of data, slipping through the air in a molecule-modifying locomotive of energy. And in there somewhere, my distorted tale, my altered details, endorsed, validated, endowed, however temporarily, with legitimacy.

I'd been given the gift of life, at least for a while. While the trick lasted, I had to do something unexpected, something that would put me into another realm, create a gulf between me and those that hunted my hide.

I made my way towards the lake front, using the tallest buildings for landmarks. I leaned against shop windows, lingered in their doorways where genie ads cajoled and captured my data. I left a data trail so deep and wide a single-cell navigation aid would have no trouble working it out.

An hour later, I stood by the lake front wall, almost opposite Orion's apartment. This is where Roxanna and her tribe would track me, this is where they'd think I'd be. I put my hand in my pocket, fondled my wad of cash. Where to run? I shut my eyes, reached into the well of inner feeling and fumbled for a glimmer of knowing.

England. The word was already there, chink, wink. That word, that place, that once-home of mine seemed to call. That little island parked by the North Sea where the fairy-tale Triton was supposed to be. Didn't the hacker, the Scarecrow, live there who was no friend of Roxanna's and who'd maybe help me? It seemed then as if this is where I'd always been headed.

The rationale was insane. The flight-time alone would give the authorities and the Great Ascension every chance to catch me in transit. The place was supposed to be arctic-like since the Gulf Stream had shifted. The security at the airports would be insurmountable. The obstacles, the distance, the terrors. It was sky-high risk, the strategy of a lunatic.

I promised myself I'd trust the irrational. The Changes had broken the back of reason, of cause and effect. In this new-made world, the unthinkable was possible. I walked up Lake side Drive and waited till a bashed-up taxi lurched into view, then brought it to a halt by the simple strategy of walking in front of it.

❧

In the first weeks of The Changes rain the color of urine fell for three weeks non-stop, leaves and lawns turned yellow, crops failed, the sun disappeared, no birds sang.

The media showed a world in chaos, people drowned in their houses. There was looting, shooting, bodies floating, refugees.

The world's markets went into freefall. In the U.S., whole cities were shocked into movement. Trails of people hiked the highways from east to west, west to east. People weaned on a four-car lifestyle had to learn to walk, to boil water before drinking, to go without. Food was strictly rationed, curfews imposed.

The first to adapt to the new environment were viruses. New strains appeared overnight, jumping eons of evolution, leaping species, crossing distances, transiting cellular defences. Ebola two and three, plague, SARS and influenza the worst of them. The young and the healthy were particularly vulnerable. News channels spewed figures: nine million dead, sixteen million sick. Scientific institutes offered explanations: trapped sub-trophic particles in the upper atmosphere, critical hydroxyl loss, carbon sink failure, ocean-bound methane release.

No explanation was adequate. Events seemed not of a chemical but a divine nature. The catastrophe appealed to the basic and primitive that only the religious had words for. The familiar frames of reference were jarred out of kilter. People rushed through the night to stand in empty fields waiting for a sign. Images of angels were found in cucumbers, corncobs, carrots; church statues of the Virgin Mary bled, cried, spoke, sighed. Long-dead wells sprung water, trees withered, a burning cross appeared in the Omaha sky.

Rumor Rumors were rife: Jehovah's Witnesses never got the virus; holy water from a church font in Nebraska guaranteed immunity from illness; a tarot reader in California cured SARS by chanting. New faiths and creeds appeared, all claimed to have the truth and the solution. All hinted at certification for a priority inoculation, extra rations, favorable treatment.

The old male gods died. The petroleum age was over. Testosterone was reviled as the fuel that drove a mechanized universe to near destruction. The United Nations declared year zero, a new era was beginning. Feminine gods, feminine values would offer salvation. Folk formed networks, new webs of loyalties, new connections. *The providers adapted, forged intimate and exclusive relationships with the new tribes.*

People seemed to disappear overnight, power and water were intermittent, the trash wasn't taken away. Inoculations began and stopped, the rumble of military vehicles was heard in the darkness, contradictory statements were made by the authorities.

Our little town of Marlborough was evacuated early one morning. Almost all complied with the loudspeaker appeals except Alvina and I. We later heard from a neighbor how they'd been taken to a storage silo some eight miles outside of town. Nurses and volunteers with armbands and a few army personnel gave them hot drinks and blankets, vitamin tablets. Then the officials disappeared. After forty-eight hours people drifted back home.

We sat in our house, fighting the personal disintegration that overcame so many. Washing was difficult, food a matter of eating whatever was available—tinned sardines or week-old bread. We sat opposite each other through dark evenings making silent prayers for each other's safety.

I fabricated seed-sprouters from anaplastic funnels, made a hand-cranked washing machine, ground corn from dried husks, wasted nothing.

"You were made for this emergency," Alvina said. "You've always been a survivor, a make-doer." She smiled ruefully, pulled me to her. "I married a man made for hard times. If anyone lives through this, you will."

"It's you," I replied. "You give me the hunger to live."

FOURTEEN

THE AIRPORT WAS A NIGHTMARE OF CROWDS, MONITOR beams, spangled uniforms and jabbering genie-ads leaping from every tangent. People hurried under untidy light clutching cases like refugees.

A screen display announced that a flight for London Heathrow was departing in ninety minutes. It took half that time to get myself cleaned up in the rest room and to find the check-in. A single passenger stood in line in a coat that shussed with grainy movie clips. He dabbed his index finger in a depression on the counter and said his name, Bernie Aster. Then he walked through to the boarding barrier.

I visualized Roxanna's driver racing for the airport, the boys huddled together in the back, hoarse-voiced and furious. Back in the zone, a guard or automonitor would detect my empty shackle and beam my escape to every chunk of technology on the planet. The taxi I'd used had been so decrepit it seemed surveillance-free, but since I'd been at the airport I'd been detected a trillion times.

The steward nodded me forward. I paused to unclench my clammy fists and purge my body of lie giveaways. Take it easy, you can do this, didn't you cool it through the DATCHO screen? I let my breath out slow, like a balloon deflating. When my digit touched the depression on the counter, blue letters spiralled up, "Med. T. OK. I.D. Mick Tarn. No reservation. No credit facility."

The steward's smile faltered. He regarded my ragged suit, my face.

"We have stand-by seats available, Mr. Tarn. You have no travel restrictions and your protocols are fine, but there appears to be some difficulty with your credit. I fear we can't offer you a flight with us today."

"Payment presents no difficulties," I said, slapping a pile of notes on the counter. "I got hard cash."

He examined my face. "We haven't accepted cash for over a decade, sir."

"Holy horseshit, you can't do this! These are good American dollars..." That's where I ran dry. I couldn't seem to summon the right tone of outrage. It was such a relief not to get arrested on the spot.

The bills lay strewn on the counter, grimy and crumpled from the compost that had buried them. The steward sniffed like they were contaminated.

"It's imperative I get on that flight," I said

"Like I said, sir. We can't accept cash."

I leaned on the counter, sighed, summoned my best authoritarian voice. "Be attentive. I am the lord high master of the Unbelievers. Our tribe does not trust technology or aesthetics or any kind, nor do we believe in credit in any shape or form." I held a wodge of notes under his aquiline nose. "'Let you not a borrower nor a lender be,' sayeth the lord, and this creed is well known. I demand you respect my human rights granted by the good offices of this land. A complaint will be forthcoming. What is your name?"

Forty seconds later, I was moving towards the departure gate, past smiling security guards, their designer weapons beautifully formed, words cool in their mouths. "Enjoy your journey sir. Travel Am-Air again soon."

I felt flushed with success. I'd promised myself I wouldn't be recaptured. I'd die first. And a memory popped into my head then of another time, another place when I'd made another promise at least as important.

⚜

Sitting on the back steps of the house during our first autumn together. Hidden behind the Berkshire Hills in deepest Massachusetts. All around us neat lawns, hazy fields, hickory, sycamore and maple. The mist of pollution was almost unnoticeable, the trees resplendent with saffron and claret. Their leaves dripped to the ground constantly like a blessing.

Alvina came out to sit beside me, shielding her eyes as she looked to the horizon.

I stared at her with her hair still damp from the shower, my married-to-me wife. I was still in the disbelieving stage, as if it were amazing that this beautiful woman walked and talked, shared her life with me.

"They said yes," she said.

"They'll sell your paintings on commission? That's fabulous."

"Yes," she repeated uncertainly.

"Which store?"

She blinked her bottomless brown eyes, cleared her throat. "It's that tiny boutique with hand-made jewelry near the top of Main Street, 'The New Curiosity Shop.'" She sighed.

"What's wrong?"

"It's too perfect." She brought her knees up, dropped her chin onto them. "I can't bear all this happiness. I can feel it trickling through my fingers. Now we're in this fabulous place. The first time I ask if someone will take my paintings, they say yes. You abandon your A-list clients, but they fly up here to see you anyway.

It's perfect, the house, you, everything. My life's never had so much good in it all at once. Terrible things will happen, I know it."

"Nonsense," I said, taking her hand. "This is how it will be, now. We got good health, everything. Things change for the better sometimes. Relax and enjoy it."

I said the words against the tide of my own feelings. I knew even better than Alvina that beautiful things don't fall from the sky into an ugly life.

She looked up. "Maybe that's why I was in the film business. It's for liquid people, we can be anything. But not you. You're my roots. You're fixed in the compass of yourself. You could never pretend to be anyone other than who you are."

I stroked her forehead. "My home is where you are."

She trapped my hand in both of hers. "If anything happens to us, anytime in the future, if we get separated for any reason, you'd never stop waiting for me, would you?"

It was a typical statement of hers. She was always voicing contingency measures: "if I don't get back on time and my network is down, sit in the car and wait outside the house." A sudden breeze tugged at her hair, her eyes glistened.

"Nothing will separate us," I said. "We're in this for the duration."

"Don't tempt the evil eye." She shivered, rubbed her arms, turned to face me. "If we were ever separated. Promise you'd wait for me. Your watching and waiting would save me, I could survive anything knowing you were there."

"Hey, relax." I rubbed the back of her neck. "This is all a bit over-dramatic for a trip to the laundrette."

But the set of her jaw demanded an answer.

I sighed. "Of course, I'd wait. I'd never stop waiting. I promise."

⟜❦⟞

The leviathan, lozenge-shaped ship bore the name *Merlin ll*. I leaned out of my puffed-up cradle seat and dredged through the goodies in the armrest: a set of wrap-around spex, damp towels, vitamin sweets, a look-book.

As the seconds ticked by before undocking, I checked my useless watch repetitively in some pathetic Pavlovian reflex.

With a lurch and a suffocated roar we undocked. The deck quivered, there was a ticklish sensation in the pit of my stomach. For a moment I had a sense of being incredibly heavy. Within minutes, the illuminated docking piers of O'Hare were far below, airships nudging against them like larvae feeding.

Chicago was a galaxy of activity and moving light, car followed car in long processions, buildings blazed, rooftop landing-platforms throbbed, street signs twinkled in the pollution haze. Then there was something else. My mouth dried, my eyes locked as we passed an unlit quadrangle crowded with yellow buildings where no traffic moved. I shuddered as the primal darkness of the DATCHO zone slipped below, ringed by sparkling sensa-wire.

How many years had I watched a procession of blimps from the confines of my cell? How many times had I wished on every invisible star to be on one of them? Now it was happening. Maybe wishes could come true, if you wished hard enough. I sat stunned at the wonder of it.

Uniformed attendants slipped between seats, whispering with hushed reverence, "Refreshments? Entertainments?"

I was ravenous.

"No cash sir, credit only," cawed the attendant when I proffered the notes. It didn't seem worth making another scene.

I knocked back the vitamin sweets, they wouldn't keep me going for the eighteen-hour long flight.

On the back of the seat in front, the "You may remove your seat belts" sign came on.

In the toilets, cold water revived me a little. When I re-emerged, bleary-eyed, the "Get High" bar had opened. A woman with purple eyes fisting a pink drink gawped as I passed. I read her lips as she leaned over her friend and said, "His face!"

The barman hooked my eyes, gave me a "why worry" kind of smile accompanied by a shrug that pulled his epaulets to his ears. I remembered that smile as I ran the gauntlet of averted eyes back to my seat.

Through the four-foot porthole, inky clouds mottled with orange, a glistening river lit like lightning.

My eyes latched onto a roll in the hand of a woman slumped in the end seat of the next aisle. Rice bread, succulent spun yeast, yellow bean sprouts. I could eat that. My stomach yowled at the sight, the seeds speckling the brown crust, a vision of gold.

The woman was long and honed, wearing a pleated black one-piece that nipped her waist ultra-tight with supportive staywear. Though African of feature her skin was bleached bone-white, her hair so black it seemed to absorb all light. Her lips pearl-tinted, her thick fingers like sausages. She caught me staring and abruptly donned her complimentary spex. It felt like a rebuff. She fiddled with her suit for a while at the ankle before slouching back.

The pilot droned out his in-flight drivel, reassured us how safe we were (though conceding he was piloting us from somewhere back on the ground). He praised the ship's solar-tiled, paper-light fuselage, the uber-strong, helium-filled buoyancy tanks, the speed, the wonder.

I picked up my spex. When I pressed the "instructions" button the thing told me I needed a credit transfer for five hours use and then blathered on about the lupe's 3D technology.

I jumped as the black-haired woman's seat bumped back to almost horizontal. She'd donned a pair of gloves and hidden the lower part of her face under a close-fitting, flesh-colored mask. Her spex were blasting miniature rainbows on her cheekbones. Mouth hanging, limbs unstrung, she'd vacated this realm completely.

After ten minutes or so, I guessed she'd fallen asleep, the untouched roll still in her hand. A fingertip-sized depression appeared in the material of her suit. It slid slowly across the front of her shoulder. More puckers appeared, moving in spiralling clusters over her upper arms. I wondered if I should call a steward, whether this was normal.

The puckered hollows multiplied, streamed around her ribs and down the length of her arms. She groaned and rolled her head side-to-side as if trying to shake them off. No one seemed to pay her any attention. The guy next to her guffawed under his own spex. Others slept, some milled around the bar or mumbled into blog-files. She seemed possessed by her clothing. It twitched fitfully about her torso, depressions cupped her biceps, squeezed them out of shape.

She snapped her head back, her seat shuddered. I felt depraved, an intruder, but didn't look away.

Hollows crawled up her ankles, circled her knees and played around her thighs, rotating, stroking. She bathed in her pool of private pleasure. Her lover, real or created, teased, pleased, stirred her hunger.

I watched the roll, saw it swing in her hand nearer and nearer the floor, the fingers loosening. She began to move—just a subtle nudge of the hips at first, but then a regular ripple of movement. Above the murmur of conversation, a soft moan.

She accelerated the pace.

I watched the roll tremble. It slipped as her grip loosened, swung pendulum-like by the tips of her fingers.

With a grunt, she stopped moving. The roll dropped into the aisle. With one smooth movement, I leaned forwards, swept it up and put it under my jacket. Contented, she stretched and softened into her seat and I sank, equally contented, into my own.

When I opened my eyes, an attendant was shuffling down the darkened aisle with a coffee trolley. Most of the other passengers were sleeping. I checked the time readouts on the console above the bar. It took a while, but I calculated we'd be landing within half-an-hour. I'd slept for fourteen hours straight.

Through the window in diluted light, blue-black shreds of cloud lingered over a sea of gray silk with seeming muscles writhing beneath. Two near-identical container ships navigated between enormous icebergs leaving twin white trails. As I watched, the sea was replaced by patchy terrain with vein-like rivers breaking its surface.

How changed would this land be since last I knew it? How changed would Alvina be if I ever saw her again? I visualized her doing all the Alvina things— painting furiously with her pink tongue protruding, jumping up and down when she got excited, devastating a room with her untidiness. It was hard to see her clearly, harder still to believe in the possibility of ever holding her again. I padded around my pockets for her photo.

It wasn't there. It must have got lost in the basement of Roxanna's house. I groaned, now I had no DNA to track her with. The last evidence of Alvina had gone.

FIFTEEN

AT HEATHROW, A QUARTER-MILE QUEUE OF PEOPLE shuffled through an array of processing stations. After passing the first few scans in a state of fright, I relaxed, calculating they'd have shackled me on the spot if the alarm had been raised. Over forty-eight hours after it was created, the fake ID was still in place.

Customs was a line of officials behind highly audible anxiety sniffers and lie-detector screens. Growing more confident of my deceptions, I slipped my mind into neutral and blanked the blue uniforms with vague answers to their clipped questions, "I'm on vacation. Probably two weeks, but maybe longer, you know." No body signs betrayed me. Loose limbed and limpid-eyed, I smiled with all my face while visualizing myself alone on an endless beach with two suns in the sky at once.

Approaching the arrivals gate I ducked behind the man in the movie coat, panning around for a Great Ascension waiting committee. No one in the crowd had an illuminated third eye, no one reacted to my passing except a gaggle of Angels of the Female Christ screeching about redemption.

The airport shuttle rattled and moaned as it moved through the earth under the metropolis. After the flight, the experience was almost mediaeval, hurtling through black, cob-webbed tunnels.

Stations flashed by, oases of piercing light—Hammersmith, Maida Vale, Baron's Court,

Fifteen years confined to a room and now constant motion. Only the vaguest of plans picked from the air and no idea if it made sense or not.

I changed to the Northern line. Inexplicably, just before Camden Town station, the carriage stopped, ticking ominously. The lights dimmed. Now what? I waited with jangling nerves for the hand on my shoulder, the harsh voice. Lupe lenses crackled in the dark. A gold-haired, ebony-skinned man stood two inches away and stared into space with that peculiarly English air of faint embarrassment. Above us the distant rumble of traffic, or perhaps a more subtle resonance—that of the city itself, grinding out the relentless rhythm of human activity.

Getting off the train at Camden Town, I changed my cash into Euros in a platform auto-booth that asked no questions. It wasn't till I emerged from the station that I got my first smack of icy English air.

My paper-thin, real-cotton suit was utterly useless against the bone-cracking cold. Yellow snow tumbled from a purple sky, thickening the roofs and lining the roadside. Photons lanced across rooftops like lightning. Beards of blue moss hung from railings, gutters and overhead wires. In the bleached light all seemed surreal. Cars and buses crept by silently, the only sound the sluicing of wet snow, a hiss of heating vents and the castanet clatter of a loose manhole cover.

People moved in eddies, signalling tribe loyalty by skin pigment, body adornment, or clothing. No sign of crystal-embedded foreheads. The Great Ascension's power center was probably the U.S. If they'd had the numbers, they would have surely got me at the airport. Maybe after all, it was only the cops I had to worry about. Legions of police might be checking their weapons, boots clanking on metal stairwells, my name spat from their lips.

Everything seemed smaller, shabbier, neglected. I felt a sense of something indefinable—crumbling brick, old churches, damp, history, the past—a sense of England itself. When I'd left this country it was in fast decline, you didn't need to be a fortune-teller to see the way things were going. There'd been no-one to say goodbye to, nothing to hold me. America was a place to live out fictions. You could lose yourself there, hide behind your mask.

Frigid sensations crept down my spine. Holy crap, was it cold. I wouldn't survive without a huna suit. I had to get clothed, connected, mobile.

I crossed the street, shuffling past the mock-Georgian, fake Gothic and imitation Tudor buildings of Camden High road. I stopped at a haze of heat around a holo-cast of sparking lights and illuminated snowflakes outside an enhancement parlor. Through the glass, two men stared—burnish-eyed, beautifully drawn brows, hair glistening with oily light. Words flitted across the window between us: "New skin in nine days. Regrow your hair, any length any color. Breast re-shaping. Buttock lifts. Give your man the ultimate gift of manhood—penile enlargements a specialty. No appointment necessary."

Further down the road, smart-clothed people steamed and stomped behind ramshackle stalls selling roses with heads the size of cauliflowers, silver apples with words of pink blooming in the skin, "Cardiocure—The fruits of love!'

Snowflakes fell faster, the cold intensified. A yellow-tiled path crossed the pavement, a pair of dome-helmeted beardy-weirdies on silent powered-cycles almost knocked me flying.

A square-jawed rejuvenile with a pointed hat and an eye painted on his forehead stood in the entrance of a Taiwanese take-away. As I passed him, something clicked, maybe his eyes, a moment of recognition. Unnerved, I upped the pace, feet splashing wetly.

At a junction, a huge pub, "The Feckless Horse," dominated a crowded shopping plaza, the whole a swathe of color.

Two maybe-youths, a male and a female stood immobile on the corner, each with dots painted on their brow.

Drawing abreast of me, they glanced at each other and turned away. I crossed the road, went left at the corner. In a shadowed alley, a wall scrawled with blazing graffiti. In the dimness beyond, a sinuous darker movement, a cat, ears pricked, amber eyes.

When I looked back, the couple rounded the corner, heads nodding together. I stopped by a shop-front venting warm air.

I watched my reflection as the couple passed. They didn't glance in my direction. They're not following, fool. They're no Great Ascension tribesters. Relax, you're paranoid.

I stopped at a pavement ministry of Bodhisattva warriors—yellow robes, rattling tins, bald heads. Since they cured baldness, everyone's got a shaved head. A blazing panel of heat at a portable stand. Three bored-looking citizens and I stood close to the panel. The snow thinned to a desultory spattering. A man in a long green coat shouted, waving his arms.

"There are still were too many of us," he bawled. "Gaia groans at each new birth. Nine billion of the most rapacious creatures ever to infest the earth. We need population curbs, now. Join the Boddissatvas."

At the edge of my vision stood a tall girl, features too small for her face, black dot on her brow, silver codpiece at her crotch. She edged closer. Then I saw the couple again, further ahead, looking in a shop window. I moved on, overtook them, turned left, moving as fast as possible without actually running. My eyes streamed with toxic snow, my feet were numb. Glacial-cheeked, I glanced behind. All three were close on my heels.

I broke into a run. Ahead, the shopping plaza and the Boddisattva warriors. I'd walked around in a square. A shop to my right, "Holistic Health and Beauty," its door gliding open:

"Welcome, Mick."

Inside a fog of warm air and a reek of chemicals. Assistants in white trouser suits stood behind displays. Grim-faced customers picked over products. I lingered by a stack of cosmetics, watching the door. No one followed me in. Before me a dazzling armory in the battle against decay: bullet-like phials of wrinkle-eliminating hexapeptides and cell-reprogram serums; cannisters of Skinrevive; the heavy weaponry of cell regeneration creams.

I picked a rainproof coat off a shelf in plaid, shiny material. In a basket, a pile of fits-all, air-filtering face-masks. Perfect. I took them to the nearest assistant.

"Eighty euros," she said, watching snow melt off my eyebrows with an air of distaste.

At the back of the shop was an area screened off for skin treatments. Slinking behind the screen, a place of couches, lockers and darkened booths where clients and therapists muttered conspiratorially. I buttoned on the raincoat, spent clammy minutes getting the face mask on. Naturally, the fits-all face mask didn't fit my face, the eyeholes too small, the fastener too tight.

As I strode for the main door, some techno-bastard voice ordered me to enjoy my purchases. Then out on the ice-bound street.

Through the mask's narrowed eyeholes the scene—the snow-crusted buildings, the careering cars—looked smeary and opaque like a painting.

No ambush, no cops, no three-eyed creatures visible. Walking quickly, knocking against people not in my line of sight. After half a block, a cream-colored, steam-belching bus filled my eyeholes.

Joining the end of the queue, I jogged in place to keep my blood from freezing. As we filed on board, the suspension groaned, adjusting itself. No driver, just an ugly data-cruncher at the front. A glimmering sign, "Free City Bus—Sponsored by Cyberdelic." Maybe the dice were falling for me at last.

SIXTEEN

THE BUS AMBLED ALONG THE TOTTENHAM COURT road, power unit whining, marzipan slush sluicing from the wheels. Ads leaped off their roadside hoardings into the windows. Each time the vehicle moved off, an orchestra of springs yawed from the seats. I urged it onward with my buttocks. The mask began to feel clammy as I thawed out. I stretched the eyeholes with my fingers, loosened the raincoat around my neck.

As we passed through Hammersmith, I took stock of myself. Every limb complained, no part seemed free of ache or strain.

Somewhere near the M25, the bus stopped by the "Stellar Shopping Experience," a cluster of temple-like domes and discount kiosks. I left the bus, bent double in the maw of a blizzard.

Doric columns stood at the entrance, sheathed in frozen snow. A rush of heat, a whiff of anxiety as the doors opened. Years of frantic purchasing had accumulated unease in the fake rock of the grotto-like interior. Perhaps buildings have memories too.

Shop fronts were set in rock crags between channelled streams. A six-foot golden fish spouted into a finger-shaped pool. People wandered wearing spex and lenses. Children paddled in the water, their uninhibited squeals and the thunder of water filled me with an insatiable sadness, a sense of having been disconnected from the stream of life too long.

Scents drifted, windows swirled with sleek invention. A trembling tree of knotted tubers beckoned with its branches, pointed to a spring that wrought itself into a word, Artemis. A line of one, two and three-wheeled powered cycles trundled up and down a shop-front, handsome couples astride them.

A powered bike would work. It offered mobility, invisibility and it could go where cars couldn't. With an all-body huna suit, helmet, hands and gloves, there'd be no bare skin to trickle DNA.

The shop was an Aladdin's cave of consumerism, everywhere the gloss and killer curves of designer gadgetry. Spex and suits, boots and gizmos, every kind of clever clothing.

The heron-thin assistant regarded my masked face with her odd-colored eyes. I refused to remove it, even when she scanned my skull for helmet size. She complimented me as I pointed out a vermilion suit of arachnid scales with trillions of follicle-like papillary nodules on the inside. It looked to be able to do everything except fly.

"Your taste, sir, is exquisite," she twittered, "the suit is fully-wired, self-powering, self-repairing and self-cleaning with active bacteria, multi-networked, biofeedback enabled, intelligent and multi-facilitated."

The suit had a clam-zipped, ribbed jacket with built-in cuff portal, temperature override and tag-on trousers that sagged like a sail when I held them against me.

"Have no cares," the assistant assured me as I made for the changing booth, "wear it next to bare skin, it'll learn your body shape and mold itself to fit."

I got a full-face, full-function, ultra-lightweight, air-sealed, smart-view crash helmet, high-grade micro-vented nostril filters, protective eyeball lenses, heated acu-stim gloves, bio-fed boots, circulation-stimulating socks. I acquired a Honda velo, as the assistant insisted electro-cycles were called. It was a red metal-flake affair with a wrap-around windscreen, sit-up-and-beg handlebars, molded seat, a grooved cowling over the power unit and fold-away pedals.

I was a lifestyle enhancer, a brand-hungry hunter, a product potentializer. I bought light and sound, heat and air, speed and vision. I felt... empowered, uplifted, almost holy. All my hard-earned stash was burned but for a few euros. I hustled from the shop, the assistant's thanks and after-sales patter following me out. I pushed the gleaming velo by its handlebars, squeaking and stretching in the strange suit, its inner sleeve clinging to my flesh. A recycle bin had the audacity to complain when I dumped my old rags in it, that it was for food-grade materials only.

I made a quick stop in the cleft between two shops, donning socks and boots, eyeball lenses and helmet, getting everything zipped and sealed.

Outside the blizzard had turned to sleet. The scene seemed crystal clear thanks to the smart-vision, tinted helmet visor. One click of the sliding switch on the cuff of my suit and warmth woozed into my skin.

I punted the velo over a car park with my feet, then across a road and behind an ugly mound of organically-formed housing complexes. Then a bright yellow velo-way beckoned with no-car warning markers.

The velo powered off with one twist of the throttle, wheels shushed through snow, the seat molding itself to my backside. Fresh air seeped over the top of the screen and into my nostrils and a burden seemed to have fallen away. A hot rush ran up my backbone. It was a shock to feel exhilarated. "I'm alive," I said. "I live and breathe."

I stuck to the tiled veloway, buzzing across busy streets, careening across car parks, zigzagging around pedestrian zones and shopping malls. To be moving under my own power was a revelation, a sense of being, at last, truly free.

Serried rows of warehouses whipped by, their roofs stacked with containers, their docking-cradles like scribbled lines against the sky. Light-gathering generators were stuck on buildings at all angles. The urban hinterland seemed endless. Here and there a hybrid tree appeared, ring-fenced in case it tried to escape.

The occasional pedestrian crossed my path. Not one head turned to observe me, I'd become invisible. Other velos overtook or passed in the opposite direction.

Colors were vivid, outlines bold, every object seemed more tangible. The odd dusting of yellow snow was thrown from banks of blood-red cloud with black streaks bleeding through. It was terrifying, that sky. Such a sky in ancient times foretold the death of kings.

I gained speed, gaining confidence in the velo, in its gyroscopic balance and effortless power. Only problem was it wouldn't shut up.

"Welcome to the Overlander, by Honda," it brayed. The voice male, English, well-bred, tingled against my collarbone and rang around inside the helmet. "I am equipped with a low output, six watt draw, air-cooled velocipede system. I have an environmental compensation coefficient of two point eight. Apart from my hydraulic assisted pedal action, there is a choice of manual, solar-charged, or fuel-cell power sources. My wheels are puncture-proofed, anaplastic-tired, recyclable duralamin..."

"Be quiet!"

"Operator, I need to learn your voice patterns for accurate speech-to-code recognition. Allowances will be made for motion distortion. Please repeat these words..."

Unable to find any way of turning the on-board computer off, I relented at the umpteenth request and repeated parrot-like a litany of ludicrous utterances—'Argentina. Leviathan. Constantinople.'

When eventually the thing was satisfied, it said: "I'm ready to receive your directions now, Mick Tarn. My navigation system is on-stream."

"How did you know who I am?"

The machine hesitated for a few seconds making insect clicks before answering. "By purchase-input warranty records, biometrics and a DNA trace within your suit. Do you wish your name as your default address?"

"No, not that one. Call me Zach. What about communications?"

"Various portals are available, Zach. One is located in your helmet, one in your suit and of course I have my own on-board device. All will be cross-networked, updated and online shortly."

"Okay. For now, guide me towards the city of Cambridge."

The machine gave directions, "Left at next junction, careful of motor traffic approaching, second exit on the right..." Then, "Zach, would you like to choose my default address?"

"Meaning what?"

"Do you wish to give me a name?"

"A name? Oh, okay. I'll call you, er...Tinman."

"Thank you."

My sight went flat without depth or distance. The snow stopped, the sky went blue and the sun came out. The wonderful, not-seen-for-decades old sun scorched my eyes. Buildings basked in bright light, overbold color colors slapped my retina. The dashboard flickered, my jacket sleeve flashed blue warnings.

"Tinman, what's going on?"

"As my processing power is superior, I've assumed default cross-platform control over i-wear, optical devices and networks. I'm presently establishing power-sharing capacity and collecting data."

"What happened to my eyes?"

"I've set your helmet screen optical enhancement to clear view, the most popular mode. Do you wish another vision?"

"You mean it's just an effect?"

"Your vis-eye enabled screen is set to overlay optimum weather conditions on present landscape. Do you wish another view?"

"No, it's fine. But don't do anything else without my permission. It makes me nervous."

A shimmer of heat lifted from the roofs of a line of parked cars. If I reached out and touched the bodywork it would surely be hot to my fingertips. With the yellow orb in the sky and the suit warming my bones, I might have been enjoying a summer's day in the beforetime. The velo asked if the suspension was adjusted to my liking and I felt in my bones a sense of sheer pleasure.

SEVENTEEN

BY LATE MORNING A FEW SQUARE MILES OF undeveloped land had opened up. According to the velo I was twenty-two miles south of Cambridge. Brick and building had given way to blisters of grow-domes emblazoned with provider names. I rode a ribbon of concrete by the side of a canal, part of the system of flood dykes that crisscrossed The Levels, as this area was called. The velo did a good line in tourist information. The dark water moved with sinuous power, all eddies and runnels like some formless animal.

"Communications on line," said the velo. "Connecting to stream."

Flutes and strings flitted about my ears and a waxen-faced woman with hair down to her feet appeared beside me. I braked hard, slewed to a stop. The woman stood in the air, slightly transparent, glistening water visible through the hanks of hair. Her face long and mournful, a tiara of glinting stones around her forehead.

"May I ask you if your current provider has truly raised your consciousness?" Her voice gentle, eyebrows lifted in concern. "Mick, we at Artemis can provide an intimate network of individuals with close cross-match predispositions to your own character within tactile-world Arthurian-myth rendering. These clients are signed to us and available to you. Online starter property provided free. Of course this can be integrated with Ultimata, our lifestyle drug, moderating synapse response to produce a serotonin euphoria of unlimited duration."

Nearby domes mutated into a series of scaled and vine-clad castles with towers and battlements, every one identical. Mist steamed from the earth, the soil burgeoned with the greenest grass I'd ever seen. My head reeled. The woman rose from the dyke's surface, extended her arms, her smile reflected in her sparkling eyes.

"Join us, my darling."

My hands released the handlebars as I felt her grip on my wrists.

"Tinman," I whispered, "what's happening?" A double-edged sword with a mirror-bright blade emerged dripping from the water. It was borne by a white hand clad in gold chain mail.

'Spam-ad in progress. Do you wish to apply spam filtering?'

My wrists were gripped tighter, the woman's face now inches from mine. "We are your world, Mick. Do not desert us." Two green dragons were soaring in the sky above her head, toothy leers, thin flames spouting from their snouts.

"Yes, apply filtering now."

The effects vanished. Beside me, the fast running dyke, the domes—the same sun-baked landscape as before. I waited for some moments for my heart to slow down to normal. I watched the water till I was sure the woman wouldn't appear again.

"Tinman." I took a deep breath, let my breathing return to normal. "Now I'm on-stream, I want you to get me The Scarecrow. He's a hacker or something, on the Authentus network. Can you connect me?"

"Searching."

I waited while the velo processed. Over in the distance was a ruined sycamore, leafless, bark peeling, it didn't look capable of regeneration.

"Connection refused. Caller-code not recognized," the velo said. "No access to this network."

I felt myself shrink. "Is there some other way to get a message to this person?"

"The Authentus are not provider associated. They are seeking members. Their homepage site has an enquiries portal. Do wish me to place a message there?"

"Yeah."

"Connection established. Begin message."

"Should I speak now?"

"Yes. Connection established."

"Okay, hi. You don't know me, but I'm Zachary Crowe. A healer and seer, check my profile out on-stream, you'll see. The Shaman, I'm sometimes called. I, well, I'm interested in joining up with you people. I have some privileged data about a Great Ascension elder, Roxanna DeLancia. I wonder if it's possible to meet the Scarecrow or one of your people personally to discuss this? I'm arriving in Cambridge later today. Maybe we could meet in say... Tinman, give me the name of a café in Cambridge."

"The following is a sponsored message: the Metropole is an experience in leisure and refreshment not to be missed. You can..."

"Shut up. Not you, I'm talking to my... Can we meet in the Metropole at say, five o'clock today? I'll await your..."

A blue line leaped over the landscape. It snaked around the sky, morphed into a woman's face. Roxanna, hot-eyed and furious. She seemed formed from the clouds, filling the horizon.

"You think after all the trouble it took to get you out you can just take off, you cretin?" Her perfect, furious face. "You're mine. I'm going to get you, you ancient crock of shit. You haven't got a chance." Her voice so loud the earth seemed to shake.

"Close file."

She remained glowering from horizon to horizon. "I got enough processing power to break any code. I know you. I can find you anywhere."

"How the hell do I stop this, Tinman?" My voice trembled.

The sun darkened with her frown. "You're nothing. Bigger things than your puny life are at stake. The combined power of our whole tribe, the inevitability of karma that matched your cells to mine, you can't fight it. I got hundreds on your data trail, hunting you down."

Tinman's voice interrupted, "A mutating gorgon-type virus has assumed control of certain functions. Do you wish me to terminate all connections and virtual effects?"

A dry retch in my throat. "Yeah, now."

Thunder, lightening. Roxanna's forehead corrugated. "I curse you with the Great Ascension curse of unmaking—your days are short and your suffering will be..."

Roxanna disappeared. The sky swelled, became purple and black. Now flakes of snow were melting into the dyke water. The domes were capped with white. The bleak landscape seemed more alien, less real than before.

I sat there, stunned, my senses jarred out of kilter. I pulled off the glove on my right hand, opened it to the falling snow. I felt the cold kiss in the center of my palm as snowflakes collected there, felt them melt as I curled my fist and held it closed. I hesitated, turned around, back towards London, twitchy, swallowing hard. I shuddered. Roxanna would've hacked my message to the Scarecrow. She knew I was headed for Cambridge.

I followed my own tracks in the snow, it seemed harder to remain upright. A wind came from nowhere, harried the velo from all sides. Nature itself seemed under Roxanna's power. Despite the suit's heat settings, I shivered.

It took a mile of deep breathing to get myself under control. Where else could I head to? The Scarecrow was the only individual I knew who might make an ally against Roxanna. An idea popped into my head, one I should have had as soon as I got connected.

I hauled on the brakes. "Tinman, can you go back online?"

"I have disabled all connections to..."

"Go on-stream and connect to a train booking service. Don't allow any other connections to come through. Keep all effects off. Make this call and then disable again."

"Concurring."

Flecks of ash and snow clung to the helmet screen. Dead trees and oxygen-fixing bluegrass seemed the only living vegetation. The dyke's cracked concrete walls looked barely able to contain its weight of water.

"Connected to Vitesse services, Zach."

"Book me a train or a bus or any kind of public transport from London to Newcastle this afternoon."

"I can get you a reservation on the two o'clock super-shuttle from Kings Cross. However, as you lack credit facilities, this will not be a confirmed transaction."

"Okay, go ahead."

I sat there, thinking. Would this send Roxanna's people off track? It was probably far too obvious. My DATCHO deviousness was redundant in this digitized world. It needed a technological trickery I was slow to learn. With a sigh, I hauled the handlebars around, back in the direction of Cambridge.

Some miles further on, buildings appeared, warehouses, themed housing developments, gated communities with guards in sentry booths.

Then the spires and towers of Cambridge were visible on the horizon. The velo path joined a four-lane traffic-free thoroughfare which eventually split into various directions. I took one for the city center, passing a pebble-dashed tower block of tiny apartments that reminded me of my cell block back in the penal zone. Surely by now they'd have found the broken shackle.

How safe I'd been in the zone, wrapped away with my illusions intact. Alvina had been enclosed in the amber of memory.

"I am a man, somewhere in England, looking for his long lost wife."

It seemed easier, made some kind of sense. Perhaps that's all I needed to do. Make everything into words—Alvina and Zach, the beginning and the end of the alphabet and everything precious in between.

EIGHTEEN

I PARKED THE VELO IN A RACK AT THE END OF A pedestrianised, cobbled lane. On either side, ancient buildings and colleges in flint, brick and stone.

Keeping the helmet on, buttocks bruised from long hours of riding, I waddled towards the Metropole to which the velo had given me directions.

Roxanna came into view across the lane fifty feet away in a flurry of genie ads. Completely self-possessed, a soft smile on her face, she held her head high as she glided in my direction. She wore the cream bodice and loose pants she'd worn at our first meeting. I stood transfixed, my desert-dry purse of a mouth trembled. She surely couldn't recognize me? My skin sealed, my face hidden by the mask. I carried on walking, hoping to bluff it out. The distance between us closed quickly, an array of jewelled rings on her fingers snagged the light.

Her eyes remained fixed ahead as she walked past me.

I stood, watching her back when it hit that this woman was taller and thinner than Roxanna. It was simply someone who'd replicated her look.

I scuttled off, moving faster.

It was 4:30 p.m., the "Nirvana" café, Bridge street. Me huddled in a corner, the only other customers three male trans-tribesters dressed as females and an obese African-looking woman in a white fake-fur. I watched the Metropole bar's entrance opposite. People passed the window, tribe types, dons in strange hats, students wearing jokey tops—'I thunk. Therefore I woz."

I sat steaming and edgy, wearing the helmet and gloves so I wouldn't dribble DNA. "Balance—purity—perfection" the menu blathered when I held it close to my face. Blisters of condensation dripped down the inside of the window, an aura of sugar crystals surrounded the condiment tray on my table.

The place was stuffed with leaf, bud and succulents. What looked like an oak tree grew through the marble counter.

I daren't enter the Metropole in case Roxanna's people were there. I hoped by some intuition to know when someone with the look of the master hacker walked in or out of there. Exactly what that look was, I couldn't say.

A waiter with a geometric beard of laser-cut squares came over. He stood with the fulsome freshness of true youth, waiting for me to remove the helmet, which I did with great reluctance.

When I asked for a menu, he advised me to go for the "optimum energy egg and bean salad." The eggs originated from chickens breathing oxygen-enriched air, whose auras indicated a state of contentment. Their eggs were enriched with antioxidants and organic minerals. The beans were so pumped with immune-boosting elements, long-chain amino acids and pure natural energy it was a wonder they didn't walk right off the plate.

"Give me a fried egg sandwich and a caffeinated coffee." I barked, desperate to advertise my high-octane, non Zachary Crowe credentials.

The waiter examined my face carefully. "These foods sir, are illegal. We have simulated versions, but the free-radical content is extremely high and potentially life shortening."

"Okay, go ahead."

"But," he said, flapping his antibacterial apron, "free radicals are far more destructive to anyone of your..."

"Yes?"

"Experience."

'Experience?'

"Development."

"Developed how?"

"Life rich, established, well grown."

"Do you mean *old*?"

He winced. "'Chrono-confronting," he said.

"I have a rare condition," I said, "incurable. Archaic dodderiss."

"Archaic?" He backed off, shaking his head.

Despite a lifetime of fresh, unadulterated, organic slowfood, never having necked so much as an aspirin, I dunked down the near-caffeine coffee in four mouthfuls. What an idiot. My heart rattled, my brain accelerated. I couldn't keep still, repetitively, idiotically, checking my stopped watch and rubbing the mark on my face.

A long-stored memory flashed up, figures in olive-green all-body suits washing the tarmac of Main Street in Marlborough. Stiff brooms in their hands and chemicals of smelly foam. Their faces were hidden by masks with bulging, multifaceted eyes. This must have been after a virus outbreak sometime in the middle of The Changes. All these things in my head. Things I didn't know were there.

I kept scanning both the café opposite and the fat woman sitting nearby.

Occasionally she sniffed the air and looked in my direction, as if I'd changed the atmosphere somehow. She was the first fat person I'd seen outside the zone and she looked over-inflated. Rather than the milky coffee pigment that most Afros opted for, she had tar-black skin. Her hair was piled high on her head, bound in a sort of wrap. The reflection of my thin, drawn face hung in the window aligned perfectly with hers. I watched the woman's reflection till it hurt my eyes, till she seemed to morph into something else. With a start, I realized the face of Alvina was staring back at me. But this was a different Alvina, stark and serious. The luster in her eyes like candles in a dark room. Her whole head was wrapped in a layer of viscous, transparent material. I knew if I moved or looked directly, the vision would go, so sat still, with the apparition captured in some strange prism of my mind, not wanting to break the spell.

A gang entered the Metropole and I snapped back to the present. They were student types, loose limbed, casual clothing, lookbooks, none seemed to give off the right vibe. Next to me, one of the cross-dressers abruptly stood, flapping his arms in some gamescape only he could see. I saw how ridiculous my situation was. I was waiting in the wrong place for someone I didn't know and wouldn't recognize, who had no reason to be interested in me. My plan, such as it was, expired here.

What a risk I'd taken. My hands were quivering with caffeine substitute. I envisioned muscular tribesters bounding down nearby streets, ranks of cops, stun batons raised, running in my direction. It was miraculous I'd made it this far.

"Sir, your bill." The waiter touched my shoulder.

When he moved off, threw my last couple of euros on the table, knowing it was well short. I donned the helmet and walked out. The sky was black, shadows pooled in doorways, orange light caught in liquefying snow underfoot.

I scanned the Metropole's entrance. Two men in heavy boots emerged, one tall, the other shorter with pointed ears sculpted like an elf's. Bolstered bodies, luminous eyes and a glimmer at their brows. The distance between us was closing fast.

I ran, pushing through pedestrians, skidding on the cobbles. The velo unlocked itself as I neared it. Opening the throttle, riding away, looking behind, I almost collided with two nuns of Wicca.

"Celebrate! It's Beltane!" They were accosting passers-by at the entrance to the Fitzwilliam Museum, their pink faces surrounded by tight-fitting coifs.

As I turned into a street busy with slow moving car traffic, the two men from the Metropole stood at the next junction. One of them stepped into the road. "Hey friend, can I talk with you?"

I rode straight for him. His eyes swelled and his re-modelled cheeks puckered as he went rigid. In that moment I swerved between him and a parked car, ducking the hand that paddled for my head. I grazed the car door, handlebars jumping momentarily from my hands. The velo veered across the road. The sound of footsteps slammed through my head, panic pounded in my throat. I peddled like fury, assisting the straining motor. A sign flashed, warning me I'd broken the speed restriction. A scream of brakes as a car from the opposite direction brushed my knee. The road reeled, the engine revved, the velo bolted forwards. I daren't look back till I was sure the footsteps were gone. Then over my shoulder I saw him standing in the middle of the street.

The side roads were slimy and poorly lit, ancient walls with gargoyles leering, a glimpse of dark water, silhouetted figures. Full of uncertain energy, I turned left then right, no direction in mind. In a doorway, the glint of light on metal. Pith helmets, chrome buttons, batons and armor. The cops exchanged looks, moved forward out of the shadows.

The alarm had been raised. Numb with dread, I turned into a sharply-inclined velo-way between railings and Victorian-themed shop fronts. The velo's power died.

"Zack," it said, "I have received a request to stop for a police check. I am complying."

"I told you to log off all networks, you idiot," I yelled, freewheeling down the incline. "Ignore it! Carry on!"

"Zach, the signal was aimed through a line-of-sight photon port and has overridden operator controls via the security facility."

"Shit, piss, bastard." I kept moving, pumping the pedals furiously until the brakes locked on.

"Zach, I am unable to continue this journey."

The velo was a lump of metal, cold in my hands.

I got off the machine. Dragged it with locked wheels squeaking through an archway into a paved shopping plaza.

"Where is the security facility?" My lungs were raw from mouth-breathing the poisonous air.

"Mounted below the seat, but it is of course illegal for anyone but the security services to attempt maintenance of the unit."

My fingers clutched at a hot tin cube under the saddle. It squealed as I wrenched the thing off, then it went silent as I crunched it underfoot. When I remounted and twisted the throttle, the machine surged forwards. A crowd emerged from a doorway, scattering as I shot through them.

"Zach, I cannot comply with a police check. The override solenoid is dysfunctional. May I report this to the authorities and arrange a service appointment?"

"No, keep logged off all networks."

Teeth aching, I realized my jaw had been clenched tight.

The plaza wasn't zoned for velos. I wove among groups of pedestrians, drawing unwanted attention. A narrow alley on my left, I made for it, past the back of a college with high railings. The velo's power unit echoed. A junction ahead, I jammed on the brakes. Buildings spun. Screeching metal, pain in my knee, the smell of damp stone. I looked up into a circle of streetlight. I'd gone over the handlebars, lay on my back in the road. Car tires hissed inches from my head. The velo had come to rest on its side, thirty feet away.

Two figures lumbered towards me down the guidance beam in the center of the road. Their foreheads blinked. Cars swerved to avoid them. Further back, two policemen rounded the corner. I scrabbled on all fours towards the velo, cursing. The velo flashed its lights, a pair of steel rods shot out from under the saddle. The rods extended telescopically to the road surface, pushed the velo upright. It looked like a giant insect preening itself. The velo rolled towards me, unmanned. I clambered into the saddle and pushed off, peddling madly, winding the throttle.

I took two left turns in quick succession, wobbled into a narrow alley by a transparent dome with ribs of white. "Tinman, how did you do that?"

"I have emergency body-signal alarm response systems in place in case of an accident."

I buzzed down a busy street. Horns blared, brakes squealed. Turning off at the sign of a veloway, I followed a broad concourse for a short distance till I found myself at the back of a restaurant in a dead-end of doorways and fermenting bins. As I manoeuvred the machine around in a circle with my legs, a shadow leaped from a doorway. It was the fat woman from the cafe.

"You can't escape!"

Her chubby mitts around the handlebars, full lips, perfect teeth.

"Please, let me pass."

"A moment, my man, of your tender patience." Her words melded in a buttery burr.

"I don't have a moment—get out of the way!"

Footsteps echoed behind me. Any second I'd be surrounded. When I tried to turn the handlebars she held them with surprising strength.

"You're Zachary Crowe, the ju-ju man, the guy they all lookin' for?"

"Who the hell are you?"

The sound of footsteps came closer.

"Relax. I mean you no harm."

Two men pushed by, laughing. A shirt flashing merrily, "Let's make love online at Erotica 786." A door opened to admit them and banged shut.

I tried to push panic from my voice. "What do you want?"

"I might help you," she said. "If I knew what it is *you* want."

"I need to find the Scarecrow. Do you know where he is?"

"How about this for a question?" A glint of animal energy in her eyes. "Why are we standing here with gangs of Great Ascension hunting your hide? Better let me aboard and get of here 'fore you get us both in trouble."

Sighing, I shifted forwards on the velo, offering the pillion. The machine groaned as its springs compressed. Her strong arms enveloped my waist. We scuttled off at slow speed, Tinman complaining, "Operator, my floating hydrolastic suspension system is overloaded, damage may result if this journey continues. Please consult my on-line manual."

"Shut up."

The velo lurched onward. Astonished faces went by, bars, shops, bollards, old houses leaning drunkenly against each other.

"Hey," I said, "who are you, anyway?"

The woman leaned forward so her chin rested on my shoulder. "I'm called all sorts of names. Fatso usually."

"Zach," said Tinman, "do you wish navigation?"

"No," she gripped my waist tighter. "I'll navigate. Turn left at the next junction."

"Zach?"

"Do as she says, Tinman. Where are we headed, anyway?"

"The Scarecrow's house. That's where you're aiming, ain't it?"

A cobbled lane made the velo wallow perilously, I slowed to a crawl. "How come you know so much?"

"Same way as anyone knows anything, by being who I am."

I half-turned, glanced into her dark face. "And who might that be?"

"The Scarecrow of course. C'mon, we're nearly there."

NINETEEN

WE RODE DOWN A WELL-LIT RESIDENTIAL STREET, windows aglow with light from entertainment centers. My wrists ached from fighting the handlebars.

"Stop here," the woman said. As we braked to a halt, she pointed ahead. "This street leads to Charteris Avenue, where my place is, number Forty Nine. The velo may be trackable, best be careful. Let me off here, wait five minutes, then come around the back. Hide that thing in the hedge of the next-door house, it's derelict."

As she waddled away, I waited, twitchy, feeling vulnerable. Her presence had lent some sense of protection. A woman tottered by on ten-inch heels. As she passed I noticed dagger-like nails, overbuilt breasts. She smiled invitingly. "Howya doin." Wanna have fun?"

"No. No credit. Thanks for offering."

I watched her till she was out of sight, waited a minute longer and then moved off.

Forty Nine Charteris street was a two-story Georgian terrace with stone-clad walls. The house on one side of it had been converted into flats with chromed metal stairways. The place on the other side was half-hidden by a huge rhododendron hedge. When I pushed the velo up its gravel drive I saw sheet metal blinding the windows and much of the brickwork was blackened by smoke. I stuffed the machine as deep as I could into the hedge. After strapping the helmet to the machine, I shuffled around back to number Forty-Nine's open gate.

Without the helmet, even through filters the air tasted foul, freezing and hostile. The back door scanned me and noisily unlocked itself. The hallway was pitch-black with constellations of stars sprinkled in the ceiling. It opened into a large room containing primitive furniture, colored crystals on shelves and a table around which were four chairs.

A cherub-faced young man with gold metallic hair came into the room from a door on the opposite side. He nodded, pulled out a chair and draped himself over it. Seconds later, the woman entered, removing her coat to reveal a red dress that billowed around her like a marquee. The wrap had gone from her head leaving a coil of black braids. She smiled at the young man.

"Azimund, you're back already. Be a good boy and make us some tea."

Azimund swanned away. She indicated a chair. "Make yourself comfortable."

"Why are you called the Scarecrow?" I asked, sitting down.

She cocked her head to one side. "It's Epiphany, actually. There are whole lot of stories for that Scarecrow thing. How 'bout the one where a gang of us refugees landed in a beat-up ship off the south coast of England, just after The Changes? We'd fought through the blockade to fortress Europe while the ice pack thickened all around. We were one of the last groups they allowed to disembark, diseased and froze near to death. My ma stuffed my clothes with straw to keep me warm and the hospital nurses gave me that name."

"Is it true?"

"Hell, no. Good story though. I was taught English by a U.S. emergency aid worker. She told me that in The Beforetime, when food was grown in the open, farmers used to put straw dummies in fields to frighten away the birds. At night the scarecrows would come to life and dance in the moonlight. I loved that story. You want some food or is that on-stream stuff about you living on chi for real?"

"I'm not hungry, thank you." The fried egg sandwich still squirmed in my gut. "You're the head of the Authentus?"

She shrugged. "You could say that."

The young man returned with a steaming clay teapot, cups and so-milk on a tray. She poured, then handed me a cup. They both watched me as I sipped the hot liquid. There was a long silence during which they continued to regard me. Why, I wondered, had I never mastered the art of conversation that wasn't about anything?

"Azimund," she said after a while, "go now, sweetness." The young man withdrew and closed the door silently. Her eyes returned to me as she sat down. "So why do you want to join us? And who the hell are you anyway?"

"Someone who wants to join your tribe and who's in need of your help. I need to trace someone. She disappeared a long time ago and now she's turned up, apparently alive and well and sailing around on a Triton, a kind of floating hospital or something. I've heard you're a brilliant hacker. I got to get in contact with her."

She lowered her head, stared into her tea. "The Triton network happens to be the most exclusive one there is. But before we get into that I need to know about you. Why should I help you? Why of all the portals in the world did you pick on mine?"

"That's easy. I found a blog-file extract you'd hacked from Roxanna DeLancia, the diva. I got difficulties with that woman. I assumed if you could hack into that, the Triton network wouldn't be too difficult."

She looked up. "Roxanna. Yeah, I remember. The Great Ascension demigod. But as far as you're concerned, there are holes in my understandin'. Why don't I tell you what I know, and you can fill in the gaps?"

There was a deliberation in her speech—she wouldn't be easily fooled.

"I get a message," she said, "from the notorious shaman, Zachary Crowe, wanting to meet with me. On-stream official records tell me this Zach is an attempted murderer, incarcerated in some U.S. DATCHO zone." She yawned, luxuriously, stretching her arms upward. "Okay, it's not like anyone believes the government line on anything, but it's kinda worrying. Other tribe's sites and blogs say you walk on water, you're a healer and prophet and you're over one hundred and twenty years old, with no immuno treatments. Now, I happen to know that the Great Ascension people are puttin' your face around, highly desirous of tracking you down. Knowin' what I know about Roxanna's health, I put it together that the reason she wants you is 'cause *you* must be the matching tissue donor she needs. That right?"

I nodded. "You're very astute. Tell me; are there many Great Ascension members in the UK?"

"Not many. Less than a hundred."

"Ah."

She paused, supported her great head with her hands. "All this would all make some kind of sense, except... Except the Great Ascension network are desperate to apprehend a guy name of Mick Tarn. Not Zachary Crowe, but Mick Tarn. Yet it's *your* image and ID biometrics they're chasing around. Roxanna's sayin' this Mick's stolen some original music sample files, you're to be discretely apprehended, soon as possible. Kindly explain how Zachary Crowe is at this time languishing as a DATCHO resident in Chicago and you're Mick Tarn, according to my household security DNA scan. Tell me all, juju man, tell me do."

In the silence a series of half-plausible explanations arrayed themselves in my mind. I stirred my tea with meticulous care. "It's complicated. Er, how did you know I'd be in the Nirvana and not the Metropole," I said, stalling.

"I didn't. I had Azimund wait for you in the Metropole. I was gonna check you out from the place opposite. Guess you were thinking the same thing?"

"You got it."

"How did you get out of the DATCHO zone?"

She seemed so *weighty*, so solid and sure of herself, I wanted to confess all my deceptions. She'd surely grant some kind of absolution. But no one could risk sheltering an escaped DATCHO. For so long lies had been my cloak and my protection, already an amorphous half-truth was passing my lips.

"I'm Zachary Crowe, aged fifty-six. At the time of The Changes, I injured a national guardsman when I broke into a quarantine center looking for my missing wife, Alvina. I did time in the zone, fifteen years, till I was paroled. Roxanna traced me as a sacrificial cell donor and kidnapped me. This was the day before yesterday. I escaped her and I've been running ever since. I managed to change my ID, shifting the master codas using psychometrical energy. More important than anything though, is getting in touch with Alvina."

She leaned over and tapped her index finger against the side of my forehead as if testing its solidity. "You got quite an agenda ain't you? And you genuinely had no immuno programming?"

"None. But I don't see why Roxanna should get the benefit."

"So there's no question of you changin' ID to escape the zone? And the authorities aren't hunting you?"

I gave her my "hurt-innocent" look, stilled my twitchy eyes. "No."

She sank into herself for a moment, looked to some far horizon and said, "There's somethin' not right about this. But we'd welcome a man of your fame to our network; it might help boost numbers. We got no provider alliances so we got no medical provision, as you can probably guess."

I nodded. "I'll gladly join you... though I'd rather you didn't make it public, yet."

Her fleshy hands cradled the teapot; she splashed more tea into cups. "How did you find out where your woman is?"

I spoke with conviction, as if this would make it beyond doubt. "I found her with a DNA search which brought up a newslink. She's on a Triton."

"You said that already. If these Tritons actually exist, that is. Most networks reckon they don't."

"What do you believe?"

She looked up at the ceiling, smiled. "Well, there's a Triton network, and for years the super-rich have been disappearing somewhere."

"Can you get me connected to them?"

"It's not as simple as that. Like you, I work with the old skills. Maybe I just use 'em in new ways."

"You mean you aren't a hacker after all?"

She lifted the teapot lid and stirred, steam shrouded her face, her black eyes glistened like olives. "My family is from Nejheme, a village in northeast Swaziland. My father was an Abrosi, a witch doctor." She spoke with practiced tone, as if she'd recited this story many times. "I must have inherited my father's gift, 'cause even when I was small, I could hear people's thoughts. I was fascinated by the way a person's thoughts can shape the world around them. I walk between worlds. I infiltrate the technical with the powers of the so-called primitive."

She turned over her palm, examined the lines there for a moment and continued, "I can do this because everything is a part of nature and subject to natural law. Nothing is more powerful than the mind. Thought can change matter, even quantum data flow can be changed through thinking. This is the way of things. We Authentus are bound to the truth as we experience it. Cognition creates perception, this is our primary law."

I couldn't suppress a groan. More flatulent femi-goddess foolishness. Couldn't I for once meet someone that could offer practical help? I nodded, giving her my "serene wise one" look. "We are similar spirits," I simpered through clenched teeth. "I understand you well."

"Everything in nature is subject to universal laws and subject to the same forces. The data stream evolves, grows and decays, has moods and pulses, just as any river does."

"Yes," I muttered. "I know this. Universal law. That's just how it is."

She shifted in her seat, leaned closer. "My cells reproduce, my immune system repels invaders, my body works at its optimum because I direct it to do so." She smacked her lips. "I ain't mastered the weight issue yet, but I'm workin' on it." She gestured with her hands, as if drawing a square in the air. "I use the power of the mind to penetrate the stream. I access a person's blog file and use that as a way into a network."

I snapped to attention. "Your words are as clear as purified water."

"People get upset about me hacking and posting their blog-files. But I do it 'cause it breaks down the boundaries, it's the last weapon left." The firm line of her mouth was grim. There was a power in her, resolute and unalterable. She sniffed the air. "By posting people's blog files on stream, I'm revealing the awful truth that we're all the same."

Beyond her head, through the bay window, rain was falling from a darkening sky. "I dance in the flow of the stream," she said. "I know its rhythms and patterns. I feel my way into the most secret archives. I also got a bit of practical help. All blog-files are archived using the same protocols and locator tags for their digital assistants to access. Someone, however, left a trace of binary code impregnated in the original locator tag's structure. And that code-setter happens to be a member of our tribe."

"So you can access Alvina's blog-file?" That word, that name, that touchstone of associations.

"Well, here's the deal. The difficulty's not gettin' into her file, it's findin' out which one's hers. Her blog-file's one stacked among billions. I need a sense of Alvina to feel my way to her file. Normally, I get to know a person, read their postings, connect my mind to theirs. With Roxanna, I listened to her music, listened to her heart. Then I opened my mind to connect with her. I rode around the archive till I got a sense of where she was at. Some part of her called out to me."

My foot was tapping under the table. This virtual voodoo stuff wasn't going to work. "'Can you access Alvina, or not?"

She stood so suddenly her chair fell backwards. She moved with surprising agility out of my field of vision. "No." Her bass voice close to my ear. "Not without your help; there's not enough time. Only way forward is to place a certain thought or idea in your lady's head. Someone with an emotional connection can do that. I don't know this Alvina, I don't *experience* her. But *you* do. You got the connection. You could feel your way to her mind. You could give her an idea, so clear and tangible that she picks up on it, then she'll add it to her blog-file. When the blog-file responds with new data, I can trace the stuff going in 'cause you'll tell me what to look for. Then I'll know what file's hers."

I had to grit my teeth to hold the sneer from my lips. I turned my head but couldn't see her.

"To you this shouldn't be difficult," she said, "someone with your awareness will easily be able to transmit an ESP message. Neurotrophic psychokinesis is what the scientists call it."

I sighed. "You're telling me to send a message to Alvina by ESP? It's the most ridiculous thing I ever heard."

"Why?" I felt her breath on the back of my neck. "You, a shaman. You who changed your ID using psychometrical energy. You believe in the power of nature, you already know how to harness it. Nothing is more powerful than belief."

That's one of my lines. One I used with clients. "Problem is," I said, "there's no such thing as ESP and if there were I wouldn't need to access her network, would I? I could just communicate by thought." My eyes felt impossibly heavy.

Her head appeared at my shoulder, so close I could see the pores in her skin, her mocking eyes.

"Aren't you the wizard who's healed and humbled endless celebs? Can't you use your powers to find your lover?"

"Yes. No." I shook my head. "This psychokinesis stuff isn't on my agenda, I don't work on the supernatural level."

She laughed. "Supernatural? Lights were turned on and off by thought power in a lab back in nineteen ninety-six. The Sony corporation had developed a thought waveform machine before the end of the twentieth century. It's well established technology."

She came around to face me, leaned forward with hands on her thighs. Her tongue protruded between her teeth as she made a hissing noise, stabbing her finger at a point between my eyes. The woman was clearly mad. I'd taken incredible risks to deliver myself into the hands of a lunatic. I watched her waddle over to a wall cabinet, pull out a drawer and heft out an onyx slab with a glass bubble on top and various ports in the front. It was about two feet square, the top surface polished, the sides rough cast as if hewn from rock.

"Take a look," she said, cradling the thing in her arms, "this five-cerobite model is obsolete and way too heavy to be wearable, but it works. It learns to read simple thought-form directions and converts them to digital data. Its training program will bone up your ol' telekinesis in no time."

I stood up. "How can that lump of rubbish know what I'm thinking?"

She carried the contraption over to the table, solemnly placing one hand on my scalp to press me back down into the chair. "It works. But they stopped makin' this stuff, 'cause it took us down the dangerous road of stretchin' human abilities. There's no profit in that."

She patted the top of my head as she spoke. "The potential was there to change our cellular structure, to heal sickness by thought alone. The providers entrance, innovate and entertain, they support and perpetuate the tribes, not by givin' us real abilities, but by keepin' us constantly distracted."

My heart was flattened, my soul empty. "My mind isn't ready to leap into this. ESP seems just another nebulous tribal concept."

She raised her voice. "That so? What about the sound that a dog can hear but not a human? Is that real? What about a dream? Is that real? What of the power that flows through your hands to make the lame walk, the blind see?" She stopped tapping, leaned back, frowning. "You've got to believe it's possible. That's the first step."

I avoided her eyes, looked into the close-woven braids of her hair. Each twist seemed to stand defiantly from her scalp. As my eyes lost focus, I glimpsed something scaly, fat and eel like, squirming in her tresses.

"What do you see?"

I closed my eyes. "Er, I was thinking of Alvina. How far away she is."

"You weren't seeing anything strange in those locks of mine?" She stood, hands on hips. When I didn't answer she left the room.

Holy shit. I covered my face with my hands. These waters were beyond my depth.

TWENTY

I SAT STARING AT THE TELEKINESIS MACHINE, IF THAT'S what it was. It wasn't impressive. Its chipped graphite glistened dully, a small cracked glass dome was set on the top.

I felt confused, helpless, outmanoeuvred.

Epiphany came back into the room with a black strip of material in her hand and stood on the other side of the table. She pushed the hunk of technology over to my side. "You got a lotta learnin' to do." She handed me the black strip. It was a smart-fiber band with sensor windows running through it. "Put this around your thick head. Use the powers of the machine. Accept this new faith. When you've opened your mind we can open the network."

I couldn't keep the anger from my voice. "This is ridiculous. I don't trust it. I don't believe it."

Epiphany brought her face close to mine. "It's the only chance you got of finding your lady. Take it. You got the power."

Something inside me fell away, my breath came in waves. "I have a confession to make."

"Let's have it."

"I'm an escaped DATCHO. It was Roxanna's people that fixed me a new ID in order to get me out."

Epiphany narrowed her eyes, smacked her lips, expelled a puff of air. "And what about your powers? Your healing and seeing that everyone blabs about?"

It was terrifying, this honesty, like falling into darkness. I had to get the words out before my throat closed up. "I have a kind of natural born prescience, but I mainly use guesswork and common sense. As for my healing, it was a trick. I rigged up a low-voltage circuit that gave clients a little jolt. I let them believe it was a miracle." I was naked. Every instinct of self-preservation gone.

Her eyes closed.

"Are you going to turn me in?" The moment stretched out. "Will you still help me?"

Still Epiphany said nothing, she opened her eyes, her face unreadable.

"Please?"

"Ha!" She exploded into laughter. It was the reaction I least expected and I stared aghast as her great form doubled over. Her shoulders trembled, she hooted and heaved and slapped her hands on the table. Azimund's head appeared around the door. Then I was laughing too. It seemed years since I'd laughed and it hurt, my throat, my stomach. Everything appeared so ridiculous. Me in the zone, po-faced with my trick chair and all those poor people throwing away their crutches. The way I'd meticulously clear the cell of crumbs of food. Orion and her attempts at seduction and the argumentative velo. It was a wonder I'd managed to keep a straight face through it all. I could barely breathe for laughing. We quaked, rocked and howled. It was like a contagion, when one of us stopped the other triggered another burst. We spluttered on and on under Azimund's amazed stare.

At last, when we'd got ourselves under control, Azimund's head withdrew.

"Well now," she said, smiling broadly, exposing pink gums. "You're a real character 'ain't you?"

I leaned closer. "Will you help me?"

Her eyes rolled. "As far as the authorities are concerned, you told me you were let out on parole, understand? As for my help, that's more a question of whether you can help yourself. You got to work on that thought-form editor. Find out what's inside you. You may have natural immunity, but you've got a nasty case of cynicism. See this process as a kind of tribal initiation ceremony. We got to make a believer of you."

She strapped the fiber band around my forehead, cold against my skin. She reached behind her, showed me her fist and slowly uncurled her fingers. A tiny clear cube sat in the center of her palm. "Swallow this. It'll enhance neurological activity in a part of your brain called the lambiacasstium. It's where your psychokinesis center is located."

I placed the cube on my tongue. It instantly melted to nothing but a cold sensation in the back of my palate.

Epiphany gripped my shoulder. "It's up to you now. If you an' your woman are still bonded, this'll work, believe me. Subtle alterations will take place in the fabric of reality. You will bend the void with your mind. But you got to believe. Anythin' is possible if you believe." She released my shoulder, took a step back.

"But I don't believe. I don't see how this could possibly work."

She turned various switches "Shush." She hesitated. "You got to know, even if I get in her blog-file, I can't compel her to connect directly to you." She brushed the top of the device gently with her index finger, whispering in some strange language as if she were comforting an animal.

"I can only put messages there with your contact codes," she said. "It's up to her to respond."

"Isn't there some other way?"

"It might just about be possible to do this without your help. But it would take too long. Besides, you need to pass this test if you want any help from me. You got to trust, to open yourself. Have faith in the magic. The machine's trainin' program will teach you. Its receptors will amplify the alpha-wave signature for each notion you create, just as if you were transferring your thoughts to another person. Try to separate and hold a concept in mind as if drawin' it from memory. Then send it out, like postin' a message. You gonna need a thought or idea that's unique to the two of you, something she'll recognize."

"I can't. It doesn't seem..."

"Stop!" Her palm in front of my face, huge sensual mounts, deep red lines. "Doubt'll destroy any chance you got. Believe. Nothing is more powerful than belief."

She brought the thing to a state of readiness by waving her hand over it. The dome illuminated momentarily, then went off. After a couple of seconds the machine whined, "Welcome to the Sony ESP mind wave-form reader mark four."

I gave Ephiphany a searching look. "This is going to take years."

"You ain't got years. Roxanna ain't got years. You've got few hours at most." She leaned over the unit. "Start training program." She turned and sailed from the room, dress billowing.

I moaned, loud and long.

It was going to be a long, long night.

TWENTY ONE

"GREETINGS." THE DEVICE'S FLOATY, FEMININE VOICE said. "Please relax. Think of nothing in particular while residual mental activity is monitored. Let your thoughts drift without becoming focused on any one idea. Here is some music to help you."

Pachabel's *Canon* swelled around the room.

Entwined in the music a new male voice took me through the old relax routine rattled out in a million permutations since the early days of do-it-yourself therapy. "Loosen any tight clothing, take a deep breath and release it slowly. Visualize a beach on a warm sunny day..."

My brain spun at a hundred miles an hour. This was ludicrous. How could that pathetic piece of crap bring me closer to the living flesh of Alvina? Outside, shadows pooled in the doorways, the sky was a bank of glowing embers. A line of airships passed over the rooftops on invisible rails, giant snub-nosed transports lit like Chinese lanterns.

"Your mental activity is peaking," said the voice. "Relax, try to relax."

Come on, be positive. What if I was able to throw my thoughts and Alvina could hear them? What would it feel like if her words came into my head? What if—keep calm, fool, you're supposed to be relaxing. Switch off—count the breath—in—out, two, three, four. That's better. I shouldn't be thinking at all. Jeez, I'm hungry. Where's the breath? Yes, there, in—out... I can hear my heart beating. God, it's loud.

"Operator, your residual mental activity has been established."

"Wait! I'm not... I haven't relaxed properly yet, I...."

"Now we'll refine your thought-form transference technique. You must imagine a designated word clearly. It's important to grasp the *sense* of the word in its exact, assigned meaning. Visualize the word forming in your mind. Say the word mentally, and hold it in your imagination. Try to stay with the word, think of nothing else. The first word is "on," in the sense of active, in operation, running, performing, working. Look at the lens on the top of the machine and direct your thoughts there. Switch the lens on."

I focused. Tried to sharpen the swirls of mental current. On. On. On. On.

Nothing happened. I pondered the word again: On. On. Bringing the sense of it, the sound of it to the center of my brain. On.

Nothing.

I took a breath, held it, let it go. On. On.

Nothing. I glared at the blank dome. Come on! On. On. On!

"Try again. Relax. Clear your mind completely. Look at the glass dome, instruct it to illuminate itself. Don't visualize the light, instruct it to turn on."

"That's what I'm doing, you shithead!" On. On! My thoughts loud in my straining brain. On.

"Try again."

"Shit. Shit. Shit."

"You're becoming agitated. Try again."

"No I didn't mean..."

"Try again."

I can't do this. My mind doesn't work in this language.

"Try again."

Out of the window, the velvet night. The forces of darkness were closing in. "It's no good. I'm sorry, Alvina."

"Try again."

"You blind, block-brained bastard! Piss off. I can't, I can't, I can't."

"Try again."

ON. ON. ON. ON. ON. On, you stupid..."

"Try again."

On. On.

I'm too old a dog for this trick. It's hopeless.

"You're losing focus. Relax and try again."

I stretched myself flat on the polished, wooden floor. I'm out of synch with the world, a mammoth thawed from the permafrost, lumbering in the wrong age...

On.

"Try again."

Stilling myself, going cold inside, reaching back into the farthermost recesses of mind. On. The thought shaped softly, like a cloud. On.

"Try again,"

A tingling where my skull met my spine. A soft relaxing, an opening, as if my neck were getting longer. The drug Epiphany gave me, maybe it was helping. On. Even softer, a whisper into the blue, on.

"Try again."

"Holy Jesus! What's the use?"

"Try again, separate the thoughts, one at a time."

On, on, on.

"Try again."

Groaning, I reached back into the night, felt the softening in my neck again, held on to it, saw the word, felt the edge and shape of the word, the name and sense of the word, sent it spinning through the air.

"On!" Announced the machine, with an arpeggio of violins. The light flashed on and off. "On. Well done."

"Holy shit," I boggled at the word "on" glowing in the dome in red letters. It was like my thought had been captured in a bottle. A miracle. Perhaps this battle could be won. Perhaps there was such a thing as magic.

And so it began. On, on and on. Till I could switch the light with a flick of thought. Then off, off and off. It was like learning to walk, falling and faltering—but gradually, one step at a time, one word at a time, the trick was learned. I lumbered doggedly through that long night, over a hundred words were made and shaped in this new conceptual alphabet. Each one formed, shaped, broadcast from my belaboured brow.

The sound of rain falling outside. I reached into the sense of rain, of the water falling, made the word and there in the glass bubble— "rain." The trick seemed to be in "feel-think." To transmit the word "battle," wasn't simply the shape and sound of the word "battle'—with its brittle consonants—but in the *sense* of battle, of clashing swords and blood-soaked limbs.

As words moved from my head to be interpreted by the machine, it was both wonderful and appalling. Thoughts are so whimsical, so fleeting. And yet now they took shape in crystalline form. Now they assumed a power, a definiteness.

The door opened and Epiphany came in bearing a large bowl filled with fruit. She wore voluminous silky pyjamas covered with stars.

I rubbed my calves, urging the blood back to them. "What time is it?"

"Around 4:00 a.m.. How's it goin? You a believer now?"

"I am, I do. I believe."

She sat down, looked at me sombrely. "Now you're an Authentus. Thought is a power. Be careful what you think. Next step, you got to send a specific notion to your woman. Bring her to mind, get a sense of her, an' then send her a special thought. Use a word or image or somethin' unusual and personal. The more unique the better. If you can do that, you win the coconut."

"It seems incredible. But I'll do it. I'll try."

"What's the signal? What you gonna send her?"

I knew it already, the simple equation, $A+Z=\heartsuit\infty$.

I saw the shiny bauble around Alvina's neck with those letters engraved on it. The symbols burned in my mind, the straight masculine lines of the letters and the curvaceous solidity of the heart.

When I told Epiphany about the equation, she rolled her eyes. "Okay, we'll try it. All you got to do is think of her and send it out."

"How do we know she even keeps a blog-file?"

"We don't, but most everyone does. We'd die of loneliness, otherwise. Send your equation to her. Imagine an invisible thread from her to you and send the idea along it. Do it constantly, non-stop."

I closed my eyes and visualized Alvina. Then I sent the equation to her with every cell in my body.

TWENTY-TWO

I LAY STRETCHED OUT ON THE FLOOR. BACK HURTING, brain aching, eyes of metal and tongue of slate. The previous night seemed like some epic, inconclusive struggle remote from the realms of time. Forgotten memories crawled from the deepest caverns of my mind. Maybe it was the pill, the mind-throwing, the confusion of the last few days...

❧

I woke in semi-darkness. Alvina was propped on one elbow watching me. Her eyes moist.

"This is a change of roles," I said. "It's me that usually lies awake."

She lay back onto the pillow, staring at the ceiling. "Go to back to sleep, my love."

I raised my head "What's the matter?"

She whispered, "What's going to happen now that The Changes are here? Now that nature has turned against us?"

I reached over and stroked her hair. "We'll survive, it'll be okay."

"What if one of us got ill? What if I caught one of the new viruses?"

"I'd move heaven and earth, sacrifice my life, bribe, influence, swindle, anything to get you well."

She avoided my eyes, continued watching the ceiling. "All this time we've lived here, I've woken every morning and contentment was there, waiting like a faithful puppy." She felt for me, ran her hand along the line of my shoulder. "I want you to know that these were my best days. The most joyful of my life. Whatever happens I'll never forget these times together."

"You talk like it's all ending. In the past humans have endured plague, famine, war and disaster—worse times than these."

"Hold me," she said.

I held her till she stopped trembling and slept.

❧

I shook my head. Epiphany jerked awake in the chair opposite me. She waved her hand and a battered 3D wall unit blinked into life, projecting an array of beams into the silvered pan of its viewing deck.

"This is an old file, the only one I got of a Triton."

She poured cold tea into china cups. The unit's deck filled with a vision of a ship, a floating city of a ship shrouded in orange mist. Deck upon deck of apartment complexes, green lawns, shops and walkways were topped by airship docking cradles. Under the translucent canopy of the foredeck, tiny figures reclined by pools and modified palm trees of assorted color colors. As I watched, the scene changed to a side-on view, a small transporter took off and immediately vanished into the mist. Two streaks of rust trailed below massive anchors, water belched from ports in the side. The leaden sea seemed flattened into submission by the ship's sheer bulk.

"Latest update says this Triton's in the North Sea, eighty miles west of Scotland. It's impossible to verify. A hundred and fifty miles north of here, the sea temperature causes phenols and sulphurous oxides in the atmosphere to condense. That whole sea's blanketed by poisoned fog worse than that of the North Atlantic. Monitoring devices, communications—photon technology won't work in it."

I peered at the screen. Could one of those ant-like people be Alvina? I imagined her working away at a canvas, wearing one of her tatty t-shirts. The muscles moving in her back. Once pledged to me those muscles, my wife, my life, slapping on paint furiously. The only beautiful thing in my ugly life. When I closed my eyes, A+Z =♥∞ was emblazoned there. I'd floundered into sleep around 5:00 a.m., the symbol beating constantly from my brain. The equation continued deep into dream where I was chased through moonlit streets by some nameless pursuer, the letters A and Z marked on the pavements in huge letters.

Nothing more ludicrous could come to pass than Alvina contacting me at that moment. She seemed more remote than ever.

"Check this," said Epiphany. She wore a loose black gown with zig-zagging slashes of green.

A volcano appeared surrounded by a yellow sea, a smudge of smoke over its crater, its steep banks covered with green vegetation.

"Recognize it?"

"No."

"Combre Vehiecha."

"But that's the one that's supposed to have..."

"Blown up and triggered The Changes? Yeah, who knows? Could be a mock-up. I ain't actually been there and seen it. Just shows you can't believe anything about anything. Now watch this. This you *can* believe. Guess who's coming to dinner?" She pointed at the viewing pan which showed a 2D still of Roxanna descending the aluminium steps of an airship. A crowd of people were gathered at the bottom, watching her. In the instant the shot was taken, Roxanna's eyes were closed as if she were indifferent to everyone around her.

"One of our people took this pic. She arrived at Heathrow ten-fifty one last night. Your trail is hotly followed."

I sat up, my voice shrill. "What shall I do?"

Epiphany flapped her palm. "Absolutely nothing. Wait it out here. You're with us now, you're tribalized. They don't know where you're at. I got Azimund on lookout, just in case."

I extended my hand, touched the back of her right palm. How warm it was. "You've been incredible. I can't ever begin to repay you."

"You're an Authentus. You're bound to us and bound to tell the truth as you experience it from now on. That's reward enough. We'll protect you, and if circumstances change, you must protect us, too."

I stood up, started pacing the floor, three steps turn, three steps turn. "Suppose Alvina doesn't pick up on my mind projection, isn't there some way of physically getting out to that Triton?"

"If it's actually there, you mean? Forget it. Without an invite and definite coordinates you'd never find it. It's deadly out there. You need her to guide you in. Hacking her file's your only hope."

"I'll get through to her, one way or another. I promised."

"This is no time to honor past promises." Epiphany's brows drew closer together. "Assumin' the Triton is what it's supposed to be, your lady's in some deathless neverland. She ain't gonna want to come back. You're history. She'd be vulnerable to pass on or pick up infections anyway."

"We got company."

We both started at Azimund's voice. He stood in the open doorway, arms folded.

I went to the window, looked out, saw nothing but houses and the high hedge next door. "Where?"

"Two guys, Great Ascension tribesters, in a car further up the street."

"Shit."

Epiphany remained seated calmly. "I underestimated them. Looks like they might have found you already."

"I've got to get away."

"There aren't enough of our people within distance to protect you. We're a tiny tribe. An' it's not as if we can call the police. May as well run for it, 'fore there are more of them out there."

"If I get through this I'll always be grateful…" She sat up straight, placed her hands in her lap. "You're an escaped DATCHO with the cops and the most powerful tribe on earth coming down on you. Don't thank me. If you manage to even get out of this building it'll be a miracle. If you do, head east. Find the flood-dyke path and follow it. First town you come to is Arkton. On the outskirts of the city is an open-air market. That's where you'll find our people. We control the recycle markets in this part of the world."

"Alvina, you'll still help me to find her?"

She sighed. "Make damn sure you stay offline. I'll set up a simple slave-to-master relay and we'll keep in touch that way. You'll only be able to access a network through me. For now, the most important thing is that you disappear, digitally and physically. And for Lord's sakes, change the color of your suit."

"How do I do that?"

She groaned, rolled her eyes." "Mercy, you're so unstreet, so… Just tell the velo to do it."

She stood, turned and left the room and returned almost immediately. She grabbed my wrist and pulled me out into the hallway. "Keep away from the windows, they may have vision-master hardware that can see through one-way glass." She held up a tiny, chromed star, leaned forward and clipped it to the lobe of my left ear. "This here's a relay. Make it your default portal. It works on antique blue-ray technology. Reception ain't too good, anyone could hack into it, but it's so outdated it's a million to one they'll be scanning for it."

She squeezed my bicep. I wanted her reassuring arms around me like when she'd held me from the back of the velo. I'd been touched more times in the previous three days than I had for years and was beginning to yearn for the feel of another.

Epiphany zipped my jacket to my throat. "*If* that woman of yours is out there, *if* she responds with your code going on her blog-file, then I'm in. You just keep sending the message out."

"Shall I sneak out the back way?"

She looked up at the ceiling. "They're not that stupid. They'll have someone out back, too. Up in the roof, you can get into the neighboring place through the loft, skinny guy like you. They won't be watching that wreck of a place next door."

I'd forgotten Azimund's presence. He came forward, nudged my elbow. "Come on."

I followed as he padded up the green baize covered stairs soundlessly. My last glimpse of Epiphany was her sitting back regally in the chair, waving me away. Two flights up, Azimund stopped in the stairwell under a trapdoor in the ceiling. He looked at me with wide-stretched eyes. "You're one of us," he said. "We're family, we're always with you. Don't forget."

I'd thought him indifferent, almost hostile towards me. Tears pooled in my eyes. I stood, blinking them away and thinking now—when there's no chance—I join the human race at last.

He used a stick with a brass hook to open the hatch and drag down a folding aluminium ladder.

"Go!" he hissed.

TWENTY-THREE

LIT BY A TINY, OPAQUE SKYLIGHT, THE ATTIC WAS almost totally dark. Cobwebs clung to my face, the air smelled of mold. I blundered through an obstacle course of roof beams, boxes and clutter, cursing the Great Ascension, the police, Roxanna and everything else on the planet.

My fingertips explored the far wall, found a space at chest height. Nothing beyond but darkness and cold air. Hauling myself up, I scraped my ribs as I wriggled over the wall to crumple in a heap the other side.

Now in absolute darkness, I lumbered around on hands and knees until eventually I found the sunken square of a trapdoor.

There was no latch or any obvious means of getting the door open. Maybe it only opened from the other side. Growing nervous, I tested my weight on the boards between the roof beams. First one foot, then the other. The thin plasterboard creaked, shuddered, then gave way. I plunged down in a blizzard of plasterboard and dust. My left hand clutched at a rafter, pain wrenched my shoulder. I hung for a second, legs dangling before hitting the floorboards.

I lay sprawled on the remains of the floor, trying to get my limbs to work. Floorboards were missing, nails projected spitefully. Only when it was apparent that no bones were broken did I stand, flexing my sore shoulder. Drops of blood dribbled through the suit from a neat puncture just below my left elbow.

Feeble light leaked around metal sheets nailed over the windows. Most of the fixtures had been ripped out, doors and doorframes included. The walls were littered with shreds of wall covering. Only a steel banister was left where the staircase had been. The air in my nostrils whistled loudly.

"I'm alive," I whispered, "I live and breathe."

The house groaned as if settling deeper on its foundations. I clambered onto the banister rail and slid down, gripping it with both hands. At the bottom, I had to balance on charred shreds of floorboard.

I stood in the hallway. What the hell to do? Lie low and wait? Or make a break for it? Shadows shifted in the corner of my eye, a twist of wall covering rustled, then dropped beside me. The house seemed to resent my presence, its cold brick exuding dislike.

Something scurried against a wall upstairs. It was a signal—time to get out. I picked my way through the doorway into the ruined front room. It was littered with strings of smart circuitry and shattered furniture. Slashes of light patterned the walls. I pushed with both hands against a rusty window covering where a corner had come away. Something brushed my cheek. I pushed harder. The metal fell away, clanging. Shit, the noise!

Light flooded the room. The air stank of the grave. I clambered onto the windowsill, fine drops of mustard-colored rain on my face. The garden was clear. The velo was almost hidden, only a few inches of handlebar protruded from the hedge. When I jumped down my hips jarred and my knees clicked as I hit the gravel, drops of blood flicked onto the stones. In the tangle of hedge a blue spot of light appeared, the velo bleeped.

"Hello Zachary. I am ready to function."

"Quiet!"

The gravel crunched horribly as I crossed to the hedge. I scrabbled in the foliage and hauled the machine clear. As I strapped on the helmet, I remembered. "Change my suit's color," I hissed. "And don't speak, use quiet mode or something."

Nothing happened. I spoke louder. "Hey, Tinman! Change suit color."

The blue light flashed on the half-moon dashboard. My suit mutated. It seemed to fill with liquid pink from the ankles up. The color changed to blue, then orange.

"Okat, that one."

The letters on the velo's dash burned blue: "Do you wish helmet and helmet screen to be compatible color? Do you wish suit to make emergency repair?"

"Yes. Do it."

Little was visible through the tangle of leaves, only the shapes of parked cars. I pulled my gloves from my pocket and slipped them on. They were blemished with droplets of orange the same color as my suit which quickly enlarged. Clear liquid seeped around the hole near my elbow, hardening quickly into a crystalline blister.

I stood listening to my pulse, waiting for a sign, for the right moment to run. The hedge quivered, a shadow passed by on the other side.

The velo unlocked itself with a loud clunk. The word "Destination?" flashed on the dashboard.

I pushed the velo back into the foliage, pressed myself in beside it.

A tall bolstered man in a red suit stood thirty feet away just inside the gateway. At his brow a crescent moon flicked on and off. His long straight hair swirled as he looked over his shoulder, gestured and pointed up at the house

Again the hedge quivered.

The man prowled closer, grinding gravel underfoot, trying to walk on the sides of his boots. He stood with his back to me no more than ten feet away, staring up at the house. My breath froze in my lungs as he turned, looked past me back to the gateway. Abruptly, he moved off towards the window I'd just climbed out of. He peered inside where I'd peeled off the metal sheet. Any second he'd see me. I needed to disappear, to be invisible...

"Velo," I whispered, "does this suit have refractive mode?"

"Insufficient resources," read the dash.

As the man put one foot on the sill and started to climb in, another, squatter figure appeared from the shadows at the opposite corner of the house. Without hesitating, he made straight for me. My stomach turned to water. I went rigid, knowing he'd seen me. "Chameleon mode?" the dash registered.

"Yes, yes, anything."

"Hey," the man bawled, pounding over, his suit a freak show of shifting sepia images. "He's here!" He stopped two feet away, staring uncomprehendingly. I smelled his strawberry scent, saw the shuffling pinprick diodes on his suit. I stood stupefied as he leaned closer, reached out with his right hand. "He's here," he whispered.

He thrust his hand forward. I ducked the metallic fingernails that stabbed at my cheek. He raised his other hand. I leaned back, almost toppling into the hedge as he brushed it left and right near my chest. "Wha..?" His expression one of rapt fascination, his rinsed blue eyes impossible to hold. I heard the pop as he released air, watched his outline fade as his breath condensed against my helmet screen.

"What's up?" Red-suit had re-emerged from the window. His big bony head behind the other's shoulder.

"He was here a moment ago," said the man before me. "I saw him."

"Where?"

"I thought I saw him, standing here, I..." His hair flounced, his overlong lashes flickered. It was impossible he couldn't see me. He reached forward, both hands passing either side of my head. His left hand brushed my elbow, touched the handlebars of the velo. His suit showed a panorama of plains Indians hunting, herds of buffaloes, big skies..."His machine, the velo, it's hidden here. It's unlocked and ready to go. He must be here."

They both watched me. It was unbearable. I held my breath, closed my eyes, imagined myself invisible, tried to sink into the darkness behind my eyes.

"Might be he set up a holo image as a decoy. Try a DNA scan," the nearest voice said.

I kept my eyes shut. Something ticked rapidly, I sensed movement close to my head.

"Nothing. Wait. There's something here."

Footsteps scrunched. After an agony of waiting, a voice, "There's blood on the ground. It's his. Come on."

The crackle of stones, a vicious curse. When I opened my eyes, red suit had gone. The other man was walking towards the house reluctantly, constantly looking back.

He hesitated a moment before clambering into the house through the window.

I breathed, brought my hand to my face with infinite slowness. It was no longer part of my body. My hand was a fat knotted branch, glistening wetly, the fingers were twigs twisted with leaf and bud. As I moved, the fingers mutated, became a new part of the mass of the hedge.

I waited with galloping heart, took a couple of breaths, forced myself to move. The velo's wheels made such a row on the gravel I had to grab the saddle and carry the thing. Grunting with the effort, cursing the sound I was making, I lugged it to the gateway and leapt on board. The street was swished clean by rain and deserted apart from a line of parked cars.

The Scarecrow and Azimund, I owed them. I had to lead these hunters away, couldn't let them be in danger. Feeling selfless and stupid, I picked up a handful of gravel and threw it at the metal over the window. The clatter of stone on steel in my ears as I peddled away. Buzzing past the Scarecrow's house, a head emerged from behind a car, a woman with a crown of curly hair and panda eyes. A third eye glinted dully.

"Hey!" she said, half-heartedly, raising a hand and pointing. I had an impulse to wave back as I wrenched open the throttle, away, away!

TWENTY-FOUR

THE VELO'S DASH READ, "ZACH, I HAVE RECEIVED FORTY-one police requests to immobilize myself and reveal my position. A fault renders me unable to comply." A junction appeared ahead. Warning signals, "Major road, no two-wheeled vehicles." I aimed the velo between bollards, shot over the sensor strips and out onto the highway. Cars hurried by, inches away. Their maker's logos lingered in the air after they'd passed.

"Tinman, you can talk now."

"We are at present on a major highway illegally, Zach. This journey must be terminated."

The earth trembled, a bellow almost made me leap from the saddle. A bus careered past, roaring away to the horizon. I slowed, looked for an exit. Finding none, I mounted the bluegrass bank at the roadside, dodged between hydrants of frost-clearing chemicals. Then I was ducking under young hybrid trees, their branches slashing at my screened-off face. Beyond the trees was a flat apron of tarmac where a row of street-cleaning vehicles were parked. I slowed, sucked air. A block of apartments squatted on the corner of a long street, their slit windows like narrowed eyes.

"Zach," said Tinman, "I recommend you return me to the nearest registered dealer for an upgrade."

"Forget it, keep moving. I want this portal in my ear to be the default com port for all communications."

"Complying. New com detected. This is outdated blue-ray technology, confined to transmissions from a single portal on the Authentus network. Superior hardware is available. Do you still wish to install it?"

"Yes, get on with it."

"Complying. However, with no-stream access, my navigation is now limited to road-sign recognition and on-board compass."

"Fine—carry on. Head east for the city of Arcton. Follow the flood-dyke path if you can find it." My gloved hands melted into the yellow webbing of the handlebar grips. My suit's legs were the same color as the velo's paintwork. "And change all smart clothing from chameleon-mode to black. "

We passed housing enclaves and domes. We rattled through an underpass and down a long straight veloway.

The air was thick with beads of sticky moisture. My nerves were stretched tight. Every time a human figure appeared, my heart beat wildly. I felt exposed, as if the helmet and suit no longer concealed me. Two pale faces glared malevolently from an upper floor window in an apartment block. A short woman with a child's face stepped out of my path reluctantly, her eyebrows two question marks over elongated eyes.

"Do I know you?" The question reverberated in my head, yet the words were not my own. Where did they come from? I pressed my lips together and hummed loudly, filling my mind with sound. That damned pill Epiphany gave me, what had it done to my mind?

The pathway became paved with yellow tiles, broadening out till it was twelve feet across. Traffic signals and monitors became scarcer. Housing enclaves gave way to ranks of dwellings mounted first on concrete blocks, then on reinforced legs six feet above the earth. All were built to the same drab design, a rectangular cinder slab with a flat roof and large glass frontage. Grow domes were set in clumps behind the houses like mushrooms.

When I closed my eyes I saw the coda. I continually brought the pattern to mind, saw the letters A+Z, the heart and infinity symbols rippling through the misty air. Mind-throwing felt like an appeal to transcend myself, to take on some mythical dimension I didn't possess. I saw Alvina's broad forehead reflected on a water recycling tower. Then in a puddle of snowmelt she was there again, pale and serious, dark hollows instead of eyes. I repeatedly shook my head as if to shake something loose.

The air had warmed since the previous day, most of the snow had melted leaving smears of slush. Above, the heavens gathered indigo clouds, shaped them into an anvil. There was a flicker in the firmament, a rumble of thunder. My breath steamed through the helmet's air vents; pressure seemed to be building in my head.

A dark line appeared on the horizon. A cluster of signs called out, warned of obstructions, a likelihood of flooding, advising all manner of alternatives. I stuck to the path, moving east. Soon the edges of the path were obliterated by sand. The dark line in the distance got thicker, morphing into a massive wall. A straggled line of stilt-legged houses were arrayed to my right, the wall looming ever larger on my left. Behind the houses was a system of drainage dykes, earth banks and channels. Wind-powered pumps thumped out a lazy rhythm, piles of bricks and the derricks of cranes showed building work in progress. Scruffs of marram grass sprouted from streaks of sand ringed with mud.

Soon I was alongside the wall. Its surface bloomed with a blanket of moss. For a moment I seemed to be merging into the wall, as if its mass exerted a gravitational pull that would draw me into itself.

No signs of any town, just an endless line of houses. My shin hurt, my shoulder throbbed, my mind struggled against waves of exhaustion. Belatedly, I remembered the relay.

"Hi, Epiphany. You there?" I slowed to a crawl.

"This is a simple relay device," said the velo. "Do you wish me to go online with alternative hardware?"

"Not under any circumstances. Just use that one ..."

"Hey Ju-Ju man!"

"Epiphany! It's great to hear your voice. You okay?"

"Yup. You're still holding on?"

"Just. Did the Great Ascension posse give you any grief?"

"Nope. They shot away from here like there was a fire somewhere. How did you get by 'em?"

"I used the suit, but it was touch and go. You pick up anything on the Triton network?"

"Hell no, not yet. Gimme time. It'll take a while. You jest keep on thinking your way into Alvina's head."

A couple in ballooning patchwork suits side-by-side on green velos approached from the opposite direction. Only their eyes were visible as they split apart and passed either side of me. I looked down, saw saffron-colored mud splattered about the velo's frame.

"You'll let me know as soon as you get anything?"

"If I crack her file, you'll be the first to know. Where the hell you at? I can't locate you with this relay."

"On a track by a huge wall."

"Great. It's the dyke path through the East Anglian flood plain. Only nine miles further along to Arkton. Find the market there and you'll find our people. Hey, better keep transmissions short, just in case. Checking out."

Epiphany had said *If* I crack her file. Now it's if—not when.

A sluice channel with brick sides cut across the path. Water gurgled in a drain as if in some giant throat. The path crossed over the drain via a ramp so steep I had to peddle to assist the motor. When I got to the top, the vista beyond the wall filled me with horror.

A huge expanse of gray mud extended to a glistening ribbon of sea hissing on the horizon. The landscape was broken by the outline of angled roofs and lumpy projections encrusted with slime, slabs of blackened ice and seaweed. A series of near-submerged pylons with wires still attached looped in lazy short-hand into a smudge of yellow mist over to my left. Rivulets streamed in a glistening web between pools of dark water. Strange black birds with long necks preened themselves on the projecting roof-beams of a collapsed building in the near distance.

Bloody hell—England had shrunk. From what I remembered of East Anglia, the coastline used to be some fifty miles further north. The sea had drowned the land.

TWENTY-FIVE

"WHAT ARE YOU DOING?" ALVINA'S VOICE IN ABSOLUTE clarity resounded through my skull. The velo wobbled, I seesawed, wrestled with the handlebars. I feathered the brakes, relaxed my rigid arms, allowed the velo to rebalance itself.

"Alvina?"

I listened for a response for half-a-mile. My mind seemed to be softening. Memories, impressions, snatches of conversation arose at will. I'd lost all sense of time. The days since my escape pooled into one endless day peopled with a panorama of characters: Orion with her slotted nose, Roxanna's flawless skin, Epiphany's glistening eyes. I saw the fretted hole in the straightjacket I toiled so hard to free myself of, glittering gadgets displayed in the shopping center, the marbled expanse of the counter in the Nirvana café.

A half-hearted wind came up, throwing sand and dust. According to the signs, it was five more miles to Arkton. The path began to get crowded. People wandered along it on foot, or rode on velos, or simply stood and watched traffic from the balconies of houses. Most wore the markers of non-exclusive provider networks: Redeemers, Datasoft, Ace-Familias. Skin regrowths were low grade, the enhancements unsophisticated. They wore diode tattoos, implanted jewelry, illuminated hair—all the trademarks of the dispossessed.

The straggled procession of buildings were hurriedly made—hardened cement oozed between bricks, their simple construction bore no elaboration. They stood on stilted legs, patches of blackened mold and bluegrass smeared over the walls. I made slow progress on the skiddy path, continually checking behind to see if I was being followed.

"Who are you?" A vision of Alvina's full lips, a sense of her anxiety. I lurched, the front wheel skittered. What was happening? I slowed, stopped, listened, emptied my mind. A minute passed while a pair of airpods swooped low overhead. Another minute, nothing...

The wind intensified. Slowly the air thickened, the helmet trembling. A whisper-soft caress on the back of my neck. The wind became enraged, shaking the velo. Something was about to happen.

I heard the velo complain as I dropped it to the sand at the side of the path and bolted towards the line of houses. Diving headlong into dry sand under a house, I clutched one of the support legs with both hands. In a roll of thunder, a force seemed to root me to the spot. I lowered my head to the ground. Epiphany's excited voice yowled on the wind. Then no sound but the asthmatic wheeze of a water-pump. I got to my knees. The wind stopped, the air became still. I waited.

"How did you get to be there? I feel so afraid. This isn't real. How can you play these tricks on me? What did you..."

Alvina. Her voice sounded reedy and thinner than I remembered, but I would have know it instantly—a hint of something exotic in the light Californian tones.

"God, Alvina is it you?" Collapsing headlong, my voice rasping over hers. "It's not a trick, it's me, Alvina, it's me. They locked me in a penal zone. I thought I'd never see you again. I'm so glad you're alive."

The voice continued "...put a message in my head? Who's the Scarecrow? I don't understand. How did you access my blog-file?"

"I'm here, Alvina. I'm coming to find you."

"Zachary, these tricks must stop. You're programmed specifically not to do this. My blog-file is not to be altered, added to, or otherwise changed without my permission. Is that clear?"

"Alvina." My mouth parched, my chest empty, my soul shriven and wasted. "This is me. I'm in England. They put me in a DATCHO zone. Why did you leave? Speak to me, keep talking."

"..don't need these tricks." Hysteria rising in her voice. "No more Scarecrow and no more unauthorized additions to my blog-file and please, no more messages appearing in my head. I think I might be going crazy."

"No Alvina, you're not crazy. This is me, the real flesh and blood Zach, Alvina!"

No answer but the rustle of sand against the helmet screen.

"No, Alvina, no!"

I don't know how long I slumped there, calling her name, stomach a dry stone, agony in my heart. The house above me creaked and sighed, sending down a shower of white dust. I watched orange ant-sized insects with lobster-like claws carrying particles of weed down a ragged hole, saw wisps of sand scud over the dunes. The strangled cry of birds came from beyond the dyke wall.

A spume of sand and bits of grass whipped itself into a spiral. Slowly the column rose, grew fatter, higher. It became denser, mutated into the shape of a coiled serpent. I watched, numbly, as it hissed, shuffling its dry coils, raising its flat head over mine.

The wind dropped. The image disintegrated, became a ripple of sand.

Epiphany's voice was deafening. "You get that message?"

I was unable to answer.

"Hey, Shaman, are you okay?"

Wisps of sand curled around me, I watched it, warily in case it played any more tricks.

"Zach. Get back to me, what's happening?"

I got up on all fours, slid around to the lee side of the pillar. "Epiphany, tell me. Am I going mad?"

"Course not. You heard your woman's voice, didn't you?"

I pulled off the glove on my right hand, opened my palm and looked into it. The same lines, the same creases, the same patterns. I'd expected it to have changed. "I'm not sure. Was it really her?"

"Sure it was. It was her all right."

"Can I speak to her again?"

"It's not so simple. She was communicatin' to her blog-file while we accessed it. She was confused. We can't communicate to her directly, it's up to her."

"She said I was programmed not to play tricks, what did she mean?"

"She's didn't understand what was going on, who knows? Be positive. We're in. We can leave any message on her file you like an' she's sure to get it."

The boards under the house above me creaked, losing more dust. "But what use is it if she thinks it's all a trick?"

"Course she does! Who knows what the Triton's belief system is? It sure won't have thought-transference in their philosophy. Throwin' thoughts in someone's head and shovin' data in the secure vault of their blog-file's not an everyday occurrence. She don't believe it's you. Not yet. You got through though, hell, ain't that somethin?"

"I'm not sure of anything right now."

"What does it take to convince you, fool? Hell, it's all a waste of time anyway. I told you before, she sure ain't comin' back."

I thought for a moment. "Please put a message on her file. Ask her who but I would know the rune spell?"

"That it?"

"Yeah, I don't know what else to say."

"How about if I have a poke around in her file? At least you can find what happened when she disappeared."

"Can you do that?"

"Sure I can. If she kept a blog record of the event, I can retrieve the info now."

"Yes. Do it, please, if you can."

"I'll get back to you. Checking out."

I emerged from under the house and straightened, putting my glove back on, dusting sand from my suit. A couple of temple tribesters stood on the balcony of the next-door house, staring down. They looked smug up there with their serene expressions, golden gowns and white hair. Like they knew all the answers. I had so much weight in my mind, so many imponderables. Had the voice really been Alvina's? Had she really picked up my thoughts? Making a connection couldn't be so easy. Maybe it had been a voice-synth. Nothing could be known for sure.

Out of the clouds in a crackling tinderbox sky, an airpod emerged. Hunchbacked, narrow-waisted, white and black, it moved wasp-like across the mid-horizon, occasionally hidden behind the dyke wall.

As I watched, it stopped moving, then its glass-bullet head tipped downward and it swung slowly in my direction. I saw the contraption of sensors slung underneath, the number 78H, the word, "Police."

I ducked back under the house, out the other side, placing it between me and the pod.

Close by, staring into a mud-filled hole, were two men in gray zylex suits and red helmets. Next to them, a whirring, mud-encrusted wind pump dribbled gray slime into the hole.

The sound of the police pod's power unit got louder. As I approached, the men were engrossed in conversation, their backs to me. "Change suit color to gray," I said. "And helmet color to red, make its screen transparent."

"Complying," came Tinman's response.

The shadow of the police pod slid around the side of the house.

Both men turned as I got close. I gesticulated with both hands like a fellow worker, giving instructions. The pod moved over us, the whirr of its engines made conversation difficult.

"What you want?" one of the men shouted. His face bore a kindly expression, slick with sweat, large pores on the re-formed nose. "What's happened to your face?"

"Hi!" My voice over-jovial, hysterical. "Jesus saves!"

"Jesus?" A flicker of concern crossed his face.

"He certainly saved me a fortune, a two-dollar saving on every product while the promotion lasts."

"What's happening?" the other man said.

The sound of the pod's power unit softened, it began moving off. Nonsense was issuing from my mouth as if words would protect me. "Jesus Junkies, that's my tribe. He came down to earth in a flying saucer and signed me up. We're allied to Fistulla instant foods, full of energy and nutrients."

I glanced up, the pod was disappearing into the clouds. Stepping backwards, I warded the men off with lunatic language. "Optima provides the ultimate euphoric high," I bawled. "Enjoy your lifestyle!"

I turned and lumbered back towards the line of houses when it was clear the men weren't going to follow me.

"Oh, the Unbelievers' mystic prophecy," I sang in tuneless frenzy, "You got to buy into our philosophy." I kept the song going as I passed the temple tribesters on the balcony. I ducked beneath the house, lurched back up to the path, grabbed the velo by the handlebars.

"A system review has revealed sand contamination, causing a blocked oilway," Tinman said. "This will result in overheating of the main driveshaft bearings. A seizure is predicted within five miles. Please make an appointment with your Honda main dealer. If you will permit me to go on-stream I can locate the closest service center."

"Forget it." I said, as we moved off.

"My immobolizer is dysfunctional, I suggest you..."

"Shut up! Shut up! Shut up!"

I drove along the dyke path, aware of eyes boring into my back and an animal panic only just under control. I needed the support of my tribe now, my newfound brothers and sisters. How much further was this bloody town? How much longer could I last? My reason rambled, I saw Roxanna's face lit momentarily in the sky, heard a thought, "We'll get him."

My brain was melting. I took a lungful of air, increased speed, forced my eyeballs to hold the pathway. Sand made the going slippery, riders and walkers clogged the path. Ahead in the distance, I glimpsed a gaggle of buildings and towers. Then a sign, "Arkton—you're nearly there."

TWENTY-SIX

THE PATH CHANGED, BECAME A TARMAC ROAD EDGED
with blue-tiled pedestrian strips either side. The dyke wall became shorter till
it was only six feet high. Houses along the side of the path became denser, lost
their stilts. I could hear the whoosh of air that signalled a major road nearby.
An ad cried out, "One mile to Arkton, a new city of hope and renewal—renew
yourself in Madonna's health center."

Every fifty feet the towers of wind power generators appeared above the
rooftops, their white blades slicing the air. I couldn't move above five miles
per hour as the path was full of traffic. Ahead of me a line of two-person velos
dodged and maneuvred for position, their riders bellowing into coms above
the drone. I watched their trembling mudguards, shadowing my brakes, not
getting too close.

Would the Authentus be able to offer any protection? They didn't have
any Provider deal, which meant they had no technology worth the name. They
were short on numbers. Chances are they'd be a gang of grungers with corrupted ID records or faulty genetic code. It might be that I'd only bring them
trouble.

Above the dyke wall, the sky was pregnant with purple cloud. A prickling
sensation spread across my skin.

Alvina's voice sounded hollow as if she were in an empty space.

"Is it you? Are you real?"

I slithered to a halt, the rear wheel skitting sideways. A huddle of people
pushed around me, a horn blared, someone cursed.

"Yes! Alvina! I'm here!" I shunted to the tiles at the side of the path.

"I think maybe it is you. But you're supposed to be dead! They told me
you were dead. How like you this is. Only you could defy them all. You keep
coming into my head in symbols and signs like you're haunting me. Only you
would come for me through time and distance, through fire and water, through
everything."

Walkers jostled against my elbows, a metallic clang as someone clipped
the rear wheel. I pulled further off the path, my knee touching the dyke wall.
"I've been locked away, Alvina. But now I'm free, and I'm coming to find you.

I made you a promise. I said I'd wait for you, do you remember?" My voice a croak. Barely able to speak for wanting to say so much.

"Promise? Yes, I remember. But Zachary, it's wonderful you're alive. I don't know how you found me. But you must forget me. I have no words of comfort for you."

I had an urge to remove the helmet, as if this would bring her closer. "What do you mean?"

"I'm so far away. You can't reach me here and I can never return. Everything is different now. Even you can't change things."

A long pause and then a whimper. I saw the flare of an image forming in the helmet's screen. When I turned to the darkness of the dyke wall she was there. Her hair short, her eyes glistening, her face unchanged. If only I could abandon my leaden body and fly to her! "Alvina, I'm coming to find you. I'll get to you somehow, I'll will."

"No. Listen to me. I set you free from your promise. Give me up. Don't try to find me. This is so painful. I must be strong. I can't bear to speak to you knowing I can't ever be with you—it hurts too much."

"What's happened? Where are you?"

Her image faded to a glimmer of orange then was gone. Her voice was dying, too. "Goodbye my gentle, wonderful man. We didn't kiss, did we? That last time? Goodbye. I'll never ever forget..."

"No, Alvina no!"

My heart was screeching, tearing itself to pieces against the cage of my ribs. I sat on the velo as people hurried by, oblivious. My eyes bled tears till I was blinded by them.

I can never return, she'd said. Things are different now. She'd cast me off. It was over. I could make no mark on the future, on its polished, finished surface.

I felt insignificant. A freezing sensation chilled my bones. She no longer loved me. I formed the shape of her name with my lips, the name that had sustained me for so long. I thought of her words over and over. We didn't kiss that last time. This was the proof, as if I needed any, that this Alvina was real.

For so long I'd entertained her ghost. Now she was effectively dead to me. I felt the last remnants of hope die inside me.

I sat still a long time. The wind keened, fat drops of rain slapped against my shoulders. A clap of low-level thunder echoed off the dyke wall. The path streamed with water, became a stream. It swirled over my feet—full of sand and cotton-thin spiral worms congregating around fast-decaying air filters and clumps of spinning moss.

How stupid, how vain, how utterly foolish I'd been. The Changes changed everything. Alvina, our love, all our pasts covered by the waters. Alvina had gone on living, enhancing, evolving, becoming someone else.

All was done.

I looked up, flitting away tears with my eyelids. The path had become almost deserted. A flare of lightening illuminated two riders further back along the path. They sat immobile in the rain on their bright-green machines, loose suits slick with water and a glow at their brows just visible through their helmet screens. These were the two that had passed me some time back. Idiotically, I'd forgotten to darken the helmet screen to hide my face; anyone could see who I was.

In the next slash of lightening, my mind became illuminated. It was clear what my destination was—I was going to die.

How comforting the knowledge was after so many uncertainties. Death felt like an old companion. No longer the terrible chariot winging down, no longer the archenemy to be dodged and outsmarted. Death was a faithful friend, waiting to escort me home.

The realization settled in me silently. Joining a tribe couldn't protect me. Alvina was a kind of touchstone, a confirmation of what had gone before. Not a beginning but an end.

It seemed to me then, that even without regrown organs, cell-renewal serums or immune enhancements, I'd lived a very long time. The Changes were a kind of death to a way of being, to an illusion of reason and permanence. What was it that Orion said? "We live in a permanent, ever-changing present."

No one could keep their promises. Everyone changed and upgraded themselves constantly. In the Darwinian jungle of the DATCHO zone I'd survived, thrived, even. But I was too backward for this strange new world. Alvina had adapted. She'd been reborn in some new manifestation of herself. I should have died with bird song and blue skies. I should have gone with The Changes as so many did. I'd lived too long, and in a matter of minutes or hours, my time would come.

"Hey, Ju-Ju man. What you doin'?" Epiphany's voice.

I watched the two riders. They continued to sit still on their machines and stare. "She's gone."

"I tried to warn you. I'm sorry."

"It's all over. There's nothing more to say."

"Get real. It's understandable. You really think she's gonna leave some kind of freeze-dried enhancement heaven for a DATCHO on the run?"

In the crevice between two houses, a sliver of road. A line of cars moved bumper-to-bumper along it.

"There's nothing left for me now. At least I know she survived."

Epiphany raised her voice. "There's everything! You got to start again. You're a genius at thought transference. A few hours trainin' and you get a connection. No one's got the ability you got. You find our people quickly now and put all this behind you."

"It's not that simple."

"You're not giving up on me are you?"

I didn't answer. The rain washed down the dyke wall.

"Keep going. Just a little longer."

I idly pulled the brakes on and off, turned the handlebars back and forth. "Thank you, Epiphany for all you've done. The Great Ascension are right behind me. The cops are sweeping the area. I can't run anymore."

"Yes you can. Change the color of your suit every ten minutes. Change direction all the time. Get to our people. They're waiting for you. How far are you from Arkton?"

"Not far." I stood on the pedals and looked down the path at the blaze of signs, signals and tower blocks ahead.

"Get to town. Find the tribe. Keep yourself sealed up. Don't do anything crazy, huh?"

"Maybe."

"The Authentus are your future, you belong with us."

"I hear you. Checking out."

I sighed, sat and watched rivulets of water running down the wall. It didn't matter, whatever I did now wouldn't make any difference. I waited for the two riders to come for me. They leaned together, heads almost touching. They seemed hesitant, unwilling to come closer. I waited till the rain eased and traffic again populated the path. Still the riders remained immobile. Eventually, I sunk into the saddle, screwed the throttle open and moved off.

How liberating the imminence of death. I wasn't afraid. All my life I'd been fearful of so many things: the contempt of others, the violence of men, of losing what I loved. Fear became in the end a habit, like the habit of survival.

It seemed an impossible weight had slipped from my shoulders. After a final flurry, the rain stopped. The sky fermented a cauldron of mud-colored, chemical cloud. Now the path was clear, I gained speed. The suit's heating sent wisps of steam floating off my arms.

The dyke wall ended. Now there was housing on both sides of the path. My senses seemed sharpened, everything I saw, I saw for the last time and it seemed terribly important to see it properly. A spray of fine droplets spun from the front wheel, a line of nettles by the dyke wall trailed into the rainwater. The housing grew denser, more permanent looking, most of the buildings were set on the earth with no legs. There were pots of flowers in bulb-shaped domes on trellises, marble inlays in the walls, virtual curtains, solar panels. Looking back, the two riders followed, keeping their distance.

Slow-moving velo traffic appeared ahead, clumps of pedestrians in garish-colored clothing. The cave-like darkness of an underpass. In the gloom, shadows and shouted conversations, the pitiless yowl of engines while ads bolted and crackled.

Emerging up a steep ramp into murky daylight, I joined heavy traffic, cars, people. A roundabout had a glass dome mounted on its center with flowers within it. Momentarily, I saw a yellow-scalloped, bell-like daffodil head, its dark interior hinting at something sensual and secret.

Now in the environs of Arkton proper, I turned at random down a residential road zoned for velos only.

"Zachary, a drive-shaft failure is imminent. I suggest you terminate this journey immediately."

"Sing to me, Tinman."

"I have only a basic music program loaded of religious ceremonial music. If you wish more...'"

"Anything will be fine."

"I have the anthem of the Sisters of the Female Christ, *Rock of Ages*."

"That'll do."

"Rock of ages cleft for me—let me hide myself in thee."

The velo's polite vocals and tinny musical accompaniment were almost a parody, but brought tears to my eyes. The words seemed to echo along the street, where canopied buildings crouched low to the ground. The sky opened into two mauve drapes of cloud with a yellow band in the center, like a vista of the great hereafter.

TWENTY-SEVEN

I SAT ASTRIDE THE VELO AT A JUNCTION BY A "HEAVENLY Health Ice Cream" stand. Behind it a paved square and a line of mock-Tudor houses with exterior timbers and battlements. I lacked the heart to continue any further.

The velo was still singing, "...could my tears forever flow..."

The two riders were nowhere in sight. I sat, unable to summon the will to search the streets for the market, unable to do anything. All the buildings pretended to be something else. Everything was fake. No one appeared as they really were, no scars, wrinkles or...

"I got the file," Epiphany's voice distorting with urgency. "The day she left your house for the last time, back in Marlborough, USA. I'm sending it through."

"No. Not now. I don't want it. Stop."

Tinman's song faded, the helmet layered a squall of burning dots across the screen. The rooftop battlements faded out, the image swirled and solidified into the form a line of stores in Marlborough's main street. Alvina was strolling down it thousands of miles and fifteen years distant. In the corner of the screen a clock—nine minutes past eight in the morning.

Alvina overtook slower groups of people in purposeful strides. Her hair bounced as she waved to someone. She wore a nose-clip air filter that everyone wore just after The Changes.

Epiphany said, "This is from her blog-file, it's grabbed data from security cams, genie ads and stuff. You wanna see it or not?"

Alvina's image was so crisp I felt I could reach out and touch her. How many times had I imagined these moments? Let me see this, let me know the truth. "Yes. Okay, yes, I'm ready."

Something wasn't right. The straight line between Alvina's brows, the tight face. She looked furtive, disjointed. She speeded up, passing the craft stores and peeling paint of the old bakery on the north part of town. I remembered that the Wal-Mart was in the opposite direction.

The frame flickered, the time jumped to ten-fifteen. A series of ghostly close-ups of the backs of heads and shop windows. Giant chess pieces carved in soapstone, a rack of smog glasses. Then a glimpse of Alvina looking across a pedestrian crossing, but this was another town, not any place I recognized. The view moved along a street empty of traffic. These new shots were via her earring com port, the fuzz of her white pullover at the edge of the image.

"Now see this." Epiphany's voice felt like an intrusion. She must have seen this already.

The scene became inverted, the pavement loomed up, hugely magnified. I saw cavern-like cracks between paving stones. Then the scene disappeared, I again saw the scurried aluminium sheen over the ice cream booth. A man with orange skin and hair that looked painted on served a couple with huge cones.

"It took me a while, but I worked it out," said Epiphany. "She removed the com at this point."

"Holy shit."

"The remaining source material of this section has since been wiped with data-destroying software. She knew what she was doing. She was running away. She wanted to disappear."

I felt utterly spent.

Epiphany's voice softened. "You want to send her a message?"

"Tell her goodbye."

"That it?"

"Yep."

"You in Arkton now?"

"Yeah."

"Okay. Follow the main street and keep on till you find a market. Our people are there. Ask for Duke."

"Could you just show me Alvina again? Anything. Just an image of her being normal."

"Sure. I got half her life down here. Wait up.....Here, there you go."

In a blink, dots filled the helmet screen and Alvina materialized again, standing outside the arts shop in Marlborough. Behind her shoulder, one of her paintings in the window, a pattern of concentric circles interwoven with the graphic waves of a pea-green sea. She was laughing, showing the gap in her teeth.

"Going plenty cheap, mister you wanna buy? Then I can get me some food in the 'All You K'neat.'" She held out her hand. I heard the rumble of my own laughter—then I remembered a dull day of oppressive heat. I'd shot this scene on Alvina's minicam, holding it between finger and thumb.

I felt dislocated, not quite complete. I tried to sense the world moving beyond the scene I was immersed in: the saddle of the velo beneath me, traffic moving close by and people standing near.

Alvina took on a half-dozen poses, spread her arms, bowed, stood on one leg dangling her heavy-booted foot. She looked down and up and then pulled her face into an exaggerated grin with stretched lips and knitted brows. I loved her, that woman. For a few years at least, I'd made her happy. Her eyes shone with happiness.

My memory of that day was tinged with a sense of anxiety. In some part of myself perhaps even then I knew what a chance I was taking. This love, this woman, this frail butterfly of hope I'd invested everything in. I watched her posturing with a tremulous heart and thought, yes, I did treasure it, every moment. I cherished and tasted our time like I knew it wouldn't last.

Harsh breath, a guttural shout, a clank of metal. Heat behind my eyes, an ache in my chest. As the image faded, something hardened in my gut, a ball of rage that crackled though the grid of my nervous system. She'd betrayed me. She'd run away and hidden herself and made sure I couldn't follow.

Josh was six feet away, dismounting from his green velo, enormous in his baggy suit. He'd taken his helmet off, his face shiny with sweat or rain or the sheer gloss of the newly-made. As I backed away, my heel hit the shin of the other one, a smaller, slighter figure, still wearing his helmet.

Almost gibbering with rage, I stepped sideways and squeezed between a half-timbered building and the ice cream booth. I stood in a small square of graffiti-splattered flagstones with a couple of recycle bins and a velo rack. This would be perfect. I wanted no monitors, no witnesses to what would happen here. I saw the diamond in Josh's grin, the purpose in his extended jaw as he came for me. I saw and I was glad. In a red mist of ferocity I wanted revenge.

Josh burst through the gap between booth and wall and lunged at me with both hands. I kicked wildly, my foot finding thin air as he put both paws around the back of my head. My crash helmet was torn off, the vacuum seal popped, the relay was ripped from my earlobe, spinning to the flagstones. A roar of pain like my ear had been shredded. The air tasted of metal. My suit scrunched as he snatched two handfuls near my armpits and hoisted me up. Everything seemed to slow down. An eerie calmness claimed me as I watched the top of his trembling head, the padded knee bumping up and down, pounding the relay into powder.

When he threw me down, I hit the ground doubled up with cracking knees, but managed to stay upright. Where was the other one? I scanned quickly, no sign of him or her. Josh leaned down, picked up my helmet with one hand, swung it in an arc and bounced it off my forehead. I heard the *thunk*, my head jerked, but I felt nothing. He uttered a throaty roar and grabbed my hair, pulled me to him. The whites of his eyes were huge; his lips pulled back revealing magnificent teeth. A small black cylinder was in his hand inches from my face. I watched his thumb find the button on top of the cylinder, at the same time my gloved, snakelike hand, index finger pointed, whiplashed out and stabbed his eye.

"Oh," he grunted. His arm swung uselessly, the cylinder dropping from his fingers.

Something popped onto his cheek and stuck there, a protective lens. I pounded his face with my fist, his hot breath and saliva spraying my face. I felt unstoppable, rigid with rage. Then he abruptly pulled back. I stumbled forwards, my head colliding with his chest. An uppercut from a flailing hand collided with my jawbone, knocking me backwards. A shard of shattered tooth fell from my mouth, a ringing sound filled my ears.

I stood, stunned. Josh was doubled over, both palms covering his eye. His head aligned perfectly with my kick, which cracked him on the cheekbone. He looked astonished as he flipped onto his back, arms swinging. A hot surge shot through me, why had I been so afraid? Pounding my feet into his sides, feeling ribs give way, the exquisite pleasure of breaking bones.

I jumped up and down on him with both feet. "Die, you dipshit!"

Then I was on my knees, unsure how I got to be there. Had he knocked my legs from under me? He was up already, towering over me, big hands grabbing my head and throwing it at the ground. A flash of flagstones, starbursts of pain, droplets of blood. I was aware of my raw, horrible breath, my shrill voice, shrieking like a girl's. A blow caught me behind my ear. I'd been blinded. I was on my back being crushed, his terrible weight. He was invincible. He'd put out my eyes. A hand seized my throat, I'm going to die, right here, right now. Sudden light, opening my eyes, I realized I'd held them tight shut. A flash—maybe lightning, maybe in my head.

"Got him!" The word bursting like a bubble in my mind.

Both his hands were on my windpipe, his face in my face, the intimacy of it. I saw pores of re-plumped skin, the blood-red gem in his brow, his bloodshot eye. This was the last thing I'd see. He pulled his head back, kept the pressure on my throat as he slid off me and crouched low. Retching for air, for breath, for life. I didn't want to die. Didn't they need me alive? He couldn't kill me. I needed to live!

My vision was going for real, waves of purple darkness, Josh's furious face fading. Hallucinations came in those last seconds, a horrible clacking sound in my chest. Between Josh's trembling arms, Tinman appeared. Tinman, majestically moving, wheels spinning, lights flashing.

Closer came the machine, the front wheel slamming between Josh's legs. Josh fell forwards on top of me, his face pushing against mine, our noses touching. Air, breath, life. Chest heaving as once again, his fingers fumbled for my throat. Sucking at the air, craning my neck, my teeth seized his perfect nose and bit. Snarling, growling in my ears.

All my fury, all my frustration, all the wasted, pent-up years, the betrayal of Alvina, of all it, he'd pay. His sucking breath, crunching cartilage. I'd never let go. My savage teeth biting down, my jackal jaws. He screamed. The hurt in that raw, terrible scream shocked me into letting go. He rolled off and curled up beside me. I lay there, breathing heavily, listening to the blubbing, drowning noise he was making.

When at last I got up, he didn't move. Both hands covered his face. He quivered like some pacified beast, dribbling snot and blood between his fingers.

Josh's accomplice had vanished.

TWENTY-EIGHT

I'D LOST MY HELMET. THERE'D BEEN NO TIME TO LOOK for it when I'd fled the scene with Josh lying there, cops and tribesters likely to arrive at any moment. Cold air froze my face, agitated the pain in my jaw. I envisioned specks of DNA like dandruff trailing from my cheeks. I was lost in a quagmire of traffic-free compressed housing developments, the buildings clung giddily together in clusters like termite mounds.

I felt alive, full of quick, furious potency. I had to find the tribe. How could I have ever thought of giving up? I'd fight them all, the cops, the three-eyed monsters, Roxanna; struggle on till my heart stopped beating.

It was almost reassuring to see the faze-eyed fascination in people's eyes as I passed, like coming back to myself after a long absence.

The velo shuddered as it rolled, squeaking with every revolution of the wheels. A reek of burning oil, smudges of smoke from the back wheel.

"Tinman, how much longer can you keep going?"

"Breakdown is imminent, Zachary. My main-shaft bearings will fail within a mile."

"You saved me, back there, Tinman. You're amazing. A true friend."

"As you know, Zach, I am programmed to respond whenever I detect trauma in your life-sign responses. Do you wish me to list my various functions and add-ons?"

I was aware of a trickle of blood from the vicinity of my left ear, a hot feeling at my forehead. "No. I'm going to have to abandon you now. It's terrible. I hate to let you go, but there's no other way."

"I understand. Please make sure to power-down and remove any personal items."

I parked the velo by a purple-roofed recycling center with an array of skips and hoppers aligned along the front. I switched off the velo, walked quickly away without looking back.

A gang of kids sitting on a wall zapping rocket ships projected in the air by a groaning Gamestation dropped their weapons when they saw me.

"Hey you got funny face!" yelled a raven-haired girl with a gummy grin.

"Look at him nose. All gone red!" bawled a blonde boy with a perfect face.

The figure ahead stood out on the other side of the street by his flabby, padded suit and the glowing dot between his eyebrows. He leaned against a wall like he was propping it up. His helmet-less head was askew as if listening for some sound. There was no sign of his green velo. I crossed the road. It was the driver who had waited for me outside the zone, Siddharta. Even when close enough to see the web of creases on his pale face, I didn't pause. I made a fist to strike him fast and hard. His casualness betrayed something, maybe a weapon, maybe there were others close by. I didn't care. I wouldn't be afraid ever again.

I tightened, took a breath as I drew level, watched his thin face.

"Please," he said, turning his palms outward.

I raised my closed hand; one good swing at that narrow skull should do it. I clenched my teeth, a roar of pain surging from my sore mouth. I swung down hard, felt my shoulder wrench, but he'd gone. He'd crumpled to his knees so suddenly the impact of his knees on the pavement was audible.

My arm hung by my side as he made a sort of bow and looked up. The face had been refleshed so many times, layers of skin formed an overlapping tide mark beneath his chin. His cheeks were pockmarked with overlarge pores like a pickled walnut and blooms of blue veins stood out on his forehead. Baleful gray-blue eyes matched the baleful gray-blue bindi that pulsed intermittently. I stood, waiting for him to say something.

"It's me," he said. "I was with Josh, I was keeping watch, stopping anyone from..."

"So what?"

"I ran away. I didn't help him. I let the velo get past me. I could have called on tribe people like he told me to, but I didn't. I knew he wouldn't beat you. I know how powerful you are."

"Then you know more than I do."

"You're the shaman, the wizard. No one's gonna beat you, no one's gonna catch you, it's impossible. Orion, she's one of us now. She tells everyone that despite what Roxanna says, you're the real deal, your powers are infinite."

A familiar tiredness in my voice, "Bullshit, it's all bullshit."

"I knew I'd locate you. I *felt* you coming. It was me that said we should look for you on the dyke path. I'd been in trance-dance and I saw you and me here in this place, this town. You're my destiny. I got no right to ask this, but I need your help."

I laughed, a wheezy, crooked laughter. "You're right. You got no right to ask me anything. Who else is with you?"

He looked away and said, "I'm Siddharta. I knew you had something special when I met you outside the zone. My feelings are always true, why didn't

I trust them before?" He looked up into my eyes. "I'm sick. I want you to cure me." He proffered his palms which bore a multitude of finely sketched lines.

"It was trick. I never healed anyone in my life."

His nose twitched. "This is a test, right? A faith test. You healed so many. I've seen all them citations on-stream."

My forehead throbbed. "Why are you so hungry for lies? I can't help you. Are you alone?"

The kids that I'd passed earlier came by on the other side of the road with an angular woman. They called out as they ambled along, "Red nose!" "Hey, funny-face!"

"You left Josh alive," Siddharta said. "He put a call out a minute ago. Our people will be flushing this area right now."

"Where's Roxanna, where's AT? How have you been tracking me?"

His eyes continued to look into mine. "You been giving us a load of trouble. You've been careful—no DNA trail, you kept offline. We know you hid out with some Authentus people. We can hack household entry security systems but it takes a long time to process. Roxanna's nearby, in a home bus. She's ready for when you're caught, so they can do the op straight off. Only they won't catch you, will they?"

"How much longer has Roxanna got?"

"Not long. The medical file the Scarecrow put on the tribal site, lots of our people seen that, before they took it down. Rumor is that Roxanna's not a true immortal. Some are talking about removing her elder status, some are leaving the tribe. But me, I got this thing in my brain, a kind of tumor. They can remove it by creating a one-off, cell-specific drug, but it causes brain damage, and it's too expensive anyway. I'd like for you to tell the tumor to go away."

"That's ridiculous. I can't do any such thing."

"It's my crown chakra," he said, flattening his palms together as if praying. "I've stayed too long in the higher spheres. Repeated aura cleansing didn't work. You got the power. You lived so long, all that time in the zone with no drugs, no immune bolstering. You got the power, please, I beg you."

"No. It's not like that. I used to con people. It was just the power of suggestion."

"I've seen the spirit light around you. I know your strength. I'm only seventy-one. You been around over a century. Have mercy on me, great wizard."

"Jeez, this is crazy." I looked away, checked for figures with flashing foreheads. Nothing but three spindly women further down the street. When I looked back, he was waiting silently with head bowed. Sighing, I leaned down, took the glove off my right hand and touched his head. As I did, his head dropped even further. The three women had contraptions of flapping silks around their heads, they were standing there like lamp stands, watching. I had to move.

Under my hand, his re-grown hair was thick as a rug and incredibly dry without its natural sebum. It felt ridiculous, this pantomime, but I did it anyway. Emptying my mind, I sent him waves of imagined golden light. I visualized the dark lump in his brain dispersing under the rays radiating from my palm. Thought is a power, it changes things. I looked across the street, the women were still watching. I kept my hand there, worked my mind some more. A sense of something passing between my hand and his head like a spark. The inside of my palm grew distinctly warm.

"Your faith has healed you," I said. "Go in peace."

He didn't answer, just stayed there on his knees. Then he tried to make some words, spluttered a bit, gave up. Tears glistened on his cheeks. I couldn't speak either. There was such a confusion of feelings. I *had* felt something. Maybe there'd been more to my healings than mere suggestion. Maybe I was going mad.

Back aching, stiff legged, bruised and shaken, I shambled on past him.

TWENTY-NINE

I WALKED DOWN AN AVENUE WHERE LOW HOUSES covered in solar panels were arranged around small squares and cul-de-sacs. Metal gates sectioned off each block. A man with a new face and old eyes leaned on a gate, a watering can in his hand.

I stopped. "Do you know where I can find the market. Or for that matter the Authentus tribespeople?"

He looked surprised, thought a minute, closed his eyes and chewed his lip. "The Authentus? They're weird. I found happiness with the Kaballah people. They'll take you, too. We're old. We got no time to mess around."

"Can you tell me where I can find the Authentus anyway?"

He swung the watering can to his left. "Down there, back toward the town center. By the new memorial there's a market. You'll find 'em there, on the stalls."

A ring of lasers danced around an ancient stone cross. Behind it was a piazza filled with market stalls, families, cars. I moved through the press of people, their breath making frosty clouds. Hand-painted signs were slung between poles. A yellow truck selling hot food belched steam. A bare patch of brown earth under my feet was covered with tire tracks. The place reeked of cooking vegetables, coffee, damp cloth and cheap mood sprays. Ragged stall holders leaned over tables piled high with ancient technology.

A large, hairy man with mismatched lips—the top much thicker than the lower—leaned over a stall running a meaty hand through a clutter of ancient PC parts. He dragged out an ancient laptop and plugged it into a power-cell feed. The screen displayed a 2D black-and-white image.

He glanced over at me. "All sterilized and genuine, sir. No retro copies." His voice was high-pitched, wrong. On the screen a horse's eyeballs bulged with effort while a jockey whipped it on, beating its sides.

On the next stall, a woman with lank hair hawked pens, "Lookie 'ere, all a real ting, all a real ting." Pens of tortoiseshell, brushed steel and mother-of-pearl were aligned before her flanked by bottles of blue ink. Other stalls sold paper, books and hand-held mobile phones, spectacles, chromed bumpers from cars of the petroleum age.

"All real, antique," read a tatty banner, "cash only" on another. The people behind the stalls looked second-hand, with wrinkles, spots, asymmetry of face and body, crooked teeth. Punters carried off chunks of archaic metal, clutched them to their chests like trophies.

A small wheezing man with a bald patch sat behind a stall loaded with cameras, primitive, fist-sized devices covered with buttons. His nails were chipped and black with grime. He had a face like a well-worn shoe, a face that wouldn't be surprised at anything. He looked me up and down.

"Young sir," he said in a flat voice. "You'd be Zachary, wouldn't ye?" A press of sleek-faced soulsters jostled past.

"Yes. I'm he."

He leaned forward, spoke in a half-whisper. "Heeh, you're even uglier than me. Scarecrow told us you were coming. Welcome, brother. You better get back here wi' me, I'll see you're secure."

I squeezed through the space between his stall and the next, ducking under the awning.

The man passed me a long grubby scarf. "Get this around yer mug and keep hid best you can." I wrapped it around my face leaving only my eyes exposed.

I sat on a stool behind a flap of cloth, trying to stay out of sight. Time passed. I examined my suit, it was already fraying at the elbows and knees, spots of dried mud and bloodstains down the front. The repetitive patter of the man's breathy voice was like a mantra, "A touch of the real past there, young sir. Authentic history. Feel the solidness, feel the mechanicals of 'em." Rattles and clicks resounded as people rummaged.

A rhythmic throb thrummed through my jaw, a dull pain was fixed in my shoulder. I leaned back against a support strut and sought solace in slumber that swept over me in waves. Time seemed to move in cycles of diminishing light; darkness pooled at my feet. At some point, lights were clipped to the stall. They sizzled and spat, cast spoke-like beams.

It became very cold, a half-moon of ice formed in the earth at my feet.

When I awoke there was only darkness. I felt a thousand years old. My left foot was completely numb. I looked up. Metal bars ran over my head, lit against the sky. I groaned and stood, saw the stall's awning had gone. Boxes were stacked in four walls to shoulder height around me like a makeshift fortress. I leaned over the boxes and watched shadowy figures dismantle arc-lit stalls with grunts and casual efficiency. Someone somewhere sold real tea and its tawny smell lingered irresistibly on the air.

"Tea," said Shoe-Face, appearing like a genie and placing a steaming cup of brown liquid in my palm. "Thought you could do wi' a cup."

"Thanks." I looked at him with amazement.

He grabbed my other hand. "Duke's the name," he turned and stuffed cameras into a large box. "Look sharp, Mr. Crowe." He said over his shoulder. "Get tea down yer, then get yourself into the truck over there."

I swallowed the tea in grateful gulps. Then I limped with my foot still numb through the chaos of collapsing stalls to the battered yellow truck. The back doors were wide open.

When I clambered inside, there were five other people already there, sitting on a bench against a wall of stacked boxes. Duke slammed the doors shut and a set of lights came on in the roof. I sat next to the girl from the fountain-pen stall who leered at me, her mouth full of precious stones.

"How ya'll doin?" she said.

"Alive."

"Shit day, huh?" Her laughing mouth was like a Christmas tree.

Everyone else babbled madly, ignoring me. I groaned as my shoulder brushed the side of the truck.

"So you're the shaman-fellah that's wiv us now?" continued Jewelled Teeth. "You gonna do a trick or something?"

I shook my head. "Believe me, staying in one piece is trick enough."

"I'm Jess," she said. She pointed to the woman next to her with over-enlarged breasts and odd-colored eyes who smiled lasciviously. "And that's Derah." Another woman with blue hair and acetylene eyes leaned forward and nodded.

"I'm Star."

"Howdy," said a gruff, bearded man in a long coat, half standing, "Ranji."

Ranji leaned across the others and offered me a cigarette, the illegal, real tobacco kind. As he prised open the packet with his thumb, the front of the box burst into life with an image of a diseased lung. "Warning" said the pack, "Cigarette smoking invalidates your health provision and will cause a painful and certain death."

"Thank you, no."

The acrid reek of burning tobacco seemed to offend no one and it took me a while to define an underlying odor—human sweat. I was the only one with a huna suit, the others wore thick clothing, fake furs, padded vests, lined jackets. Their chatter rattled around the hollow space.

"I'm not working Tuesday, ain't worth it."

"What's he gonna charge us for 'em?"

"I don't want him near me, he's poison."

I sat back, lulled by the lilt of conversation, immersed in the friendly fog of enclosed air. This was my tribe—my family.

THIRTY

WE'D GONE NO MORE THAN A COUPLE OF MILES WHEN the van lurched to a halt. The brakes squealed, I nearly slid off the bench.

"It's drinking time!" Jess shouted as the back doors were hauled open. The group stood as one and stampeded out into the cold night air.

When I emerged, everyone had gone. The vehicle was parked outside a two-story, red brick building with a waist-high, algae-stained flood wall around it. The windows were filthy, half the solar panels were gone and a lopsided sign bore the legend "The Rampant Lion."

Yellow light leaked from an open side door. Inside, at least thirty people were crammed into a low-ceilinged, L-shaped room with a bar at one end. The air was thick with smoke, heat and chatter. The walls were covered with ancient sporting implements: skates with vicious blades, skis with spiked poles, baseball bats, golf clubs.

Duke shouldered his way through the press of people to where I hovered in the doorway. "What you drinkin?"

"You don't understand," I said. "The Great Ascension tribe, the police, they're after me. This is no time for me to be in a public place. I can't just..."

"Hey, take it easy." He patted my shoulder. "No one's gonna come for you here. This place got no monitoring devices. You're invisible. Hey, it's Saturday night!" Duke turned and made his way back to the bar.

Jess, Derah, Duke and half a dozen others shouted for drinks. The albino barman's pink eyes scrunched as he roared for order.

If this tribe was bound to the truth it didn't seem to do them much good. Most were unmodified, and any enhancements they did have had been hacked-up in some black-market boutique. Their skin colors ranged from jet to milk-white, their features a fusion of every racial and cultural element: oriental eyes, frizzy hair, Negroid noses. They sported an excess of jewelry and facial hair.

"Hey Wizard," shouted Jess, presenting her palm with fingers outstretched. "You can read palms can't ya? Read me. Tell me about Dray, is he coming back or what?"

I glanced at her palm, at her striated heart line. "Dray's not coming back," I told her downcast eyes, "but another will take his place soon," (and another and another, but I didn't mention that).

Derah sauntered over with a foaming drink in one hand. "You tell me any'ting?" Her palms were square, her Venus mount full with a set of crosses at the base.

"You're an extremely sensual creature."

"You got it right there," said Star, leaning over my shoulder. Half a dozen people gathered around.

"You live a life of the body. Libido-boosting treatments have put you in a state of permanent arousal. A little restraint in your love-life might prove beneficial." I said this to roars of laughter.

Smoke stung my eyes. Everyone was sloshing down alcohol as if it were a drinking competition.

A man with bushy eyebrows and a battered face stretched his palm over the gaggle of heads. "I'm Mahler! My turn!" he said.

While I read for him, Derah slopped a metal tankard full of amber liquid on the glass-topped table in front of me. It smelled of earth, rotting apples and autumn in the time before the changes. "Cider!" she said.

On the man's hand were two head lines, one bent, one straight.

"You see everything two ways," I said. "And can never make your mind up."

He nodded sadly. "Had some dodgy neural implants. Makes me crazy sometimes."

"Me!" yelled a girl with a blonde frizz. "Do me!"

The cider tasted both sweet and sharp. Each sip made me thirstier, tasting better than the last. I passed light-hearted comments over the outstretched hands, just a couple of sentences on each to laughter and general approval. The whole bar watched, listened and commented.

Ranji leaned toward me, his thin beard studded with sapphires. "You got to get yourself a stall, Zach. You could make a wad."

I couldn't remember if I'd read his hand already or not. "It's easy," I said. "Anyone could do it."

He banged a full glass of cider on the table.

"No thanks, I don't drink." My words sounded unfamiliar, slipped too easily from the side of my mouth.

"No." He laughed with big, uneven teeth, pointing to the empty tankard beside the full glass. "Neither do I."

Surely I hadn't drunk it all?

"Dance!" shouted Duke. "Git it clear!"

Though the screen-wall was peeling, the floor uneven and the air scrubbers barely functioning, the wall-mounted jukebox looked state-of-the-art. "Multiformat, multi-effect moog warrior" it sang as it warmed up. The machine sliced the air with laser beams. Ella Fitzgerald wafted into in the middle of the room with her head cut off at the forehead and her feet missing. Her body was big as a barrel and wrapped in a gold silk wrap. "Don't treat me mean, baby," she sang in her buttery bassoon voice. Figures walked through the hologram, shifting tables and chairs to one side of the room.

I thought I was moving backwards, but it was actually the table in front of me sliding away. Someone politely asked me to stand and I realized I'd been sitting down. When I got to my feet, the chair had gone. Ella's lovely voice kept repeating "Don't treat me mean" to a syncopated rhythm that throbbed through the floorboards.

Another full glass miraculously appeared in my hand. People's faces took on a luminous quality. Ranji was telling me something. "She never wanted to know me after that. A new face and a couple of clicks up the IQ register. She was gone, hombre."

I sat on one of the tables in a corner of the room while everyone else stood. Derah removed her coat and began testing her limbs, shaking them out.

The music changed, reggae-ja fusion boomed, balls of color danced over our heads. Ella was replaced by a cartoon, a clown with red eyes and a pointed face who moved among us, urging us to dance. Lenses on the ceiling sprayed hoses of light. Derah's face leaned into mine. "You wanna dance, Zachry?"

"I'm sorry. I never dance."

The room trembled with sound. "Do ya feel in your soul, is your soul your own?" sang the mad clown.

"How's about a stagger then?" said Derah, still standing close. "Try this!"

I stared stupidly at her fingers till I could focus on the pill she held under my nose. "It's a special—for 'Siren' in wave sound. Coming on next—I got the accompanying tabs for the whole 'Elevation' series. Try it, you'll blow."

Siren. How familiar, that word! "I don't take tablets," I said. How pompous I sounded.

"Take it," she pressed the blue pill to my lips. "Limbic part of the brain they work on." She rocked back on her heels. "The pill will make the sound," she tapped her head, "an event."

The pill dissolved instantly on my tongue. Derah disappeared. Now Jess stood before me, smiling a bejewelled smile as she placed yet another drink in my hand.

"Oh yes. He's gettin' there!"

Jess turned and pushed her way over to Ranji, dragging him into a dance. They threw themselves around, kicking their feet high. Mahler came up, wriggling his bushy brows. "Look," he said, pointing at Duke who was in a clinch with a stocky oriental girl. "They gave him a regrown heart, but his new heart rejected 'im."

Laughter bubbled from me uncontrollably, drink spilled over my shoes. In the racket, Duke heard, looked up, leaned towards us. The girl's face moved with his as he said in a low voice, "Try to be nice to Mahler, you got to show respect for the dead."

He stretched over and shook my hand. Somehow, I was standing again. I didn't consciously stand up. Perhaps some internal gyroscope had gone.

A woman with holographic earrings said, "Don't take no notice. He ain't finished evolving yet."

The room jumped and reeled, full of firecracker light, shifting shadows, raised voices. "C'mon old man!" Jess bawled, pulling me to her. How perfect her lips were.

"I'd rather not."

Words were useless, the floor seemed to tilt, shifting me into her. I moved easily, as if swimming, my legs and hands knew what to do. Jess's joint less body against me, her flailing hands above me.

"Gee up!" she roared. The room revolved, a kaleidoscope of color and moving faces. I felt the color, saw the sound swirling. Faster and faster went my legs, quicker and quicker my arms, picking up the beat. I never danced before, never knew I could. Jess moved in close as the tempo changed, put her arms around me and we sashayed sideways.

Everyone was dancing including the cartoon man who flashed into any vacant space. A man shouted, neck wagging, repeating the same word, over and over, "Siren, siren, siren."

Next to me, Ranji danced with a hyper-flexible woman who wound herself about him. Star tapped my shoulder. "Remember me?" She grabbed my elbow. I floated with her like a whisper could carry me away. "Shall I accept you as you are—or do you want me to like you?" she said.

The song shifted gear, something changed. I was inside the song. I knew this mantra, knew every nuance. "Take me away, take me inside—siren song, siren song." Star's arms around me, the muscles writhing in her back.

A drink materialized in my hand, the liquid dribbling over Star's shoulder. My legs seemed longer than before. Someone stood on my foot. Star's mouth brushed mine, her tongue flicked out, touched my cheek.

"I pinched the protocols, y'know," she whispered. "It was me who did that. When I worked for Sun Systems software, I planted the code to access blog-files."

Roxanna's voice suffused the room. A gollup of air forced its way from my lungs like she'd stolen my breath. The music rained down like a balm and we were helpless. We danced as one, rocking and swaying, anticipating the beat, knowing the moves, my voice raw in my throat, calling the words I seemed to know, "baby maybe, maybe I can ho—ld on, ho—ld on." The faces around me were shining as if lit from within. We were carried by the music, rare and beautiful filling every cavern of mind, "got nobody, got nobody, got nobody, but me-ee-ee," the words a golden thread moving through my brain. I seemed to know everyone's thoughts, and all thoughts were one with the music. Roxanna caressed me with words, soothed away my suffering. She knew my pain. I'd known this song forever. I loved everyone. Most of all I loved Roxanna.

Star bounced against me, a set of purple pulsing spex on her head. "It's even better wi' these, they got scent-a-rama."

As she turned, I lifted the spex off her head, put them on. My vision changed. Now everyone had fine hairs of magnetic fiber around them. The aura around each person throbbed and contracted with the beat. I tasted the scent of roses and the sap of new grass. Astonishingly, up where the roof should have been, the stars and moon were shining bright. The moon! Hadn't seen it for decades, how huge it was. The chalk-white globe had a face on it, joining in the song, the mouth a giant "O." The sugar-crystal stars looked down.

All motion slowed down.

"It's trance-dance! You ready?" Star's words seemed out of sync. I heard someone's thoughts in my head, "take me away!" I'd left my body, I watched myself from above, my gray head nodding, my red-splotched face with a smile at the corner of the lips. An old silver-maned jackal, battered and scarred but still skulking. I moved in a syrupy sea. I felt the tug of the moon's gravity, beads of frozen gas falling on some far-off planet, cosmic winds brushing the infinite vastness of space.

"Roxanna, come take me," I called, knowing she heard me. My head had so much space in it. The faces whirled around me—Jess's glittering mouth, Derah's deranged eyes, Star pointing up at the heavens. We saw into each other's minds and we all thought the same, we knew the secrets of the universe.

The room reeled, softened and pulsated. Seconds, days, lifetimes passed. I was the sound, anywhere and nowhere at once. I wanted to stay there in that place forever where no pain could touch me. The music got louder, a table fell, the room went upside down, someone's hand touched mine.

"You got mindstretch," said Star shooting rods of electricity in all directions, pulling an empty glass from my hand.

"The music, it's sublime."

"It's just the pill you took."

"Roxanna, I've got to save her."

"Uh, huh." Star looked around, shadows on her face, her tongue a fluorescent flame that licked her lips. The spex were still on my head, the stars still out. I could fly to Roxanna. I weighed nothing at all. I raised my arms. Nothing happened.

"I have to go." I said. I saw the door, the peeling wire-wall covering on it, but couldn't move, my feet didn't work. It took me some moments to realize Star had grabbed hold of the back of my suit.

"You're too far gone, old man. Sit down."

She pulled me back onto a chair, sat heavily on my lap.

I sat pinned there, watching the party revolve around us. It was like being in the eye of a hurricane, stars in my eyes and a delicious fainting weakness in my limbs.

The room faded. Someone's knees nudged me. Star shouted in my ear, "You had enough?"

She stood and I remained slumped in the chair. Through the fuzz I could just make out bodies throwing themselves around, the cartoon man leering.

I felt suddenly feeble, sick, sodden with drink and stretched thin as a hair.

"He's blissed out," Star said as Ranji leaned over me. She and Ranji pulled me up and led me from the room.

"I need more drink," I spluttered, "another pill." They pulled me into a dark room. A couple of thermablankets on top of thin mattresses were on the floor.

Star lowered me onto a mattress, pulled off my shoes. She threw the blanket over me and tucked it around my middle. "There now, sleep."

I'd never sleep again. My mind roared and crackled, the row from the next room was tremendous.

"Leave the spex on," she said. "I'll put 'em in sleep mode, help you switch off." Closing my eyes, even the darkness behind them was spinning. When I opened them again the door was shut, only a slat of shifting light remained.

The stars still shone up above, the spex released a scent like lavender, a pulsing hypnotic tone thrummed into my ears.

"Come take me, Roxanna," I murmured. "Take this worthless trunk. You're welcome to whatever you can extract from these bones."

THIRTY-ONE

EYES STOPPED UP BY SLEEP, STOMACH A CESSPIT OF poison, my head full of blazing coals. My bladder was bursting, but every attempt at movement made me want to throw up.

The sliver of light under the door no longer pulsed, the music had stopped. However terrible the consequences, I had to pee. A soft snoring betrayed someone curled on the other mattress. It was just discernible as Star, her face innocent in sleep. I felt like a poison toad, festering beside her.

Standing wasn't possible. Only by rolling in slow, agonizing motion onto hands and knees could I manoeuvre myself off the mattress. I kneeled on something sharp, but the sensation was vague, removed.

My head exploded with puffballs of pain. By holding tight to the door-handle and waiting till my stomach stopped heaving, I managed to get to my feet. The hard light of the bar pricked my eyes, the aroma of beer and cigarettes hit my guts. I had to vomit. Bodies were strewn everywhere, on tables, over the floor. Duke sat at the bar in a pool of smoke and pink light with two others muttering darkly.

"Hey! It's the soothsayer!"

Incapable of speech, my tongue a dry rag too big for my mouth, I stumbled for the toilet door. I retched a stream of orange liquid and saliva onto the mortuary-white tiles. My face looked grotesque in the mirror, cut out and stuck on at the wrong angle.

Back in the bar, Duke gestured me over, holding a white dot between finger and thumb. "Here. No-hangover pill, you should a took it before. Drink plenty water, take it an' sleep. You'll be fine in morning."

"Isn't it morning now?" I managed to say, necking back the pill.

"Naw. Only 5:00 a.m."

"How could I have poisoned myself like this?"

Talk was too much effort. I'd never felt so appalling in my life. Hunch-backed, spex askew, I staggered back to bed. The blanket still held my warmth as I cowered, desperate for unconsciousness.

A prickly sensation crept down my legs. Pulses of heat and cold were running up my back. The light under the door had gone. I seemed to be spinning slowly. Is this conscious dreaming? Some trick of the spex? Hadn't I taken them off?

The sensations intensified. Then all was tarmac black. Perhaps this was the astral plane. Or alcoholic poisoning. Maybe it was the effect of the pill. I'd taken too many pills. I fumbled around with my hands, but there was nothing there. I had no idea which way was up.

The black diffused into a million light fragments, reformed, becoming the deepest blue. The color had thickness and texture, like liquid paint. I couldn't say whether it was cold or hot, night or day, where body ended and sensation began. The blue gave birth to a yellow dot which grew in size, glowed brighter till it was impossible to look at it directly for more than a few seconds.

With a gasp I saw I was in the beforetime. The sun shining up there, clouds like puffs of steam across the radiant blue. Invisible waves pushed against me slowly, thickened into syrupy viscosity. Then a yellow landscape materialized, rolling with majestic slowness. A great wave loomed and solidified against me, a bank of dry granules. I was part of the landscape, beached on a solid mound of sand. The dunes undulated for miles in every direction, pock-marked by indentations. The sun had become amplified, was bigger, hotter.

The scene burned, super-lit, the shadows hard. Heat radiated up from the sand, almost unbearably hot. I was stretched out flat like a starfish. When I raised my arm, I saw it was adorned with a white cotton sleeve. I was wearing a white suit.

"Would you like to go somewhere else?" That luxurious voice... I'd know anywhere. Alvina stood next to me, smiling, as self-possessed as a Buddha. Her big forehead and gap-toothed grin, her wild hair. She seemed to glow with energy. Too stunned to respond, I simply stared up at her.

She leaned over me so that her face filled my horizon. "Is this a good place for you?"

I continued to watch her, mesmerized.

She bent down and prodded me on the chest. I felt the pressure of her finger on my sternum.

"Oh Alvina! Where am I? Am I dead? Is this heaven?"

Her laugh—the same, ready, Alvina-laugh. Her face was the same Alvina face. She wore silk pants and a yellow bodice with ribbons streaming in a breeze which sprung out of nowhere.

"Hello, my love." She seemed fleshier than I remembered, more self-assured. "We're not in heaven, and we're not in the physical world, either. We're somewhere in between."

I motioned for her to come closer. "I love you, wherever we are."

She smiled and reached for my arm. "Come."

She helped me up. I concentrated on the feel of her hand on my bicep. The pressure was greatest from her thumb, lessening along the fingertips.

"I have much to tell you," she said. "Can you hear me okay?"

"I can hear you—it's like this is really happening."

Her eyebrows lifted. "Of course it's really happening. Can't you feel my touch, too?"

Her arms stretched around to hug me. God, this was no dream! I felt her ribs give, her heart pound out its rhythm.

"There are strange rules with this dream," I said, "but I know I must keep watching you, or you'll disappear."

"Those aren't the rules," she laughed. "This isn't a dream. I won't disappear. Look!" She pointed at the sun. I squinted at it, saw a slither of black radiating from the center to the outer edge of the golden orb. When I looked back she was still there.

"We don't have much time."

"Let's make time, Alvina. Can we go somewhere where there's more time?"

"Ha-ha." Her life-affirming laugh the sweetest music on earth. "This must be your first time, meeting someone like this. Don't worry, couples do this all the time, and never get together in the meatworld. There are time constraints, but no other rules."

"So can we fly?"

"Yes, of course we can fly, we can move through any world you like. Where would you like to go? Would you like to see how I live?"

"Perhaps. But first I need to know what happened to you, to us."

She looked down momentarily. "Yes, of course. That's one of many things I must tell you."

She flapped her outstretched arms like a conductor leading an orchestra and began to lift off the sand. I held her around her waist. We both floated quickly above the dunes through wisps of cloud. A ragged coastline rolled by, the sea glistened far below. Cool air ripped at my clothes. This was the most incredible, exhilarating ride of my life. I didn't want to let it ever stop.

My shirt flapped open. I noticed the sparse hairs on my chest were black instead of gray.

Alvina, her hair full of eddies and currents, pointed. "Look!"

On the water before us, the Triton. I recognized it from the images I'd seen at Epiphany's house. A colossus of a ship with cliff-like sides, endless gantries, decks and accommodation blocks. It seemed impossible the thing could float. Lights burned from a thousand points, airships milled around the upper decks.

"Home."

Alvina stared into my face, in the gloaming coral of her eyes a look of pure rapture. My eyes were prickly with tears as I pressed my face against hers. I realized with alarm I couldn't feel her against my cheek, nor could I sense anything with my hands. Alvina lifted one arm and used little movements of her fingers to swim us up into the air alongside the hull, pushing aside the nose-cone of a two-person airpod. Decks crowded with people swept by, we floated up to hover before a steel door.

"I waited for you, Alvina. I kept my promise. I won't ever leave you now."

She pressed the heel of her palm against my chest. "I know. You've always been with me, you know. Wait, I'll show you."

She pulled at her thumb like it was a joystick and everything stopped: the people roaming the decks, the airships, the clouds in the sky.

"What's happening?" It was unbearable that this should all disintegrate now.

A flash and everything started moving again. A man stood in the air before us, the sea at his back. It was myself as I used to be. His thin face, my face, his sad eyes, my own eyes. The hair jet, the skin unwrinkled. I recognized the charcoal-colored suit I used to wear decades ago. It was a favorite of Alvina's.

"I have assimilated all known aspects of your character with close-match personality profiling," the man said in my voice. He smiled—not with his mouth but with his eyes, and I felt a wave of sadness like I'd lost something important. He vanished in one touch of Alvina's thumb.

"I created him in your image," she said "He gives me advice, consoles me, makes me laugh, interacts with us all the time. I thought you were him when you first connected through my blog- file—I didn't know what was happening."

"I don't know whether to be glad or sorry you've created a digital assistant in my image."

She squeezed my elbow. "There isn't time for regrets—look!" The blackness had eaten a bigger slice of the sun. Almost a quarter of its mass had gone. Alvina pulled me towards the doorway. I wanted to stop and kiss her so much.

"Come."

I tried to concentrate on what I could feel—the jacket's tightness between my shoulders, the moving flannel around my legs. I heard the squeak of hinges as Alvina opened the thick metal door. The ship's metallic bulk enfolded us. As we walked down a well-lit corridor, I heard the muffled pounding of our footsteps, sensed the movement of air around my neck, the jolt in my ankle at each step. I saw Alvina's hand in my own, caught the vanilla scent of her, but felt nothing with my fingers.

The corridor had little marble statuettes posing in alcoves in the sheen-coated walls. Soon we emerged into a broader corridor with large windows through which a crowd of people were gathered.

"Recognize our star resident?" she said, stopping.

I did. Through the glass we looked down on a stage on which an ex-US president was performing. His skin was gray, like cement, his panda eyes set in an unwrinkled mask. That shucksy cowboy countenance was still there; that overdone, feminine mouth unchanged. A mouth that had declared endless states of emergency and weasel words. His feet slapped out a ragged routine, his limbs jumping with unnatural energy. No sound reached us but the muted schuss of the rhythm section. The small crowd that was gathered around him seemed to be mostly talking to themselves.

"Here everyone has a second chance. Even heads of state have their dreams. We're the everlasting elite of the world—look!"

A momentary shadow and we were in a different section of the ship. The ceiling was lower, the walls painted metal, tinted portholes replaced the windows. Through the nearest window a pig was visible, rooting around in a stainless-steel pen. Its body was slender and un-bestial, the graceful structure of the ribs and knobbly undulations of the vertebrae visible through human-like skin.

"These animals are gene-spliced with humanoid elements and internal organs developed for individual immune system profiles. You could say, truthfully, that they're almost human." Her voice became hard. "Everyone will tell you that pigs are ideal hosts for such use—they're the nearest mammalian match to humans in terms of organ suitability. But the truth is, they use them because all cultures are contemptuous of pigs."

I turned to her, placed both my unfeeling hands on her shoulders. "What's happened to you, Alvina? Why did you leave me? What are you doing here?"

Her face pulled in on itself, two creases appeared between her eyes. "You don't know?"

"No, please tell me, tell me everything."

Alvina closed her eyes and everything went black as the darkest night.

THIRTY-TWO

WE WERE IN ALVINA'S ROOM. WE DIDN'T WALK TO THE place; after a few seconds of darkness we were simply there. It was a small chamber with a statuette of Shiva on a shelf in a corner. A barely begun painting with just four bold green lines slashed down the canvas rested on an easel beside a single bed.

A hologram of myself was propped up by the bedside, looking serious, standing outside the house in Marlborough. On the wall was another man's face, one that I seemed to know. I trawled through the sludge of memories until I recognized him as the man standing with Alvina on the deck of the Triton in the image I'd seen at Orion's apartment.

"Zachary, please believe me," she said, placing both her hands on my shoulders so we stood facing one another. "I had no choice but to leave you all those years ago. I was sick. I had the worst kind of mutating virus, the strep five flu strain." She leaned forward and kissed me quickly on the cheek, but I didn't feel it.

"I couldn't kiss you, that last time,. You must have wondered why I'd kept my distance. I couldn't tell you. You'd never have let me go. It's so contagious, this disease. It's amazing you didn't get it, too. I decided to go away and seek medical help, almost certain that I would die. It was all I could do. I walked to the edge of town and caught a sealed cab to the nearest specialist flu isolation center—Jessop Hills."

A slap of recognition. The center where I'd been arrested. A whispering in my ears, a hollow feeling in my throat. "You were ill?"

"Yes, terribly ill. I should have died. I almost did."

A charge detonating within me, a shift in everything I thought I'd known. "You didn't leave me? I mean you still... you hadn't... you didn't want to go?"

"Of course I didn't want to go! I'd have done anything to stay. What else could I have done?"

My knees buckled. I clung to her, pressed my forehead against her. "I'd have stayed beside you whatever happened."

When I looked up, she'd covered her face with her hands. "I know I should have told you," she whispered behind her hands. "I tell myself a thousand times over I left to save you, so you didn't catch it. But... but it's not true. I'm weak,

I was so scared. I'd have done anything to save myself—that's why I ended up here."

I stretched up, kissed the back of her hands. "I went there, to Jessup Hills. That's why I was arrested. I tried to break in, looking for you."

It was a long time before she took her hands away and answered, throat trembling, eyelids fluttering. "I'm so terribly, terribly sorry. You'll never forgive me. I didn't know what had happened to you. I fell into a coma a few hours after I arrived. I was out for months. I expected never to wake again. They should have told you I was there. I told them to inform you, once I was safely in quarantine."

I felt a flood of weakness in my joints. I released her, leaned against the wall. Alvina supported me, her shoulder under my arm. We stood like this, me half-collapsed, till a coherent sentence came to my lips.

"No one told me anything. No one told me what had happened. How come you're here, on this Triton?"

She glanced over my shoulder at the door, then looked directly into my eyes. "Honestly. What do you think of our floating paradise?"

"I can't answer that. I'm so glad you're alive. It doesn't seem credible." I paused. "Who's he?" I said, pointing to the textured image of the man I'd seen holding her on the deck of the Triton, dreading her answer.

"Yoseph?" She sat on the bed. I stood, but when she reached and pulled me down beside her, it was actually the room that rolled while I remained still. "Can't you guess?"

Her face close to mine. My heart so constricted, I could barely speak. "Is he your man now, or..."

"That's my father."

"Your *father*? But you barely knew your father."

"True." She reached for my hand, held its numb form in both her own. "He was a pioneering doctor of immunology. It's he who began the Triton project. He was the first master of this ship. He got the support of certain powerful people with whom he reached an understanding. They secretly supply us with raw materials, modified stem cells and certain other materials we need for our medicines in exchange for an eventual place here with us."

She looked at the image on the wall. "Ditching morals and absolute selfishness is a prerequisite of being here. It takes enormous resources to keep each of us alive—we're living medical experiments. The Triton remains unattainable and yet highly desirable to the people who might try to eliminate us as a source of new infections." She turned to me. "Yoseph left my mother when I was little. He searched for me when The Changes came. He traced me to the isolation center through privileged access to health and disease monitoring records. He pulled strings and cashed in favors and somehow got me out of the center and brought me here. I suppose he felt he owed me something."

I shivered, hanging somewhere between hysterical laughter and bitter tears. "It's all so strange. I'm... I'm so glad to know you've survived. I don't know that this place is a good place to be. But if it saved you, I'm glad of it. In all this time, couldn't you have got a message to me? In all the years? I thought you were dead."

Alivina's face seemed to stiffen, her lips barely moving. "When you came through on my blog-file, it was the biggest shock of my life. I'd begged my father to find you. For security reasons, no one but a couple of elders have access to networks. He told me you'd succumbed to the flu virus while I was in a coma, and that I should forget you. I had no way of checking." Alvina pinched the skin at the back of my hand as if checking its quality. "Darling, you must understand, I can't ever come back. Don't spend any more time looking for me, you'll never find me. Now I have the pain of knowing you survived and not being able to be with you." She released my hand, wrapped her arms about herself. "I can't believe you managed to break into my file. I can't believe you can enter my thoughts. This mind throwing thing you do—it's a kind of sorcery, it's beyond belief."

"I love you, Alvina."

My shirt had disappeared.

Her cool fingers trailed along my belly, her touch an electric jolt. "I want to tell you that I've never stopped loving you. Our being apart hasn't changed that." She spoke warily, examining my face for my reaction.

"I've spent so much of my life afraid. I'm not afraid anymore, though I have every reason to be, now." She brought her hand to her throat, to the gold globe there with the markings we both knew on it. "When I was only three or four, my father still lived with us. One morning I heard my parents arguing, my mother crying, my father shouting that he would leave. I ran screaming from the house. I climbed the wall into the next-door garden and hid there in a banyan tree. I heard my father calling, but I stayed where I was. I must have gone to sleep, because when I awoke, it was dark. The stars were bright in the sky and when I looked down, there was my father below, calling my name. I was very frightened and climbed down, thinking he would punish me, but he simply held me. It was the first and only time he did that, he held me so desperately tight. He crushed me so that I could hardly breathe, like I was something so precious. There were tears in his eyes and I felt so utterly loved in that moment.

"You make me feel like that. You would always hold me so tight, like you'd never let go, like you'd die without me."

Her hands caressed my rib cage as she spoke, fingertips barely touching the skin. Now, as if I'd wished it, I was completely naked. Alvina beside me, when I blinked and focused, was naked too. Her small juvenile breasts were exactly as I remembered them, the oblong mole near the left nipple, the dark aureole. I held my breath as my eyes explored the familiar terrain of her body.

Her fingers continued their slow advance, exploring the line of my hip, the top of my thigh. She moved over me, golden skin, the round curve of her buttocks. I surrendered to the moment, trusting it to last. I felt her breasts flatten against me, her ribs flex, her sigh in my ear.

Her out-of-focus index finger traced the hollow of my eyes.

"I love this," she said, "the detail and weather of your face."

We entered the gentle play of love, so familiar and yet so new. The moments stretched out, each second a pearl beyond price. She moaned as we went through the slow dance in which we both knew the moves. I bent my useless hands back and used the inside of my wrist to stroke the skin at her hipbone, watching it prickle expectantly. So cruelly unfair that I couldn't feel anything with my hands. I was patient, knowing she wanted me to be. She moaned. Her head dropped back and as I kissed her throat, her hand enclosed me. There was only this at the center of myself and nothing else. She seemed so childish and yet so adult and I remembered thinking these same thoughts long ago.

When we came together, it was like coming back to life, like being reborn in the divine knowledge of her. We moved to the same rhythm, my heart swelling, tears falling from my eyes, riding a roaring thunder. It was all over far too quickly and we subsided, gasping into each other's arms.

The silence went on a long time, only the creak and rattle of the ship about us. She sat up, squeezed my wrist, said: "Your arms. I love the way the muscles are knotted and the veins stand out like vines."

"Alvina. Don't ever leave me again, please. I couldn't bear it."

She threw herself against me. Her hair fell over my face as she began squeezing my shoulders. "I shan't. We can meet like this whenever you wish."

"Do you promise?"

"You kept your promise, and I'll keep mine. You said you'd wait and you did." She pinched the flesh on my shoulders painfully. "I promise you I'll come through whenever circumstances permit."

"Does it have to be in this weird place, like it's a dream? Can I come and find you in the real world?"

She smiled, sadly. "No, darling, you'd never find me. We can only meet like this."

She buried her face in my chest, hair scrunching, voice distorted. "I'm not as strong as you." Alvina flickered, faded, returned. She pulled away from me, creased her brow in annoyance, wrenched her thumb. The wall behind her disappeared to reveal the sun now a completely black disc in a mauve sky.

Her breath caught in her throat. "No time." She kissed my neck.

Her body softened, melted. I groped for her, but it was like grasping water. She slipped away, leaving only darkness.

A voice came out of the void, "I'll connect again when I can. I love you."

THIRTY-THREE

FOR HOURS, I LAY UNMOVING, SURE I'D BE SUMMONED back into the strange Alvina world at any moment. In a heartbeat, she'd return. She'd promised.

It took forever to reclaim myself. The mapping out of sensations, the awakening of awareness, the naming of things. Weak light filtered through the filthy windows, the threadbare red carpet was stained and torn, the reek of stale beer permeated the room. It was so mundane, so *real*.

In the final seconds, as Alvina's words faded, I'd snatched off the spex. I'd seen in sulphurous light the suit billowed and flattened about my middle, warped into the undulations of Alvina's body. The crotch section still enfolded my genitals in an obscene embrace. It took me hours to understand that the miracle of meeting Alvina had been fabricated by photons and smart-ware. I'd lain bathed in the lupe's tricks of light, the suit's teletactile second skin being propelled by data. Apart from my face and hands, my perceptions had been fooled utterly. Alvina and I shared the deepest of intimacies in solitary isolation. Every touch had been one of moisture-saturated micro-fibers, each caress a contraction of smart-friction material.

I felt translucent, a mess of nerves and blood vessels. A sense of rapture and loss, of terror and amazement were all gathered behind a wrecking ball swinging through my mind. My disintegration was complete.

"Tings a happinin' while you lyin' there in an interotic."

Jess's ghostly head around the door, eyes pickled, flesh loose on her face.

"She still loves me," I said, unsure if this was illusion or not. "Alvina was ill. That's why she left."

Jess's lips formed a straight line. "Who?"

"Alvina." I sat up. "My wife."

"I don't know shit, 'cept that somehow you been tracked here. You bin flyin' in 'at suit for hours. Better come wi' me."

I waited, reluctant to react. Was this really happening?

I rubbed the carpet with my palm, sensed sticky fibers, grit. I put my finger in my mouth, bit hard. A shock of pain from my shattered tooth, the blood throbbed in my finger. Blinking away images of Alvina, of her face, her hands, I got up and fumbled for the door.

The bar seemed smaller than before, washed with orange light. Everyone was gathered there. The place reverberated with the aftershock of violence. An upside-down table had one leg missing, smashed chairs and bottles littered the floor. The main door hung lopsidedly from one hinge. Everyone was talking at once.

The room subsided into silence as Duke stood and regarded me with a bleary eye, a fine scratch of blood on his cheek.

"Some Great Ascension people came 'ere wanting to take you off. We had a hard time askin' 'em to leave."

My mouth struggled to work as if I'd forgotten how to speak. I swallowed hard, "I'm sorry. I've been on-stream; they must have tracked me. I seem to bring trouble wherever I go. I'll leave before they come back."

"You can't," Mahler said. "They're outside. Lot's of 'em."

Duke squeezed his head between both palms as if trying to expel something. "Oh crap, my brain aches. Why's the Great Ascension so hot for you?"

"Didn't Epiphany explain?"

"Nope, only said you were one of us, and that was enough."

A lie was on my lips immediately. I was Roxanna's song-writer till I got addicted to Euphora, then she fired me. Now Roxanna wanted to work with me again. My creativity only worked on Euphora though, and I wanted to stay clean. It was a great story, completely convincing. But I was an Authentus tribester and done with deceptions. If we mean what we say, then love is true and a promise is a promise.

"I'm an escaped DATCHO." I said. "Roxanna got me out. She did it 'cause she wants to steal organic material from me, but I'll die in the process."

Someone coughed, glasses tinkled behind the bar.

"Are we talkin' about the diva? I mean, the Roxanna DeLancia?" asked a white-faced Star.

"That's the one."

"Land of my bloody fathers," mumbled Duke.

"Holy arseholes," said Star.

"Let's all 'ave a drink," Ranji crooned, crumpled against the bar.

"We need to think about this," Duke said, pouring himself a glass of energized water. The liquid's blue hue made his hands translucent, exaggerating the veins in his wrists, the black rinds under his nails. "We gave 'em a good fight. But there's gonna be more of 'em next time."

The door trembled as it was rapped on from outside.

No one moved. The knocking began again. When no one answered, the door was forced open, its solitary hinge gave way and it fell in clouds of dust to the floor.

Half-a-dozen figures filed in silently wearing beautifully cut boots of mock leather with sure-grip soles and ankle struts sucking noisily at the floor. They split into two groups of three and lined up either side of the doorway. Pumped and primed, retinas stretched with mood elevators, they stood silently, waiting. Two of them I recognized as the men who almost caught me outside Epiphany's place.

Roxanna swept between them, hair rippling with strands of writhing s-wire. Her long neck was decorated with a line of pearls, a tang of oranges preceded her. Her pleated maroon dress had silver panels around the waist where Egyptian hieroglyphs decayed and reformed. Her stunning eyes and the naked wonder of her face was hypnotic. Any that were sitting stood up, the whole room at attention.

"Down. Please sit down all of you," she said, standing in a puddle of light in the center of the room regarding me with distaste. "Yes it is I, Roxanna DeLancia."

"Lord save us," said Derah, mouth hanging.

"You will be familiar with me through my music," Roxanna began. "I hope you feel I make good music. I'm a good person. I try to live by the heart, try to do what's right." Her voice was perfect, soft and breathy, with a sense of bafflement. "This man," she said, pointing at me, "has done me a great injustice. All I ask is that peace reign between our tribes, that you good people stand aside and let right be done."

Silence, but for her ragged breath.

"Please, one of you, answer me."

Someone coughed.

Duke spoke at last, "So, it's not as if you want to use 'im as donor-meat?"

Her perfect lips peeled back, displaying dazzling dental work. "Ha, yes. You are not the first to be seduced by his guile. Did he tell you that he's a DATCHO? That he escaped from a U.S. DATCHO zone?" All eyes turned on me, though they already knew this. "He's a convicted thief and an attempted murderer."

"It so happens that some of us 'ave done DATCHO time," said Duke.

Derah's head appeared from behind the bar, glass fragments twinkling in her hair. She was naked as far as could be seen, her buoyant breasts decorated with rings of radiant diode tattoos.

"Wha's happenin?"

Roxanna ignored her. "You may know that I'm an immortal, a tribal elder of the Great Ascension. This man has stolen my work, he's carrying original data internally. I need to retrieve it. As a reward for your cooperation, and to prevent further violence, I offer you all full membership of the Great Ascension community."

"Really? Me? All of us?" said Star.

"And me?" said Derah, hoisting a hefty fur coat around her shoulders.

"Yes." Roxanna seemed to grow taller. This was some performance. "I offer this to each and every one of you, besmirched with bad credit, penal code violations, faulty genetic markers, whatever. This includes every benefit of our label including our medical facilities, plus the most life-enhancing software on the planet. I'm talking about the quickest, most privileged path to God."

"Go to hell. Less 'ave a drink," said Ranji, yawning.

I looked around. My options were few. Every exit would surely be covered. Maybe I could use one of the sporting trophies on the wall as a weapon.

Duke held up his palm. "That's quite an offer. No one should 'ave to deal with this after a heavy night."

"I'm hungry." said Mahler, blinking stupidly.

"You really her? The goddess?" Star came in close. She tentatively extended her hand. "I love your work, it takes me way out." Star's fingers brushed Roxanna's elaborately decorated fingernails. Roxanna's lips compressed. She flinched, snatched her hand away, took a step back.

"I need an answer from you soon," she said, looking at Derah. "This offer will hold for one hour. If not we will take him by force, and we won't fail."

"What we gonna do?" said Derah, shuffling out from behind the bar, almost buried under the bear-like fur coat.

"What choice do we 'ave, when the goddess herself has come among us, offerin' salvation?" said Duke.

The whole bar jumped as the coffee machine vented a flatulent snort, blasting steam in all directions as Mahler primed it.

Roxanna flinched, took another step back. "Well?"

Duke sat heavily on a bar stool, swivelling around to face her. "Okay, people. What you think?"

"Nah," said Ranji. "How's about that drink?" There was as chorus of groans, Derah closed her eyes, shook her head.

Duke looked deep into his glass and spoke softly, almost to himself. "People like you and people like us, we don't belong to the same realm." He raised his eyes to Roxanna. "For us, findin' heaven and forever, regrowin' our internal organs and eyeballs, it just ain't gonna happen. There's no fairy-tale endings for us. If you really are Roxanna, if the gates of your tribe are really open to us, one way or another, we won't last long with you once you've got what you want. We're bound to our own way an' you know what? That's the way we like it." The bar echoed with whistles and cheers of approval.

Roxanna speared me with her eyes. Her voice dropped an octave as she pointed me out. "Would you trust his word against mine? You'd turn down your only chance of salvation? Are you really that stupid?"

Star slowly got down on her knees. Her hair spilled over her shoulders and along the filthy floor as she prostrated herself. "Ain't nobody, ain't nobody but mee-ee" she wailed, raising her arms in mock supplication.

"Jeez. Are we gonna 'ave that drink now or what?" said Ranji.

Roxanna's eyes flicked down to Star and back to me. "You fooled them all. Right and karma are on my side. You think you're so clever. In mere minutes, you'll be dead."

She backed out through the doorway, face set, head nodding as if confirming something. The troop lining the doorway looked at each other, hesitated, then filed out behind her.

"Well how 'bout that?" Duke swivelled on his stool, a grin on his face.

Derah pulled the coat tighter around herself. "What's gonna happen now?"

"I can't put you in any more danger," I said. "I'm going to get out of here before they come and get me."

"No," said Derah.

"Yes. There's no question. Either I go out or they'll come in."

"I'm comin' wi' thee," said Duke.

"An' me," said Star.

"There's gonna be a whole troop of us," said Ranji. "Ain't never gonna get that damned drink."

THIRTY-FOUR

IT WAS ME THAT SUGGESTED USING THE WALL ornaments to defend ourselves. Star pulled down a spiked skiing stick. Duke climbed onto a table, tore more items off the wall and handed them around. I got a cricket bat of splintered wood with a ribbon bound around the handle. Duke chose an aluminium javelin for himself.

I counted twenty-four of us, and a sorry lot we were with our washed-out faces and bloodshot eyes. Only the barman stayed behind with instructions to call for help. The events of the night seem to have sucked the strength from my muscles, my limbs felt slack and useless.

The outside air was chill, the sky an umber blanket. At least eighty Great Ascension were lined up, filling most of the car park. We couldn't have picked a worse place to do battle. The ground was covered by unevenly-laid paving slabs slippery with purple moss and enclosed by high walls. All I saw were blazing bindis, like a sea of colored stars. Their vibrant suits melded into one shimmering mass of smartware. Colors came and went, suit-front scenarios moved and mutated, photons shot through the air. They seemed sure of themselves, quietly waiting. We huddled together like hags, heaped in furs, coughing and spluttering.

We stood with the waist-high flood barrier just in front of us and the walls of the pub behind. Deafened by my pounding heart, my hands felt too big, the bat too heavy. We were bunched so tight I couldn't swing the thing without hitting one of our own.

The enemy closed together in two lines. As they did so their suits all took on the same blue hue. Someone moved among them handing out stun-sticks. At an unseen signal they moved as one, maintaining a perfectly straight line. The murmur of their communications filled the air. As they closed on us they raised their sticks, shiny red batons with chromed, blunt tips. They looked unstoppable, like an army of medieval pikemen. No single face was discernible, just a line of grim remodelled jaws. When only a couple of yards separated our ranks, I found I was looking at Josh. His nose was patterned with teeth marks, both eyes blackened, top lip swollen and purple. He eyed me as if I were a likely meal.

Duke began cursing, prodding the air with his shiny spear.

The approaching line stopped.

The tension was unbearable. They were so close I could see scratches on the knees of Josh's suit, smell a multitude of mood sprays, see a manga monster smirking on a padded shoulder.

It started with a quick movement to my left. The clatter of a dropped baseball bat. Derah collapsed, slumped over the flood wall. Her exposed buttocks were obscene in the open air.

More of our people started to go down. The enemy was quick, speeded up with Reactophen or similar; we were slow and too close together. One after the other, in lightning lunges of their stun sticks, we fell. Duke swore louder, stabbed his weapon at a long-legged female tribester. She easily dodged the javelin's tip, touched her baton on Duke's outstretched arm. Duke folded silently to the ground like he'd been switched off. The javelin clanged to the concrete.

"Stop! That's enough." I dropped the bat and held up my arms. "Take me. It's over, leave them alone."

The woman turned, lashed lightening-fast. I felt burning in my side, pain from my clenched jaw and then I was down.

Josh was above me. He leaned down and spat in my face. The warmth of his spittle was more of a shock than the act. The ooze dribbled down my cheek, his nails scratched my wrists as he dragged me along the ground. In my rag-doll helplessness, I could feel and think, but nothing worked, arms and legs useless.

Josh hoisted me onto his shoulder. I saw an upside-down vision of sophisticated boots, concrete slimy with moss, legs moving, the fat tire of a vehicle. There was too much blood in my head, my tongue lolling against the roof of my mouth.

A tearing sound close by my ear, a chemical smell in my nostrils. Gleeful faces congratulated each other around me. They wrapped tape around my mouth, my eyes. As the last light disappeared I saw a face that seemed familiar, unsmiling and sad-eyed. Sounds and smells became more concentrated—mood sprays, chemicals, shouts and cheers, hands pinching my flesh. My hands were taped together. Already a little movement had returned, I could make tiny twitches of my fingers.

In the black, a voice. Roxanna. "No more talk from you, you bastard. Get him in the truck, now."

My heart pumping impossibly fast.

They snagged my feet and yanked them free. The back of my hands dragged against metal, my shoulder grazed the ground. Laughter, shouting, cheers.

More hands hauled me upward. My hair got pulled tight, strands were torn away. Doors banged shut. All sound softened. They dropped me on a hard, rough surface, the air warm, moving. A hollow sound and a suck of air as another door closed. An engine whirred. I was in a vehicle, moving slowly, the suspension adjusting. Cold hands clutched my clammy skin, snatched at my suit, tearing away the zip. The suit split down the front, from collar to crotch. They tore off everything. I was naked. They scrubbed me with a strong-smelling liquid. I counted six pairs of hands.

A clink of metal. Orange scent. Roxanna close, her breathing harsh.

"How long's this gonna take?"

"Not long." A deep, male voice.

Something pierced my back, cold and sharp, deep into my spine.

"Okay, we're in," the male voice again. "Come on, hurry. Give it here."

"Sorry, I didn't know which one you..."

Who's voice was that? It sounded familiar. Heart pumping desperately fast. Roxanna's laughter loud in my ear. I turned my head, some small rotation just possible. My face rubbed against the rough surface. My forehead burned, my cheek stung, but the tape shifted a fraction. A dot of light appeared in the corner of my right eye. I saw a white sheet, instruments, a gleaming stainless-steel tray.

My blocked voice yearning to scream out—this is a crime against nature, you'll die sooner or later, you poisoned vulture. But all I could manage was "Gluh." I saw a piece of a face, gray eyes, a ridge of rebuilt skin at the neckline. Him, Siddharta. It was his voice I'd heard, the man I healed yesterday, years ago, whenever. I reached with all my senses out to him. Felt his fear, his guilt, his humility. Life had been good to him once. I placed my thoughts in his head, beamed my dwindling life-force into him. *Don't let them kill me. Don't, don't. Stop them.*

I heard a sound like air escaping. Freezing cold down the length of my spine, a deeper numbness, my muscles liquefying.

"All set. You ready?" The finality of that deep voice.

I couldn't see Siddharta now, nothing but a section of steel tray.

Don't! I screamed in my brain. *I healed you. I'm the wizard and I'll curse you. Stop them! Stop them!*

"Dispose of him as soon as we're done," Roxanna's voice softening. "Great spirit, may the will of the god consciousness be done. Give me more time, that I may do your bidding." A metallic rattle, liquid being poured.

Stop! Don't! Save me!

"I can't do this. It's wrong." Siddharta.

I craned my neck, saw the underside of his jaw, a pulse in the loose skin at the throat. No movement. No sound but harsh breathing.

172—JOHNNY FINCHAM

"What do you mean!" Roxanna's voice almost hysterical.

"It's wrong. He's got the power. He's a spiritual person. I don't want to... I can't do this."

A roar in my temples, an ache in my throat.

"Get out! Get out! Get out!" Roxanna's deafening bellow.

A shadow passed over me. I heard the sound of multiple lock-bolts springing, a loud bang. Siddharta shouted something, his voice fading to a rush of air as the door whoomped shut. I thought of his dry hair, his eyes during the healing. Something had passed between us. As I left the world, I saw how astounding were the powers of life. Perhaps there'd be something beyond this one where my soul could find rest.

Roxanna's beautifully shaped ear appeared only inches away, her head on a pillow beside me. Plastic-coated fingers pinched the skin at my neck, stretched it tight. A sharp pain, an incision in the skin. Then I was rolled over, face down.

Thank you, Alvina for loving me. It was worth it, the whole thing, the DATCHO zone, the years of loneliness, everything. You made it worthwhile. Time, you wretch, who marks all down, get that written—Alvina loved me.

A shout from outside. A piercing, artificial wail.

A growl close to my face. "Don't stop!"

Something scraped the vehicle's side. We stopped moving, the engine died. Something fell to the floor and shattered. A hand curled around my jaw, pressing against my mouth. My teeth cutting the inside of my lip. *This is stupid, I can't make a sound anyway.*

"What's going on?" A muted voice outside, a voice of authority. Something metallic rattled. An incredible pressure against my mouth.

"We committed no crime..." said a voice, barely under control.

"We picked up aggressive activity close by," the authoritarian voice again. "Stun sticks discharging, hostile body language. There's a gang of grungers out sparko in the car park of the Rampant Lion. Know anything about it?"

"You better charge us quick or let us go on. We got a legal team—the best there is."

"I'm entitled to an explanation under article forty three, section seven. And be quick about it."

"If you gotta know, we were preparing for a new moon ritual, but these Authentus people attacked us. We had to defend ourselves."

"You. Yeah, you. What happened to your head?"

"I fell out of the truck."

Siddharta. I searched for his sad eyes in my mind.

"You fell? Why isn't the safety lock functioning? That's a charge right there. Why's this vehicle moving so slowly anyway? What's in there?"

"It's one of our mobile medical centers. One of our elders is sick. It's a virus, a vitro flu strain, you can't go in there."

"Okay. I will accept your explanation. You people all ready to go?"

The back, open the back! Shooting spears of thought to Siddharta's brain. Seeing his face, feeling his sadness. *Tell the cop I'm here. Tell him I'm in the back, look in the back.*

"Yes, yeah."

"Okay. Enjoy your lifestyle."

"Thanks, sir."

The engine started, the truck rocked, the suspension settled.

Tell him to search this truck! Make him look in the back! A thunderous roar in my head.

The surface under me dragging as we pulled away. *Damn and shit!*

"STOP!" I felt Siddharta's words in my skull before I heard them. Roxanna emitted a guttural wail. I slid off the bed, bounced on the floor.

"Save him!" Siddharta pleaded. "He's in there. Open the door. They're killing him!"

Shouts, doors yawing on their hinges. Cold air. A series of shrieks from Roxanna.

I was dragged along the floor, head striking metal, a hollow ringing sound. An explosion of light. The tape torn from my eyes by enormous hands. Foul air, sky, traffic noise. A big face, brown eyes under orange lenses, blue body armor, a helmet.

"You alive?" said the cop.

I hung off the back of a white truck, a puppet with the strings cut. My head was raised, twisted gently sideways. Through the open doors I saw bottles and drips spilling liquid, two beds, Roxanna's small bare feet. A foam neck brace was sprayed around my shoulders. Beyond the big face, Siddharta was kneeling by the side of the road.

THIRTY-FIVE

WE WERE ALL ARRESTED—ROXANNA, JOSH, AND EIGHTY-four Great Ascension members. It took an hour and a half to get everyone scanned and processed at the roadside. I lay limp in a thermablanket in the back of a cop car while an army of uniforms shouted and shackled. Roxanna called in a virtual legal team who pleaded and threatened to no effect whatever. Eventually, they took us all to a mini-tower cop-shop in a desultory, dome-filled corner of Arkton.

The first three hours after my arrest were a honeymoon time when I was a victim, an innocent. John Stevas was the officer who'd dragged me from the hospital truck. He was a mass of a man, almost seven feet tall, who sucked vita-lollies that dangled like matchsticks from his fat lips. He plied me with "Reviva," gave me more blankets and scanned my skull for psychological and physical trauma. Then I was placed in a medical bay lit with antiseptic light. A medic came and fixed my teeth, extracting two ragged stumps and reseeding the gum with quick-growing molars. A healing accelerator ray ran over my face and bruised body, then I got trauma salts in a sweet, fizzy drink.

All too soon the mood of my captors hardened. I was placed in a cubicle crammed with scanners while a spare, twitchy female cop with too-small ears grilled me for four-and-a-half hours.

My data trail was recovered, the velo brought in and examined and on-stream feeds were scrutinized. Various agencies were called on: the immigration service, the F.B.I., the U.S. Department of Correction.

I told them everything, figuring they'd know it all soon enough. Backwards, forwards and sideways I told it, from the moment AT and Josh arrived in the zone. I talked till I got tired of talking, till my mouth became dry and used up. Then I moved inexorably through the various processes of imprisonment. At every phase I seemed to go down another flight of stairs, deeper into the bowels of the building.

Four floors down I was hustled into a holding room. Despite the ceiling's battery of fish-eyed monitors, faces appeared continually at a little window in the door. Then I was moved down to what must have been the deepest, dungeon level. They locked me in a cell with only a tiny, hard bed in it. I got green overalls and a thin shackle, much lighter than the one I wore in the zone.

It was almost a relief, this passive containment. No decisions, no possibility of escape, no future. The walls were a swirl of soothing green that emitted a dual-tone pulsing sound that sapped the mind. Nothing could be moved or manipulated. The yellow self-cleaning thermablanket was fixed to the mattress, the bed's metal legs welded to the floor. Passable food was brought at regular intervals. The containers and cutlery decomposed within the hour to a gray sludge and then to clear liquid that quickly evaporated. Deeply-recessed lights dimmed when presumably it was night-time outside.

The female officer came down and re-recorded my confession, checking for inconsistencies, her right foot tapping, ears pricked. It was a relief, this unburdening, as if all that had happened couldn't be true unless someone recorded it. She prowled around the cell, body armor creaking, regarding me eagerly. "Escaping the zone. You know what the penalty is?"

"I know."

"Never known anyone to jump a DATCHO zone before. Thought getting out of them was impossible."

"Will I be shipped back to the States, or will the sentence be carried out here?"

She smirked, strode around some more, purposeful movement in her buttocks. "The ultimate sentence can only be carried out back where the offense was committed. They'll initiate the process by requesting your extradition once they work out who you are and what you've done. We've only got you on a couple of minor moving traffic offenses in Cambridge so far. Back in the States, they don't seem to know you've escaped the zone yet."

I'd damned myself. My internals seemed to sag. The irony was delicious. If I'd made up a story, I may have got away with it.

"John Stevas told me you let the Great Ascension people go," I said to her back as she paced. "Including Roxanna?"

She stopped and turned, looked at me with widened eyes. "They're all wearing shackles. Can't go nowhere till the trial. Roxanna got bail on medical grounds. And that's more than you need to know." She unlocked the door and left me alone with the low-pitched hum and whisper of the air conditioning.

Each morning I was given a set of filters and lenses and let into the yard to exercise. I dragged myself around the eighty-six footstep-a-side square, listening to my shoes crunching on the gravel, peering up at the high brick walls topped with sensa-wire.

Days passed—two, three, a whole week. Each day identical to the one before. I slept most of the time, exhaustion my normal state. Everything, even thinking, was too much effort. Perhaps it was a preparation for death, this dusk of the soul, this closing down. Even for Alvina I barely spared a thought. We were forever now confined to different realms. Our virtual rendezvous had been not a coming together, but a goodbye.

On the eighth day of confinement, John Stevas walked into my cell, winked conspiratorially and dumped a pile of smart-fiber material on the floor. As the door clanked shut behind him I stared uncomprehendingly at this mound of micro-fibers, pressed-in squares of teletactile fabric and technology. Only when I straightened the thing out, inch by inch on the bed did I recognize what it was. My suit was inside out, clumsily repaired with hot-welded stitches

I checked the cuff com, which flashed "signal blocking in place." At least its power pack still functioned. I made a vow then, as I put the suit on. If there was the slightest chance, I'd get my story down and upload it somewhere. Maybe when they transported me, or before sentence was carried out, they'd let me go on-stream. I could relate my tale into the wrist portal and upload it in half-a-second. Who knew what warped and biased tale would be told officially when I'd been turned to dust? I swore to get my story down and get the data to the Scarecrow. She'd make sure Alvina got it. I could trust her and I could trust the Authentus. Belonging was a bridge that wouldn't fall down.

Later that same afternoon, the female PC walked me out of my cell and up four flights of stairs. Then I was put in a cage with a spindly, bolted-down bed and four chairs. The cage was in a big room full of cops bent over data combers, where curtains of info flowed, cross-referenced with columns of biofeedback and ID recognition. I was ignored.

The female PC and the twitchy cop wandered in occasionally and asked questions. "You got no middle names? You were born in the UK?" But they seemed subdued, the light gone from their eyes. Perhaps they'd grown bored with me already; maybe there was no advancement to be gained from my capture.

In this room there were windows with natural light and countless time displays, so I was well aware of afternoon slipping into evening and then night. I slept off and on, lying fully-clothed on the hard bed.

I woke at 5:30 a.m. and started to get undressed under the thin thermablanket. Surely, nothing would happen till the morning. Perhaps they'd take me away then, put me on a transporter. Perhaps a U.S. marshal would arrive to escort me back.

John Stevas sauntered in, smiling to himself, nodding at various people. He unlocked my cage by pointing his finger to a touchpad and beckoned me out. "How you doing?"

"Fine, I'm fine," I mumbled, hastily wriggling back into my suit.

He checked the shackle, then escorted me through a side door to a small room. This was the best place I'd been held in so far. It had wire-walls displaying river scenes, a cream-and-strawberry orchid in the corner, body-form chairs in gray fabric, a free drinks machine gurgling to itself and a cylindrical recycle bin.

He sat me down and left the room. I studied the various permutations available on the drinks machine, pulled leaves off the orchid, sniffed its scentless petals and eventually sat down. The water rippling around the walls made me drowsy.

Head nodding, I was just about asleep when John Stevas came back in, rubbing his hands together, bouncing on the balls of his feet.

"Okay. We're ready to process your case. We got everything through. It all checks out. You've got a big media profile! Palmist to the famous and all. What was it like, meeting all 'em movie stars?"

"Dull." I was in no mood to make small talk.

He leaned back against the wall, whistled feebly and looked at me. His stare was guileless, open. "You better hold onto that seat. You've got one hell of a shocker coming."

"Oh really," I said, leaning forward, pressing a button and watching a cup fill instantly. "You're going to carry out the sentence here after all?"

"You know, you're one hell of a lucky guy."

I extracted the cup, filled with cold green fluid. "Luckiest man walking this earth," I said with what I hoped was the right degree of irony.

"You know that fella, what's his name? Siddarsa or something? The one who told me to look in the truck and saved your neck? He said you kept putting words into his head and he couldn't keep you out. Said you're a shaman."

"He saved me so I could die a legitimate death. How lucky is that?"

"Oh, you have no idea just how lucky, yet."

He examined his nails momentarily, then strode over and sat next to me, the chair crumpling as it found his shape. He stretched down and hauled my shackled leg up, resting my ankle on his knees. I had to half-turn and grasp the arms of my own chair with one hand to stop myself sliding to the floor. Green fluid slopped from my cup and down my front.

"You've been took," he said, taking a code-key from his belt and inserting it in the shackle.

"What do you mean?"

"You've been had—hoaxed, duped, had one put over on you." The code key twinkled, all the diodes on the shackle lit up at once.

I gripped the chair base tighter. "Who by? How?"

He whistled between his teeth as he twisted the key and said, "No one can break the encrypted ID master codas. Not the Great Ascension, not the Authentus, not anyone. It's impossible."

"The master codas must've got broken, otherwise they couldn't have got me out of the zone. I'd have got zapped by the security screens."

Three turns, a push, two beeps of the key and the shackle separated into two neat halves that clunked softly to the floor.

I held the cup in front of me like an offering. "What now? Am I being deported?"

"Nope." He dropped my leg, waved vaguely in my direction, touched a device on his belt. "I told you the master codas can't be cracked. They've never been broken. We checked and believe me, we'd know."

"Then how did they bust me out of the zone?"

"They didn't bust you out. You got out of the zone 'cause you were cleared to leave."

Inside me, a fluttering, hollow helplessness. "Cleared to leave? Who by? How?"

"Parole. Your parole came through."

My right eyelid began to twitch, I couldn't stop it. I gulped air. "Parole?"

"You must've made an application, must've had a full hearing before the board?"

I took a long breath and held it. The hollow feeling had gone, my eyelid stilled. No sound but the thunder of my heart. "Yes, but it was refused, I mean, I assumed it would be. I didn't think they'd ever..."

"It came through. Your name was on the release list. It's simple. A Great Ascension member worked in the zone's admin department. When your parole came through, a ward guard should have escorted you out of the zone to a processing center to get acclimatized for the outside. The Great Ascension guy failed to pass on the order for a guard to take you out to the center. Josh and AT made a great performance to convince you you'd escaped, so you'd be completely dependent on them. Your name change had already been fixed as part of the parole process to build a new personality."

The cup exploded in my hand. Chlorophyll splattered over me and the chair. His words were an incantation, a spell that would fracture chains, open cages. Tears welled in my eyes, laughter gurgled in my gut.

He stood up, grinning. "You really think that flashy light show they put together was a master computer? And that they tapped into the stream with an antenna and a balloon? Sheesh, signals are blocked hundreds of feet above the zone, everyone knows that." He shook his head. "There've been enough legal incursions on your part to get you recalled for parole violations. You recorded some moving traffic offenses and there was a shortfall in a café bill. However, as your activities were a result of you being the victim of criminal activity, there aren't enough grounds in the UK for a deportation order."

He moved towards to door. *Don't stop*, I prayed. *Keep talking, don't break the spell.* "It seems that legally, we can't hold you any longer. You'll have to wear a monitoring unit and attend a hearing in a couple a days. But that's it. You're free, Mr. Tarn. Enjoy your lifestyle."

He left the room.

I sat, shattered. I'd grown wings. If this were true, I was free—legitimate, a citizen, normal. It couldn't be true.

I stood up, took deep breaths. Was this happening? Had the suit taken me to some new realm? I touched my face—dry skin, stubble, no spex.

I sat down. Stood up again. Sat and sweated out another tremulous, terrible hour. I was placed in a series of cells while two officials kitted up for a chemical attack tested me for viruses and fitted me with a permanently linked tracker unit. The cheap-looking ring was set with chips of clever crystal that looked, listened and licked the environment, broadcasting data and ID biometrics constantly.

While the processing went on, I waited for someone to walk in and announce this was a joke. If I closed my eyes for too long, I was sure I'd come back to the sticky carpet and dust of the Rampant Horse.

With John Stevas' heavy hand on my shoulder, I was steered through a fake-pine door to a reception area lustrous with impregnated glass. People were sitting there, ordinary people without uniforms. No one looked up as I passed. Beyond, automatic doors legitimized me and whanged open. Then out onto the pavement: civilization, smart faces, shops, cars breezing by, purple clouds in the sky and the heady scent of sulphur.

"Wait up!" Officer Stevas' big form lumbered behind me.

Shades of shite. I knew it.

He bent his head to stare into my face. "Where you headed? What you going to do now?"

"I don't know yet."

"You're not gonna do anything stupid are you? You know if you leave UK waters you'd break the bonds of your release and you'd end up back in the zone? You know we got trauma counselor services available?"

A thin form in a silver suit stepped between us.

"The Shaman will not require your services, thank you. He will be supplied with all the help he requires." Siddharta nodded repeatedly, eyeballs bursting from his head.

Officer Stevas shrugged, then turned and walked away.

A gaggle of Great Ascension people stood a few feet away, watching warily, all smiles and bows. A couple with identical faces spoke briefly together before coming forward to embrace me. I felt like a king, a conqueror, and the biggest fool on earth.

BOOK TWO

AND SO IT HAS COME TO PASS THAT I, SIDDHARTHA OF the Authentus, am privileged to record this, the chronicle of the Shaman. I have missed nothing: his escape from the zone, the meeting with the Scarecrow, his re-capture, and the moment he was released.

And now I place on file the events that led to Shaman's departure from this realm. Unlike the previous testimony, this section was not dictated to me. What follows is a record of events as I experienced them, for I alone accompanied the Shaman on his final journey. Despite the legends and lies propagated by rival tribes, this is the truth, for we Authentus are bound to the truth above all things.

I stood on a street corner in Arcton city, waiting. I'd been there for many hours, from the moment the rumor was posted that the Shaman would be released. It was the fourth time such a report had circulated and I was reconciled to disappointment. Others also waited nearby: ex-Great Ascension tribesters and other potential converts. No doubt they'd learned of the miraculous powers of this elevated soul—not least from my own and Orion's postings. I was careful to keep a good distance between myself and them. I felt a bond between me and the Shaman that went beyond theirs. I'd been healed, changed. His thoughts had been transmitted to me. I wasn't a mere opportunist like them.

I missed the instant he emerged from the police station, I was checking my portal for updates. I looked up to see his unassuming figure coming toward me, wearing an overstretched huna suit, scuffed at the knees and elbows. There were long slashes down the front, badly welded together so that glimpses of skin were visible. His unmodified face was drawn and tired-looking, though his eyes burned brightly. The red stain that covered his nose and part of his cheek gave him the appearance of a Native American in war paint.

I ran to him, assuring the police officer accompanying him that he required no assistance. I knew if I was to be accepted, it was essential that I demonstrated my usefulness immediately. Kneeling at the Shaman's feet, I said, "Master, allow me to serve you."

To my immense disappointment he merely laughed. A couple of Great Ascension tribesters who hurriedly embraced him were similarly rejected. He strode away, shooing us off like so many pigeons. This I knew was a test, probably one of many I'd have to endure. I dashed forward, shadowing his wiry figure.

I kept close to his heels and he strode down streets and through alleyways. Everywhere he went, people stared. He kept always to the shadows, randomly turning left and right, always following the most uninspiring looking passageways. The other followers soon gave up, but I kept close to his heels. Eventually, on a side-road full of low grade smartware shops and bustling crowds, he stopped and turned, his pink nose wrinkling. "You gonna stick to me like shit on a shoe? Go away!"

Whenever he was excited, his English accent was most pronounced. I smiled, seeing the gentleness in his amber eyes. "What would you have me do, master?"

"Bugger off!" He spun on his heel and walked back the way he'd come. It took me much longer to catch up with him this time.

"Where do you wish to go?" I said. "Let me help you." Two Temple tribesters walked up at that moment and bowed low, their silver hair touching the curbstones.

"Somewhere I can be alone!" he shouted, speeding up, almost running.

I found it hard to maintain his pace, my breath became labored. Though the Shaman had cured me of my illness, I was still weak. For a man of over one hundred years, his energy was astonishing.

"There's a café close by, master," I said, having already used my portal to scan for anything he might need. "The Arcadia. It's got private booths—I can instruct any potential followers to keep their distance."

He held up his hands. "Don't call me master, you don't owe me anything. I'm Zachary Crowe." His face softened as he saw how exhausted I was, he dropped his hands. "How far is this place?"

In the Arcadia, mood lifters misted the air smelling of new-cut grass. The tables were of real mahogany, wire-walls drew the eye into lush landscapes. Each booth was formed from pergolas of genetically modified lilies that danced to an inaudible sound.

The Shaman permitted me to stand a few feet away and guard his booth. Groups and individuals continually approached, bowing low and uttering the traditional greeting of the potential convert, "I come to you empty, I am bound to no place, position or view." I barred the way, told them to stay back. Some were reluctant to leave until I took their names and promised I'd plead their case. I ordered a selection of herbal tea infusions which I placed on the Shaman's table. He talked constantly into the com device at his sleeve, to the leader of his tribe, the one called Epiphany and to someone called Duke, re-assuring them of his safety. I was able to hear most of the conversation as his com was set, rather recklessly I thought, to open voice. He had a strange expression on his face, and spoke haltingly, as one unused to talking. I learned afterwards he'd been a lifelong loner and was technologically inept.

At one point in the conversation he asked if all members of his tribe were fine and when he received assurance, asked if they'd be happy to accept new members, including ex-Great Ascension people. Hearing this, my spirits soared. The Shaman was going to open his heart and his tribe to all that would follow him.

"Thank you," I said, leaning into the shadowed entranceway to his booth when the conversation ended. "May I assume you'll permit me to join your tribe also?"

"Don't thank me yet," he said taking a long drink of tea. "My tribe has no provider associations, and no illusions. We'll see how many of you are still keen after a taste of life in the raw. That'll sort the takers from the fakers."

"I am myself free of illusions and I know the truth. I know that you are a magician."

He laughed, bitterly. "Everything you know about me is crap. I'm fifty six, not a day older. I got no more magic in me than you have."

My faith wouldn't be shaken. "You healed me. You took away my tumor, its disappearance has been medically verified. You've survived an impossibly long time with no immune enhancements. You practice thought transference. I know this."

He pondered a moment. "Maybe there's something in that. But anyone could do what I have done."

A delivery girl in a silver stretch-suit arrived bearing a bunch of pink, tuba-shaped blooms with palm-sized heads. They came with a talking card with an ansa-link that said they were courtesy of Carriane—a Great Ascension elder known to myself who offered the Shaman instant membership and elder status. The Great Ascension, she said had been purged of Roxanna and other "negative elements" tainted by "corrupt karma."

He held the talking card to his lips and spoke carefully, "Piss off." He dropped the card to the floor and regarded me with narrowed eyes. "What do you know of the Tritons?"

I considered this a moment, hearing the rustle of the flowers, the gurgling of liquids being poured behind the bar. A Great Ascension woman stood near the bar and waved, but I pretended not to see her.

"The Tritons? It's said they're fantastic ships where an elite of undying people undergo controversial treatments that keep them alive forever. They're on a remote network and located in inhospitable parts of the world. They're probably mythical."

He nodded. "Use your com. Tell anyone who wants to join the Authentus to get to the Rampant Lion pub. There they'll be sworn in. Then go down there yourself."

"And you, master? Where will you go?"

He drained his cup, and stood up. "To a place where none can follow."

I knew his destination at once, one of many intuitions I'd had since I had come into his influence. "You're going to find a Triton. I will go with you. I will always be with you, now."

I stood aside as he emerged from the booth into the bar area of the café, adjusting the collar of his suit.

"This is my path, not yours."

"How will you get out over the ocean, master?" I said to his retreating back.

"I'll figure something out."

"I am—for the moment—still able to access all Great Ascension resources. A tribe airpod is available at a site nearby. I am qualified to pilot such a craft."

He stopped. As he turned to face me, his com device started flashing.

"Hey wiz , how ya doin?"

"Epiphany!" he answered. "I've never felt better. I arranged for new converts to go to the pub, as arranged."

"Much appreciated. Way things have turned out, maybe you're a magician after all. I hope all this praise hasn't gone to your head?"

He smiled, held his cuff com close to his mouth. "I'm turning water into wine later this afternoon."

"We're having us one hell of a party tonight to celebrate your release."

He gave me a nervous glance. "Sorry, the party will have to wait. I'm going to find Alvina."

The sound distorted as the caller raised her voice. "...fool. Haven't you had enough damn excitement?"

"She's always been my destination."

"Finding her's impossible—an' you know it. Look, you and her have been in interactive contact, right? You can carry on like that. Lots of couples do it that way and they're happy."

"No. I got to find her, there's no question."

"She's the past. We are you future. You can have a good life. You can start again."

"Sorry. You've shown me what it is to be in a family. I'm different because of you. I'll always be an Authentus, however long I've yet to live. But I got to go to her now."

"You gonna search every inch of the North Sea? How the hell you gonna find that damned thing?"

The Great Ascension woman left the bar and approached, hands in prayer position. I came forward, held up my arms to block the way. The Shaman's voice continued behind me. "I could just ask Alvina where exactly she's located. She promised to connect again. Can you access her blog file, tell her I'm shipping out in a pod to look for her? If you give her the logon details of this portal, maybe she can contact me direct. You've given me so much, I hardly dare ask more."

"Have I ever let you down? Where you gonna get a pod?"

"My number one fan, Sid." He turned and we exchanged looks. It was the first time he called me by that name, the one he used for me ever more. "Sid's got access to Great Ascension resources," he said. "He can collar me one of the tribe's mini-pods."

The voice distorted again, "...even run four hundred seater airships through the smog caps. A mini-pod's not robust enough."

"I'll have to chance it."

"Zachary, please change your mind. You'll never come back."

"I've never been more sure of anything. I'm going. Thank you. I'll never forget you."

"Nor I you, Zachary. Stay real."

"One thing. That tab you gave me, to open my mind for thought transference? It was a fake, right?"

"Multivitamin pill. Did the trick though. Goodbye, you old bullshitter."

"Goodbye, Scarecrow."

He dropped his arm, saw the Great Ascension woman standing near and hesitated. Then he turned back to the booth and beckoned for me to follow. As I sat next to him, his mesmerizing eyes held mine as he asked if I knew what I was doing. Death, he said was the likely outcome of this venture. When I replied that my life was already his, he sighed, ordered more drinks and asked me if I'd use my com to record his story. He said he wanted the truth to be known about himself before it was obscured by illusions. He wanted a transcript to be circulated to all Authentus tribesters and to various public sites around the stream where anyone who was curious could access it.

He talked then for some hours, while I recorded every word. He spoke quickly, without hesitation or pause. I listened with fascination as he told his tale. It was curious, for though events no doubt occurred similarly to the way he related them, he'd obviously made certain modifications to the actual truth. For instance, he denied his age and his healing powers. Like all true magicians, he claimed to possess no abilities beyond the average, and to have used deception rather than sorcery. Yet having spoken at length to Orion and having, like her, experienced his phenomenal magic, I had no doubt he had the capacity to change matter, to program living cells.

Another curiosity is that he denied living without food. Now, though he drank in quantity and often, I never ever saw him eat. And his great age was obvious in the wisdom and gravity of his manner. I was perplexed by these distortions at first, but came to understand that there are many shades of truth. In all spiritual texts, the reality is not obvious, it is hidden behind the words. As our Authentus tribal lore has it, "A lie is a doorway to the truth."

After he'd related his story he seemed relieved. It must have been important for him to tell it to someone. He knew, of course, what would happen. He was a seer after all, and saw how things would be.

I used my velo to transport us to an airfield of concrete and purple permagrass on reclaimed land deep in the flood plains. The Shaman carried a heavy antique com unit we'd got from some Authentus market people in Arcton, hoping to use its non-photon technology to find and connect with the Triton. The landscape was bleak—all ominous sky, hangars and communication spigots of sparking photons. We had to walk the last half-mile as the security monitors wouldn't allow any vehicle near the hangars. Pods are delicate craft, full of sensitive equipment, fuel and gasses. The going on foot was hard, and I huffed and hacked in the cold air. The line of ribbed tubular hangars before us were like giant worms, the insignia of various tribes marked on each.

I led the Shaman to the orange Great Ascension hangar. As I bent to the lock at the base of the door it registered my biometrics and shot up with a terrific clatter.

We'd hardly spoken during the journey. I had many questions I'd long wanted answering but I stayed silent, eager to impress him with my solicitude and competence. The Shaman seemed preoccupied, no doubt contemplating the awesome journey ahead of us. He may have had an intuition that it had been years since I'd flown a pod. In fact, my license had expired through lack of qualifying flying hours. It didn't seem prudent to mention it.

Inside the hangar, I saw with suppressed anxiety the pod was one of the latest mark three models which I hadn't flown. Smaller and less robust than the mark two, it looked aquatic, hardly a vessel of the air at all. The orange-and-black cylindrical body was parked on a rolling cradle with hydraulic clamps arresting the nose. It creaked occasionally in an undercurrent, as if eager to be away. I walked around it, doing a pre-flight check, familiarizing myself with the machine's layout. The Shaman watched me as I worked. The pod seemed so unsubstantial—its skin gave under my fingertip, its shiny helium tanks visible beneath the fuselage, along with aileron control rods and oxygen reservoirs. Along the sides were fin-like wings, a line of sensors and navigation gear. The cockpit was slung underneath, a bubble of transparent carbon-fiber with a hatch in the side. Behind that was the cowling with slotted grooves protecting the enclosed impellor power unit.

"It's made of ultra-light materials, a proportion of its weight being offset by helium buoyancy tanks." I said, clambering over the cradle and putting my head inside the cockpit hatch. "It's really only a short-hop pleasure craft. A three-person carrier, max. It's not made for overseas work or long hauls."

"You sure you're okay about this, Sid?" the Shaman asked. "About coming along?"

I pulled my head back out to answer him, noticing his fingers playing with the ring on his left hand. "It's a privilege." I hesitated, at loss for something else to say, then twisted around and dropped the com unit inside, before getting in myself. "You can't pilot it yourself anyway," I added.

He almost folded himself in half to place his head near the open hatch. No doubt from his many years practicing yoga with masters in India, he had remarkable physical flexibility. "Sid, listen. Isn't there an on-board tuition program I can use? Chances are, we won't be coming back."

As if I would have denied myself this opportunity! I dropped into the pilot's seat, spoke proudly. "This is what I've been saved for. This is the high point of my whole life."

"Zach," the bass notes of an official resonated around the hangar. I looked through the pod's screen, saw the ring flashing yellow on the Shaman's hand. "It's officer John Stevas," the voice continued. "Get in that ship and you're back in jail. Think about it."

The Shaman hesitated a moment before saying, "Sorry John, got to go." He pulled the ring off.

"Wait!"

"Warning." This new voice came from remote units set around the hangar, the police signals had overridden them. "If you leave the area you will violate your parole conditions and render yourself liable for arrest and imprisonment."

"Shuddup!" The ring crunched under the Shaman's heel, fragments of crystal forming a circle on the floor.

He came to the hatch, began wriggling inside. "Shit, this machine's built with midgets in mind." He struggled in and sank gratefully into one of the passenger seats as I checked the controls and primed the power unit.

"Wait," he said.

We sat, looking through the pod's screen. The hangar was cave-like, opaque and silent, occasionally disturbed by the wind's sighs. We looked through the open hangar door at the purple sky, at tangled threads of orange and black cloud.

"Could this little blimp bear me up through the heavens and on to Alvina?" he said, softly. "It doesn't seem possible, like we're sailing into a dream."

I didn't respond. I felt oddly calm. Everything that had gone before had brought me to this moment. "Shall we get started?" I said, after a couple of minutes.

The Shaman's eyes were lustrous in the gloom, lit only by dashboard effects. Slowly, he nodded.

We sat in the sky, beneath us a thousand feet of nothing. I had the familiar sensation when flying a pod of my stomach dropping through the floor. Visibility was poor, nothing but cloud roiling like black smoke. The pod's power unit screeched. The vessel had fits of the judders every couple of minutes, the screen vented fluids to clean itself of greasy deposits that continually cloaked it. We were squeezed together in our low-slung seats, the virtual dashboard a splendor of green light and dancing dials.

Thankfully, the joystick was similar to that of a mark two, though more delicate and responsive.

"Where the hell are we?" the Shaman said.

I checked the navbox. "Having just crossed the great Wash dyke barrier, we're moving out into the English Channel—we'll make faster progress when we're above the cloud. To where shall I set the navigation program?"

The Shaman's forehead was a map of lines that wriggled with concern. "No idea. Just get us out over the North Sea and wait for instructions." He leaned forward and stuck his hand through the screen display as if checking that it was solid. "How long till we're under the smog cap?"

Again I looked at the navbox. "Soon. Then our communications won't work except for radar, radio or whatever technology the elderly com unit provides. I should warn you that with the pod's emergency power pack, we've only got a maximum airtime of just over four hours. Also, I don't know how long the outer skin can resist the corrosive effect of the smog."

He pinched the skin on the bridge of his nose and took a long breath. Then he leaned back and closed his eyes. I sensed a whisper moving down my spine, an almost undetectable dialogue between my ears.

"You're using your powers, aren't you, master?" I said. "Sending Alvina your thoughts?"

He opened his eyes, an expression of amusement on his face. "Yes. I'm asking her to tell us where she is." He shut his eyes again. "You are highly perceptive," he added.

Some time later, when we'd been in the air two hours, I checked the fuel levels. In another few minutes there'd be insufficient fuel to get us back. This didn't concern me, having trust in the Shaman's purpose. When I informed him of the fuel situation, he merely nodded.

The engine seemed quieter then, or maybe I'd just gotten used to it. Above, the blinding sun. Below, mountains of charcoal-colored cloud. It seemed a place of legend, this vista of shapes. The cloud formed castles and trees, dragons and dinosaurs all eroding and mutating.

The Shaman appeared to be sleeping. Suddenly he opened his eyes wide. "Alvina, come to me now. Keep your promise. Come to me, tell me where you are."

"You want me to transmit that on all available configurations?" I said.

"Yeah. I've been sending it out in my head, might as well send it for real." He looked at the com box. "Is that thing working?"

I smiled, as reassuringly as I could. "Apparently. And there's a low-level radar that may show an outline of larger vessels. But I'm sure we won't need such devices."

We had less than two hours flying time left, assuming the emergency fuel cell held a full load. We flew just above the sea, looking for something which had appeared momentarily on the radar scan. Billowing blooms of orange vapor blinded the view ahead. Occasionally it thinned to show a fury of algae-clotted waves and scarlet spume.

I watched a vague shadow move into the center of the radar screen. "We're almost of top of it," I said, moving the joystick with the utmost care.

Something solid was emerging to our left. A rock or reef it looked like.

"A ship!" shouted the Shaman.

I saw black squares of overlapping plate, a flat, featureless deck with virtually no superstructure, scything through the water at great speed.

"That's no Triton," I said. "Just a crewless bulk container."

I pushed the stick and we watched the motorway-sized deck vanish in the mist. We ploughed upward through clouds of sticky droplets. Blooms of blue and smears of ash obscured the screen.

The Shaman kept his eyes closed, sending out his thoughts. A vein pulsed at the side of his brow. At times the contents of his mind seemed to seep into my own. His woman's name, Alvina appeared in my thoughts, requests for coordinates. I looked at the fuel register—only one hour and forty-five minutes of fuel left.

"Alvina!" The Shaman's eyes rolled like loose marbles. "I swear I heard her voice. Alvina, can you hear me? Where are you? What's your location?"

"I didn't hear anything," I said, staring into the mists. "Was it a mind message?"

"Alvina. Speak to me, where are you?" He looked around the cockpit, as if she were with us in the pod. There was no sound but that of our breathing and the power unit's whine. "Alvina, I'm listening."

A faint sound behind my seat, I stopped the machine in the air by centering the joystick, fifty feet up. I listened for the sound again, thought I heard a faint voice. We looked at each other.

"It's her," he said.

I saw an input reading on the com unit, I tuned in on the signal.

"Go back to shore, Zach."

We both lurched as a woman's voice filled the cabin.

"Alvina. Lord of Hosts, she's come through," the Shaman touched my shoulder. "Sid. Do you hear?"

I nodded reassuringly.

"You'll never find me." the voice got louder. "Go back. Save yourself. We can still meet in the virtual realm as we did before."

The Shaman looked up when he replied, as if talking to some higher deity. "Alvina, how wonderful to hear your voice."

Silence.

"Alvina." he continued. "I'm coming to find you. I'm not turning back. Tell me where you are."

Silence. Swirling cloud, the engine's screech.

"Alvina, come through. I won't turn back."

"Emergency. Ninety minutes of fuel left." The words squirmed across the screen accompanied by a voice-over that was distinctly unexcited. "Emergency landing procedure recommended." An orange light began throbbing in our faces.

"Sid. How many minutes are we from the coast?"

I checked the distance and then the port-tank indicators.

"Nearest landfall eighty-six miles. We're on the emergency power supply. With the wind blowing a westerly, by turning off the engines and drifting for a while, we might make it to shore but I doubt it."

He grabbed my wrist. His grip was extremely strong. "It was wrong to drag you into this. We could look for the bulk carrier, try to land on the deck. I could leave you there."

I tried to suppress a smile but could not. "Do you think I'll let you go on without me, master?"

"No sense in us both getting killed."

"You can't fly on alone." I spoke as resolutely as I could. "My future is with you. Where you go, I go."

"Turn back!"

Our harnesses squeaked as we jerked back simultaneously. A woman's face flooded the screen. She had coffee-colored skin, a broad forehead, full lips and wild jet hair. Her brown eyes were huge and imploring, big enough to dive into. I was shocked; this was photon technology. Somehow the signals were being received and processed, but the neither the built-in nor the antique come unit was receiving it. The Triton must use some new form of photon technology.

"Alvina." The Shaman stretched his fingers to touch the screen.

"Warning. Emergency landing procedure recommended." The words blared out in the same sonorous voice as before. The woman's face in the screen was drawn, her chin quivering.

"Go back." There was iron in her voice. "You'll never find me. Go back or you'll die."

The Shaman seemed to shrink at her words, he looked down at his bony knees. It was a while before he answered.

"You know I won't. I'm coming on. Tell me where you are."

"Eighty minutes of fuel remaining," the auto-voice said, spelled out in white lettering in the folds of Alvina's frown. Her face froze, then was gone.

"She's gone," the Shaman said.

I kept the craft immobile, watched the master processor register. It was still processing incoming signals.

"The signal's still up and running," I said.

"So she can still hear us?"

"I assume so, unless the communication was one-way."

"Could we still make it back to shore if necessary?"

I tried to look reassuring. "No chance."

We circled aimlessly for some time, precious fuel depleting as we did so. Every couple of minutes, the Shaman made an appeal to Alvina, but there was no response.

"Sid, what happens when the fuel cell expires?"

I was becoming accustomed to these tests and spoke calmly. "We'll have to use the last reserves getting down and ditching. Pointless putting out an SOS, no one would come."

The cabin began to become chill as the pod restricted auxiliary power. Our breath formed clouds of condensation.

The Shaman spoke gently. "Alvina, you made me so happy. If I had to do it all again, I would." His fists opened and closed in anguish as he spoke. "Sid." he said, looking at me levelly. "I'm so sorry to have used you like this. Ditch the pod. Save yourself."

I shook my head. Such an instruction was unworthy of an answer.

A claxon began blaring behind us. The screen and dashboard emitted a mess of warnings and red lights. I breathed deeply. If the Shaman did not use his powers to rescue us soon, some higher force would surely intervene. This was my chance to touch immortality.

"All will be well, master," I said.

The Shaman shook his head. "I'm not worthy of your confidence, Sid. This is no test. How foolish I've been." He raised his voice, almost shouted, "This is the end."

"No." Alvina's voice again, this time with no visual effects. "Forgive me, Zach. I should've known better." She sounded exhausted. "Set the navigator for bearing four-four, North, six-one-seven, East. You've got just enough fuel. It won't be what you expect. Whatever happens, look for the landing deck and get down onto it. There's no time for explanations."

"We will, we will, thank you." The Shaman looked at me, and exhaled deeply. "Praise be to heaven."

The claxon continued honking, warnings exploded in our faces: low fuel, emergency landing procedure, autopilot override. It was difficult to concentrate. The radar was a squall of shapes and code. We were just above sea level at the location Alvina had given us. The vision was hellish, great banks of mist and sea-spray.

"If this is the Triton's location code there's no sign of it," I said. "Only a small square vessel shows on the radar and it's immobile. It seems to be sitting above the water."

The Shaman turned to me. "Sid, the Tritons are going to distort their imprint to disguise their location."

I gave up on the radar. "Well, we should be able to see something."

We were so low the sound of crashing waves was audible, sea foam was flecked on the screen. The sea seemed hungry to draw us into it.

"There it is!"

Burning in the fog, a looming curtain of white light appeared. The Triton's side was a cliff of white interlocking plates. An anchor, portholes, chains were visible. The surfaces shone with unnatural luminosity like a genie ad. The hull reached up and away, a skyscraper of the sea. A waterfall gushed from a vent in the ship's side, the chromed anchor looked double the size of the pod. I manoeuvred alongside, took the pod up towards the higher decks. The engine was silent, the claxon clamoring like the clappers of hell.

I checked the radar again. Only the small square object was visible in a fuzz of interference. "This thing is far bigger than its radar profile. There's something wrong."

There was tightness in the Shaman's voice. "Alvina said it wouldn't be like we expected—just get the pod down on it."

The claxon was joined by a shrill whistle. Red dots chased each other across the dashboard. "Emergency landing" it read. "Operator override imminent—fuel-cell exhausted."

Seeing the horror in the Shaman's eyes, my faith almost failed me. "Zachary, master, save us, please!"

"Do as I say!" Alvina's voice was imperial. We looked at each other with wide-stretched eyes.

"Maintain your bearing of four-four, North."

"That'll take us straight into the hull," I said.

"Do it, Sid."

I tilted the joystick and we lurched towards the mass of metal plates. Emergency silver buoyancy spheres began inflating rapidly around the outer shell of the cockpit.

Instinctively, we both reached down and held our seat belt retaining struts as the ship's side loomed before us.

It was incredible. Unbelievable. The ship wasn't a ship at all, merely a ghost, a projection. We passed clear through its gleaming metal and into nothing. I sensed my jaw hanging slack as we thrummed on with claxons and whistles blasting, buoyancy spheres hissing, burning off our last seconds of power.

I tried to gain height, but the fuel was completely exhausted and the pod began sinking. As we spiralled downward the Shaman uttered a sigh of loss and futility.

"What an idiot. The ship's a decoy luring us to our deaths."

I saw rocks below us, a froth of water breaking against them.

"I've been tricked," the Shaman said. "How right that I end like this, totally deceived."

As we got closer it became clear that they weren't rocks, but a contraption of metal. We lost height fast, buoyancy spheres breaking off and flying in all directions. A rust-scabbed crane swirled in my eyes, mechanical grabs and derricks, steel pipes. It was a prehistoric ruin, an oil-drilling platform from the great petroleum age. A brutal construction decked in algae, rust and peeling paint. This was the object that had shown on the radar. On one side a white circular landing pad with a giant "H."

"Sid!"

I was juggling the joystick, making for it as he pointed the platform out. We almost hit a tall metal building near the landing pad, lights burning in the windows, shadows moving.

We dropped like a stone towards the white circle. The pod couldn't possibly survive the impact...

Somehow we were down. And apparently, alive. With a bone-wrenching bang, we struck the pad. Buoyancy spheres exploded. The pod's skeleton warped, the cockpit's roof pressed against our skulls. A dribble of green oozed down the cracked screen. Then there was silence but for the sound of raging waves and the hiss of escaping gas.

It took some time to extract ourselves from the pod. Unbuckling twisted harnesses, wriggling through the distorted cockpit, we checked ourselves for injuries. When we climbed out, the craft looked like a giant had trodden on it. A huge split ran down the length of the fuselage, power leads and buoyancy tanks were exposed. We used a rope from the survival kit to tie the ship to a rail but still it thrashed about like a wounded bird.

A series of steel gangways crisscrossed the strange structure. We walked down one to get off the landing platform, bent forward, grasping the corroded handrail. The wind jostled us, the air smelled foul, a mix of formaldehyde, sulphur and burned oil. The sea was crashing somewhere below but I couldn't see it. Magenta fog obscured everything beyond fifty feet away.

The drilling rig was much bigger than it looked from the pod, and even uglier close up. Another gangway climbed steeply to the large building we'd almost hit as we landed. The walls were made of corrugated, algae-streaked metal. Forty or so windows faced us with lights aglow. Scattered around were steel cylinders, heaps of aluminized containers on a raised deck, drums of chemicals, lifeboats. A battery of lenses was perched on rails overhead, blasting beams of rainbow light, presumably the 3D image of the Triton. As I watched the beams flickered and died.

We slowly approached the building. The incline was awfully steep, causing my heart to beat too fast.

There was an alcove of welded steel sheets around the entrance protecting us from the wind. The door seemed to tremble with some vital force. A window in the door had faces pressed to the glass, curious faces, mangled faces, gray hair, scars, wrinkles. *These aren't the sort of re-built people you'd expect to find on a Triton,* I thought. *They looked old, worn out.*

The Shaman's cuff flashed.

"You are in a quarantined area," a voice said. "You cannot enter this or any other part of this vessel. If you need assistance, you will be supplied with the necessary fuel and equipment to repair your craft. Then you must continue your journey."

None of the people in the window had moved their lips. Someone, some-where else, must have been speaking.

"Alvina Rohanna Khan." The Shaman spoke boldly as if, despite appear-ances, he knew we were in the right place. "I want her to come out and talk to me."

"This person is not a resident," came the reply. "Please let us know what assistance you need."

"We need no assistance save you bringing me Alvina."

One by one the faces slowly moved away from the window.

We stood waiting a long time. No one communicated and no one appeared at the door. The wind snatching about the alcove made a warbling sound.

"Sid," the Shaman said to me. "Tell me you wish you hadn't come."

"I am where I should be," I replied. "Of that I am sure."

He stepped back, staring up at the rows of windows and I moved to stand beside him. It was very cold, my suit struggled to maintain my body tem-perature. My lips, eyes and cheeks were burning in the corrosive atmosphere. I wondered how the Shaman was faring with his bare skin exposed through holes in his suit. He had such a massive accumulation of years, yet his physical endurance was superhuman. Never once did I hear him complain about bodily discomfort.

My watery eyes made out a thin silhouette three levels up. Whoever it was had their arms stretched upwards.

"It's her," the Shaman said, pointing at the figure. "Alvina. I can feel her. I know it with my bones."

The figure quickly moved away. We continued waiting.

Something was about to happen. People were gathered behind the door. They'd donned olive zylex contamination suits with molded transparent masks over their faces.

The door groaned as it opened. Three people shuffled out, the material of their suits swishing and crackling. They looked artificial, a clear pliant sheen formed a second skin over their scalps, hands, and faces and grilled valves at their lips and nostrils vented condensing air.

They emerged in a blast of warm perfume. I glimpsed the interior of the building—it looked luxurious—whisper-fine wall lining, statuettes set into the walls, a wool-look carpet.

No one said anything for a moment or two.

The tallest of the three looked familiar. His face was a checker board of coffee and milk colored skin except for a raised purple area on his cheekbone. He wore a black eye-patch over his left eye with white letters on it. He stretched out his hand and shook hands with me. It was odd, feeling the plasticky surface of his palm. He shook the Shaman's hand also but didn't let his go.

"Forgive me," he said. "You are the first unexpected guests who've landed here in some years, so you'll understand our lack of preparedness." The words slid from the corner of his mouth, controlled, Spanish-accented.

"I am Argossy," he said. "Chief physician, and captain of the Triton since the passing away of Yoseph, Alvina's father." His eye-patch and mask moved with the muscles of his face as he smiled. At that point I recognized him as an ex-President of a small South American country. He'd been embroiled in a corruption scandal many, many years back and had promptly vanished. "This," he said, pointing to a bone-faced woman with two lumps on her forehead, "is Zaphia. And this," he nodded to the one standing on his other side, "is Naji." A young guy with a handsome face and yellow eyeballs lifted his hand and shook it feebly.

"You people don't look like immortals," said the Shaman. "More like walking wounded."

Argossy chuckled, retained his grip of the Shaman's hand. "Alas, much that is said of us is not true. On-stream rendering gives us the choice of how we want to present ourselves, and images can be manipulated. Certain illusions are necessary and some are pure vanity."

"So this heap of rusty metal is a Triton? Where's Alvina?"

Argossy released the Shaman's hand to spread his palms wide. "Yes, yes, this is the Triton. There are rumor of others, but as far as I know, they are just that. In order to remain hidden and to retain our mystique, we've had to resort to certain tricks."

The Shaman's eyes were bright, his breath quick. "Where's Alvina? I'm not leaving without her."

Argossy brought his right palm up, rubbed the clear covering over his good eye. "We have gone through a great deal of trouble to make communication with you. And we have allowed you to locate and land on our little metal island. So you see, my friend, you already have our trust. Now that you have found us, now that you know the truth of the Triton, we are in your hands. We must stay hidden. Will you keep our secret?"

The Shaman looked over Argossy's shoulder through the window of the door behind him. "I insist you bring Alvina to me, now."

Argossy shook his head, looked pained. "She doesn't want to meet you. The pain of not being able to be with you will be too much. Do you understand?"

My master stepped back and looked up at the windows. "No."

Argossy hesitated before speaking, "Unlike you, none of us may leave this place." Zaphia and Naji nodded as if on cue. "We are not, as you see, a palace of luxury, more a sort of hospital." He dropped his hands to his sides as if unsure what to do with them. "Some might say a leper colony. We are beyond the end of our life cycles. Beyond immune system programming, cloning and cell replication. Through advanced age or barely containable infection, we are the living dead."

"So you don't live forever?"

"We have a kind of existence, but at the same time we are intimate with death. Every advance in medical knowledge is matched by a new form of death. Death adapts. We can trace its twists and turns, its progress through the body, its new manifestations. We are on familiar terms with death."

The Shaman put his hand on Argossy's shoulder and looked him in the eye. "Alvina is ill—is that what you're telling me?"

Argossy glanced briefly at Naji, then replied. "The disease has never left her body. All of us here are unable to remain alive without constant intervention beyond anything known in the land-bound world. Massive resources are devoted to evolving new search-and-destroy viruses. We and nature are constantly evolving, constantly at war. All of our time is spent in lab work, in research, in undergoing treatments."

As he spoke the wind rose, so I could barely hear him. "Alvina has the Strep Five Virus. It's incurable. There are side-effects of the treatment and it's terribly contagious. Alvina can never be with you, flesh to flesh."

"I will join you then." The Shaman took his hands away, waved his right hand in my direction. "Me and my friend, Siddharta..."

Argossy's eyes were evasive. "No. We are at the limit of our resources and the limit of our numbers. You could only join us when one of us dies. Our number is made up of those with wealth and influence who bring the means and connections to keep the network of secret supply ships coming to continue our research programs. Please try to understand, wealth is life to us, our lives hang in the balance, day to day."

"Either we join you, or Alvina will leave with me." The Shaman crossed his arms. "If not I'll broadcast your coordinates, tell everyone what the Triton really is, and where it's located."

"No," Argossy spoke quickly. "Please listen. If you broadcast our whereabouts, we'd be either exterminated or overwhelmed with the terminally ill. We lost Alvina's father, Yoseff—our founding patriarch—last year. Without his expertise and influence we have struggled to survive." He scratched the plastic over his chin. "You see, we die here, too. We prolong life, but not indefinitely. Yoseff told Alvina you had died. It was not a decision he made lightly. He wiped her records so you couldn't trace her. He did this because there's no going back for us, no past to hang onto. You can't meet with her. You can't stay. You must make your ship work, we will help you and then you must go."

The Shaman stepped forward. Argossy stepped back, bumping against Naji. The three Triton residents closed together, blocking the door.

"I won't go without seeing Alvina," the Shaman said, his voice rising.

Argossy's eye wandered. "She does not wish to present herself to you."

"How do I know you're not preventing her from coming out?"

"She is her own master in this. She could not bear to be so close and not to touch you."

"Don't be so bloody mad, is the world mad?" the Shaman shouted, "I can't stand anymore! Show me Alvina! Show her to me!"

He forced himself between Zaphia and Naji, began shouldering the door.

Argossy dodged around him, took my arm, drawing me away. We walked back from the door a few paces while the Shaman hammered on the window. I looked up, saw the slender figure above us in the window again.

"Please," Argossy said. "You must make him see how hopeless your position is. You cannot enter. It is in your interest to leave us in peace."

The Shaman roared in fury. He thumped, pulled, and then kicked the door.

"Please desist." Argossy said, raising his voice. "I assure you she's happy as she is."

The Shaman looked at me. I saw in his raw, torn face an animal savagery. "Alvina!" he screamed. The power of him, the fury held us all transfixed while he thumped and kicked the door till his knuckles were bleeding and his strength spent.

Time passed, I don't know how long. The Shaman lay slumped against the door. No one dared try to shift him. Argossy and the others shuffled around, muttering to each other, not looking at us. I stood back from them, leaning against the railing. I waited to see by what agency the door would eventually open. No one would stand against the Shaman's will. We would gain admittance eventually; it was as inevitable as night following day.

The Shaman seemed to recover slightly. He sat up and looked through the door's glass. "I've seen that interior before, in the virtual Triton Alvina took me to. I've seen those face masks you all wear, too. In a vision I had back in a café in Cambridge."

I heard him then in my head. It was the clearest I'd known his mind to open to me since he spoke telepathically to me from the back of the truck. "Alvina. Open the door." I heard him so well, he may as well have shouted at the top of his lungs. I watched him, hunched against the door, facing away from me. I watched him for a long time, till I was aware of the acid air burning my eyes. I squeezed them tight.

When I looked again, the Shaman had fallen into the open doorway. A thin figure in an olive protective suit held the door open with one hand, covering its face with the other. The figure bent over the Shaman and touched his side. He scrambled to his feet, reached around the figure and hauled it off the deck. I glimpsed a woman's face over his shoulder before a hand covered it again. The face looked aged, clear plastic covered her neck, scalp, her whole head.

"Don't look," she said, her voice clear and strong. "I don't want you to see my face."

"Alvina!" the Shaman bawled.

"No!" she protested as he put her back on her feet. "Don't look at me!" He ignored her, pulled her hand away from her face.

Under the clear plastic covering they all wore, wrinkles were arrayed around her eyes, brown spots mottled the loose skin on her cheeks. The hair was stuck flat to her head and riddled with gray. This was an aged form of the Alvina who appeared in the screen of the pod. Her brown eyes were still youthful though, warm and lustrous. The Shaman slid down the length of her to his knees, crushing her legs against him. She collapsed slowly on top of him, till they were entwined in the entranceway, rocking together silently.

At last we were allowed inside the building, but not before we'd been made to wear anti-viral protective suits and masks. My master and I were stripped in the freezing air and blasted with bolts of antiseptic light from hand-held tasers. Then all our exposed skin was glazed with a glutinous coating—a sticky molding covering our faces and hands like a too-thick skin.

The Shaman, Alvina and I were led to a cluttered storeroom. The place was filled to the roof with sealed sta-fresh packs with unpronounceable labels.

Alvina and the Shaman held each other so tightly they seemed welded together; neither of them spoke. I was uncomfortable with such intimacy and wished I'd been allowed to wait outside. I kept my eyes on the scene through the barred window, saw the deflated airpod drifting around the landing pad. From behind me there was only the sound of their suits flexing and a series of sighs.

A loud clatter made me turn. Alvina had stepped back against a shelf and disturbed some boxes, knocking one of them to the floor. She emitted a series of groans like a long-sealed chamber being opened. She was bent forwards, her hands moving over the Shaman's body, stroking, prodding, examining. She took his plasticized palm in both hers, folded the fingers and wrapped it into a fist. She ran her fingers along the outline of his face, concern in the crinkles of her eyes.

From outside the door came the sound of people moving along the corridor, a resonant throb emanated through the floor.

"Are you disappointed, finding me like this?" Her voice made me start, then I turned back to look through the window.

"You're here and you're alive," the Shaman's voice said. "We're together. Nothing else matters." A squeaking sound and a series of rustles. "For goodness sake, Alvina. I wish we could get out of these masks."

"Zach, I'm incredibly infectious; one touch would be enough to kill you. I'm only alive through enzyme-inhibiting anti-virals." Another rattle, shuffling feet, laughter. "Your bone-crushing cuddles—however many times I've simulated you giving me them in a sensa-suit, it's not the same."

"If you're ill, I'm going to look after you." My master's words were muffled. "Whatever time we have left, I want to spend it with you."

"I should never have tried to stop you coming here. Will you ever forgive me?"

"Oh Alvina. I love you so much, it hurts. Every second that's left is ours." Outside, something flashed in the sky above the deflated pod, a shadow appeared in the mists.

"You're amazing," Alvina said, "How strong you are. Nothing can stop you. Nothing will separate us now."

An orange torpedo shape dropped into view. I saw the Great Ascension insignia. The pod was identical to the one already there. It hesitated over the lip of the pale landing disc, swung pendulum-like as it dropped.

"Alvina," the Shaman's voice was behind me. "I've found out how powerful belief is, how it can change things. There are powers inside us that with enough belief can cure you."

The pod drifted gently across the pad and nudged against our craft, which noiselessly tumbled sideways off the platform and out of sight, spilling buoyancy spheres as it fell.

Alvina spoke. "I believe you. It's a miracle, you being here. We've both been dead to each other and now we live. I've always been so afraid, and my fear has made me obsessed with my own preservation. But I don't feel afraid anymore. I can't ever..."

"I hesitate to interrupt you," I said, turning, "but we are not the only new arrivals to this place."

They were stretched out on the floor, Alvina's head on the Shaman's chest. They both stared at me as if only then aware of my presence. A door banged somewhere, there were raised voices in the corridor.

"Who can it be?" said Alvina.

The Shaman knew, his words were heavy with a worn-out sense of dread. "The last person on this earth I want ever to see again."

Alvina was fastest to her feet, up and out of the door before either of us. I followed the Shaman's back amidst a clump of suited figures shuffling ahead, blocking the gangway.

When we eventually got outside and near the pod there were already a dozen people leaning over it, peering into the open hatch. Argossy and a woman with wire-brush hair and tubes in her nostrils were reaching in, there was the sound of snapping harness straps.

When they dragged Roxanna out by her arms, her face was slate gray, bubbles of spittle at the corner of her lips. For some reason, a quote from the Bible or some such spiritual text came to mind: "How are the mighty fallen."

Roxanna who was once bathed in light, idolized as an immortal, for whom thousands—including myself—had been prepared to die without hesitation, now seemed but a husk of a human being. I felt a stab of sympathy, even though I had seen through her and the Great Ascension's delusions.

The Shaman raised his voice. "This woman is Roxanna DeLancia. She is the head of the Great Ascension. She's a criminal, a tissue vampire. She tried to kill me for my cell material and she'll do anything to..."

His voice faded, no one took any notice and it struck me then that any of those around us would have probably been desperate enough to do what Roxanna had done. I circled the group of turned backs, leaning in for a better look.

Argossy laid Roxanna gently on the deck, talking to her in a low monotone. She gasped like a landed fish, a web of fine blue capillaries visible in her cheeks.

I stood near the Shaman. "She has somehow managed to track us here. Perhaps all Great Ascension pods are linked in some way."

We watched Argossy stroking Roxanna's forehead, rubbing the backs of her hands. Someone passed him a black cylinder, he took her jaw in his hand, opened her mouth, sprayed it down her throat.

At that point I saw Alvina among the faces on the opposite side of the group. She looked up, flashed a grim smile. Everyone leaned in closer as Roxanna struggled to speak. She coughed and spluttered, it took a long time before she got the words out.

"People of the Triton. I beg you grant me admittance. I bring gold, a complete payload, almost a hundred kilos." She coughed up bubbles of spittle. Everyone shuffled nervously as if embarrassed by this overt display of bad health. "It's in bullion bars under the seats of the pod, take a look. There's more to come." She tried to hold up her hand but only succeeded in fluttering her fingers. "I still command loyalty amongst many. People that would help you, us, in all sorts of ways. Take me. Save me. Please."

Everyone started to babble excitedly. Argossy, still kneeling over her, held his hand up for silence. "I doubt whether we can cure you," he said. "Anyway, the question is academic. We're full. I concede your assets would help us, but our overstretched medical facilities mean there aren't enough resources. Not for you, not for him," he nodded towards the Shaman. "Not for anyone."

The Shaman spoke quietly, and this time everyone listened. "It's time to face your death at last, Roxanna. Haven't you done your life justice?"

Roxanna looked vaguely in our direction, her eyes blood-filled. "At my income level and with my accumulated spirituality, death is not an option." She spoke with surprising strength. A fit of coughing, then, "I carry the hopes of many with me. I must show them it's possible to overcome death. From me they expect no less."

Someone actually applauded.

"You've outstayed your welcome this lifetime, you poisoned witch," the Shaman growled. "It's time you shuffled off. You've done enough harm."

Roxanna turned her head slightly, her ruined eyes straining to focus. She seemed to gain strength somehow, speaking ever more clearly. "Death is the ultimate failure. You'll never know how it feels to sing with a million people tuned in, knowing you're touching the hearts of every single one." She spat feebly, splattering her cheek. "Death is for losers like you."

The Shaman pushed his way through to the center of the crowd, leaned over Roxanna and Argossy. "Good Lord, you're pathetic. Face your end with dignity you self-obsessed shitbag. Death is inevitable, even for you."

She rolled onto her side, got painfully up on one elbow. "You should have saved me from this obscenity, that was your purpose."

Alvina spoke. She'd quietly made her way near the front of the crowd and stood facing the Shaman. She stood straight, while most of the crowd were stooped over Roxanna. "Death," she said, "seems to me part of living. It's death that makes life precious. If you can't acknowledge that, I don't think you can live fully and what's more I don't think you can dare to love, either." She looked across at the Shaman, the pursed lines round her lips deepening as she raised her voice over the keening wind. "Pain and death are a part of life and inseparable from love. People die here eventually. Death can be postponed, but resisting it is as futile as sticking the autumn leaves back on the trees. Death makes a mockery of all." She looked over at the carnival-orange pod. The wind moaned, her suit rustled. "If you can live with yourself, Roxanna, and I have no doubt you can," she leaned down and rested her hand on Argossy's shoulder, "and if the people here will grant you your wish, which I have no doubt they will, then you can take my place. You can stretch your days out here instead of me. My place is yours if you want it, if you're that afraid." She smiled. "'I've lied to myself long enough. I'm leaving with Zach."

Argossy snatched Alvina's hand, held it in both his. "Alvina, I promised your father to care for you always. You are the symbol of hope for us all, our patriarch's legacy. You can't go. You'll die out there. We need you."

She nodded, smiled grimly. "Since father died you have discharged your obligations with honor. But I owe Zachary his due. It's his time now. I must go." Tears pooled in flattened globules down her face, trapped there by the mask.

Argossy's shoulders shook. He still held Alvina's hand. "You can't go back to land. You'd infect everyone, you'd bring disaster with you."

Alvina took her hand from his, reached out with both hands toward the Shaman and I. Instinctively, I moved close and took her left hand, the Shaman her right.

"Take me away," she said. "Take me somewhere where there are no people. Where no winters come, where there are no chemical fogs and no illness." She stepped over Roxanna's legs. "Come on everyone," she said, turning to them all, "unload the gold. It'll buy you more years. We're leaving in Roxanna's pod."

They needed no further prompting. Roxanna was ignored as, with suits cracking, shouts and the squeak of no-slip soles, they formed a human chain. Slabs of heavy yellow metal were passed from the pod, stacked on the deck.

When they were almost done, I stood by the Shaman and Alvina in a kind of dream. It all seemed so fantastic, this place, these events. I held onto a hand-rail, felt its solidity. Soon we would leave this fabled Triton, never to return.

I heard a vague hiss at my side. I was shocked to see the Shaman's hands were bare, he'd peeled off the covering over his palms and was feeling for the seal under his collar. He tore away the tab, wrenching off his mask. He stood there, his face naked to the air, and reached for the front of Alvina's suit. She backed away, clutching the tab on the fastener under her chin, her face narrowing in surprise. He looked deep into her eyes, communicated something to her.

Alvina nodded, she dropped her hands. He peeled away her mask, rolling it into a ball and dropping it on the deck. Her hair threw a fury of dark and silver strands about her head.

They kissed. They kissed for a long time, those around us shocked into silence. There was only the sound of Roxanna's agonized groans and the buffeting breeze.

When they pulled apart, the line of patched-up, disfigured faces was aghast. Roxanna's words hissed through the air.

"So now you're infected too, idiot," she gargled like a drain. "Now you'll die. He's dying too!" She shouted. "I could have been saved by that fool, I could have made better use of those cells. That's what you're showing me, is it? How to die?"

Alvina looked at the Shaman. I knew she had the same confidence, the same trust in him that I did. He would not fail us. Her face was both ancient and youthful, wondrous and weary. "Where will you take me, my love? We can't have much time left."

He held her bare palm in his own, skin to skin, flesh to flesh.

"We must trust the powers within," he said. "There is much magic in the world. If we believe strongly enough, all things are possible."

We strapped ourselves into the pod. Before I entered I began removing my anti-viral wear, to demonstrate my confidence in the Shaman, but he insisted I keep it on. I got in the pilot's seat, went though the pre-flight check.

Outside on the deck, Argossy and two others were lifting Roxanna onto an aluminium gurney. Roxanna's head rolled side-to-side. Argossy looked exhausted, his shoulders sagging, as if bearing a terrible weight. He turned and looked up, waved.

Without her suit, Alvina was stick-thin. She wore a white, long-sleeved undergarment which covered her meager figure from neck to ankles. I noticed she still wore the globe pendant at her throat. I knew what words were written there. Rather than taking the third seat, she sat in the Shaman's lap, molded herself against him in the cramped cockpit.

"I'm so happy. I won't ever regret this," she said. "I won't waste time being sad, however little time is left."

"Who wants to live to be ninety anyway?" the Shaman said, smiling.

We lurched into the air with a rattle of released mooring clamps. Below us Roxanna was being wheeled away, one hand trailing limply along the deck.

"Everyone who's eighty-nine," Alvina answered, her eyes sparkling like diamonds.

⚜

There is little more to add. I flew the pod to the east coast of Scotland. We landed at a commercial airbase near Chanonry Point where we took on more fuel. There I and the Shaman parted. He and Alvina took off, abandoning me in that ice-bound, inhospitable place, despite my protestations. He wouldn't reveal his destination. He smiled at me sadly and charged me with telling this story faithfully, without distortion. In a rush of air, the pod vanished into the mists, never to be seen again.

I have rendered his words to all that would listen, I have fulfilled my allotted task, and more will I do—anything to serve him, the Authentus and the cause of truth.

Needless to say, I have heard the rumors. The reports of the Shaman's death, the stories that he was a liar, a trickster, a fraud. So many have an interest in debasing the truth—other tribes, the authorities, the providers. Each would deny the suggestion that one can survive without immune modification, each would deny the power of the mind. Even among our own tribe there have been suggestions that I made up the story of the Triton for my own advancement. None have been able to locate the vessel or to verify that perilous journey. As if a person of limited imagination like myself could invent such a tale!

I stand as a witness to all that the Shaman accomplished. I experienced his wonders, first-hand. His magic continues. He comes to me often. He speaks to my mind. He guides me, empowers me, offers me guidance.

Some months ago, Epiphany succeeded in hacking a police report on our tribe's activities. I present it here, as an independent document of our status and values. I find it highly amusing and it serves as a testament to the Shaman's great legacy. May all beings come to know the truth. We are what we think. Cognition creates condition.

SIDDHARTA SEVENRIVERS VERITAS

⚬❧⚬

Date: 26 11 0017.

Police log N908\87APF.

Subject: Status report on Authentus tribe.

Ref: 895Y31/PSZ

A brief summary of the result of close-monitoring of the Authentus network follows.

Extensive group and individual acts of subversive activity has been noted. Tribal membership consists of unstable and antagonistic persons many with criminal records. The Authentus have assimilated the Great Ascension, Lords of Truth and Pagan Earth tribes and are presently the largest of the pan-western European networks. They have so far refused any association with a provider, causing severe power imbalances amongst the big four and consequent economic instability. The Authentus profess non-acceptance of any creed, faith, ideal or conviction whatsoever, save their belief that reality is created by thought. The tribe bear no facial enhancements, take no immuno boosters and claim to heal themselves by mind-power modification.

The elders are Epiphany Oujimeme (aka The Scarecrow), Siddharta Sevenrivers Veritas and Duke Tulmud. Each bear purple pigment streaks across their faces. They claim that this demonstrates their contempt for the world of appearances. They promote the ludicrous fiction that their high elder, the Shaman (aka Mick Tarn, parole replacement ID of ex DATCHO, Zachary Crowe) is alive. They claim that he and his wife, Alvina Khan, are living in some luxury on a large vessel floating in the South Pacific. Zachary, it is maintained, has magical powers and is in constant contact with the tribe through telepathy.

The fate of notorious fraudster, Zachary Crowe and his wife can be found in log N908\87APF. In summary, a minipod with Great Ascension insignia was found smashed and holed, drifting a hundred yards off the Isle of Mull near Scotland on the sixth of February, zero, zero, sixteen. No bodies were recovered, but Zachary Crowe's huna suit, with portal and memory disc intact were found, also a gold pendant with runic markings scratched around its circumference. Biometric scans revealed traces of Zachary Crowe's and Alvina Khan's DNA. Worldwide cross-reference monitoring has failed to discover any evidence of Zachary Crowe and Alvina Khan extant. Consequently, death certificates were issued on the twenty-eighth of November, zero, zero, sixteen.

The two best known of the tribe's aphorisms are: "A lie is a doorway to the truth," and "Cognition creates condition." Both are said to have originated with Zachary Crowe and to have been passed to Siddharta by telepathic means.

Predictive processing suggests the tribe will have a powerful influence on future social stability, value systems, and medical advancement. The alarming effect of the tribe's propaganda on provider viability has already been mentioned

For these reasons it is strongly suggested that close digital tracking of all tribal activity continue.

- THE END -

JOHNNY FINCHAM is the UK's leading palmist and appears regularly in the US and UK media. Mr. Fincham has published many books on the subject, including *The Spellbinding Power of Palmistry* and *Palmistry: Apprentice to Pro in 24 Hours*. He holds an MA in the novel, is a winner of the Pulp fiction prize and was a commended writer for the Elevator literary award. He has contributed to various futurology websites as an advisor on the nature of society in the future.

Also in Print from Virtual Tales

Challenge of the Red Unicorn

Jack Scoltock

The Curious Accounts of the Imaginary Friend

P.S. Gifford

P.S. Gifford

Dr. Offig's Lessons from the Dark Side

DRY RAIN

B.J. Kibble

Earrings of Ixtumea

Kim Baccellia

Figgy-Dowdy

Frank Minogue

THE FIRST VAMPIRE
A NOVEL OF SAMSON & DELILAH

Alicia Benson

The Further Accounts of the Imaginary Friend

P.S. Gifford

HANNAH

Sharon Poppen

ALSO IN PRINT FROM VIRTUAL TALES

Coming Soon from Virtual Tales

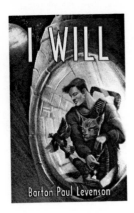

Lightning Source UK Ltd.
Milton Keynes UK
30 October 2009

145635UK00001B/7/P